Touch of a Scoundrel

TOUCH OF A SCOUNDREL

MIA MARLOWE

KENSINGTON PUBLISHING CORP.
www.kensingtonbooks.com

BRAVA BOOKS are published by

Kensington Publishing Corp.
119 West 40th Street
New York, NY 10018

All Kensington titles, imprints, and distributed lines are available at special quantity discounts for bulk purchases for sales promotions, premiums, fund-raising, educational, or institutional use.

Special book excerpts or customized printings can also be created to fit specific needs. For details, write or phone the office of the Kensington special sales manager: Kensington Publishing Corp., 119 West 40th Street, New York, NY 10018, attn: Special Sales Department; phone: 1-800-221-2647.

ISBN-13: 978-0-7582-6356-8
ISBN-10: 0-7582-6356-2

First Kensington Trade Paperback Printing: August 2012

10 9 8 7 6 5 4 3 2 1

Printed in the United States of America

Chapter 1

Devonwood Park, 1844

Griffin rarely prayed in church. He used the time when everyone else's eyes were closed to sneak a peek at Sabrina Ashcroft's rapidly growing bosom. Every fourteen-year-old boy in the shire was fascinated by the new bumps sprouting on her chest. Ogling those lovely mounds sent urgent sensations coursing through his body, driving all thought of prayer from his mind.

But he talked to God now as he urged his gelding to the top of the rise.

"Let the delay be enough," Griffin repeated. His mount's powerful haunches bunched and flexed under him as he forced it up the steep incline. He didn't say please, to the horse or the Almighty. He was his father's heir, after all, and the earldom of Devonwood was an old and venerated estate.

A peer of the realm demanded obedience from those subject to him and gave restrained courtesy to his equals. Griffin loved and feared his father as much as the vicar admonished him to love and fear God. In his mind, the two had always been intertwined so tightly, he suspected the earl spoke to the Lord as if they were on the same footing.

But a sense of urgency crowded Griffin's chest and he began to add a silent "please" to his repeated prayer.

He reined in the gelding and surveyed the rolling meadows of his family's ancestral seat. A blur of movement caught his eye. He narrowed his gaze at the lone horseman barreling down the tree-lined drive toward the haphazard castle that crowned Devonwood Park. His gut clenched with apprehension.

The sun burst from behind a westering cloud bank, dazzling with unexpected brightness for so late in the day. The sweet scent of newly cut hay wafted over the hedgerows. Larks threw their songs to the heavens. It was a moment to gladden any lad, but the eerie sense of having lived through this slice of time once before stripped away any joy Griffin might have felt.

His palms grew clammy and a hard shell formed around his hammering heart.

He didn't have to wonder what news made the horseman push his mount to such a breakneck pace.

He *knew*.

The *Sending* that morning had been so specific, he had dared break his father's rule and warned the earl about what his "gift" had shown him. Griffin hesitated to call it that, but his mother had insisted the ability to glimpse the future by touching inanimate objects was part of his birthright from her side of the family, inherited just as directly as his raven hair and storm-gray eyes.

The earl, however, didn't hold with such outlandish things. He thrashed his son every time he admitted to having a vision of the future, even though events always unraveled just as Griffin said they would.

Griffin was never able to anticipate what would set off the miasma of lights in his head. It might be an accidental brush against a scrap of leather or a piece of carved wood. A china teacup might whisper the future to him. When he and his father had shaken hands to say good-bye that morning, his father's signet ring had all but screamed what was to come.

Once Griffin had *Seen* what the morning held for his father, he'd pleaded with him to change his plans and remain in the country for another day.

"Ballocks!" his father had said, and then whipped him for "gypsy-ish nonsense." The punishment had caused a mere fifteen-minute impediment to the earl's schedule, so Griffin had slashed through the harness on his father's equipage with his belt knife. That set the earl's schedule back a full hour and earned Griffin the promise of another thrashing when Lord Devonwood returned in a sennight.

"I don't dare do it now," the earl had said through clenched teeth. "I'm too furious with you to trust myself to stop once I start."

Griffin didn't care. He'd welcome the beating if it meant his father would return. The only thing that mattered was undoing the future he'd *Seen.*

"Please let it have been enough time," he whispered as the future roared toward him with the horseman galloping toward his home.

Griffin dug his heels into his horse's flanks and charged back down the hill to meet the rider. Once he clattered over the drawbridge, under the portcullis, and into the bailey, he saw his mother had come out to greet the horseman. Baby Louisa was balanced on her hip and his brother Teddy clung to her skirts. *Maman* had never held with nannies or governesses for her little brood. It was yet another of her eccentricities that made Griffin wonder sometimes why his thoroughly conventional father had chosen her.

By the time Griffin reined in his horse and dismounted, the rider had begun his report.

"It was a deucedly freakish accident," the man said,

twisting his cap nervously. "The earl's carriage collided with the mail coach at a blind corner. I'm sorry as I can be to tell you this, milady. The driver and the footman will mend, but Lord Devonwood was trapped inside the equipage and we had the devil's own time getting him out. His lordship . . . died before a doctor could staunch the bleeding."

"But the mail coach should have gone much earlier." The words tasted of bile as they passed through Griffin's throat.

"It was delayed," the man said. "Had to replace a wheel just outside of Shiring-on-the-Green."

All the air rushed from Griffin's lungs. If he hadn't interfered . . . if he had let his father leave at the time he'd intended . . . His vision tunneled until he forced himself to inhale. The welts on his back from his thrashing stung afresh.

Tears streamed down his mother's face. When she wobbled a bit, he wrapped his arms around her to keep her upright. Since their mother was crying, little Teddy began to howl and baby Louisa offered sympathetic whimpers.

In that surreal moment, Griffin noticed suddenly how short his mother had become. The crown of her head fit neatly under his chin.

"What would ye have me do now, Master Grif—I mean, Lord Devonwood?" The rider gave his forelock a respectful tug.

Lord Devonwood. He was the earl now. The full weight of the estate and all its retainers settled onto his fourteen-year-old shoulders. Between one breath and the next, Griffin's boyhood slipped away forever.

"Ride to Shiring-on-the-Green and make arrangements to return my father's body for burial," he said, grateful his voice had not chosen that moment to break in an adolescent squeak. A pinprick of a headache began to form behind his right eye. It happened sometimes when he'd had a vision. This was the first time the onset of the migraine was so delayed. "Then call on our man of business in London and tell him to prepare an accounting of the estate within the week. There are things that require our attention."

He noticed he'd already adopted his father's habit of speaking of himself in the plural.

As he helped his mother back into the house, Mr. Abercrombie's lesson from last week haunted him. His tutor had told him that theologians and philosophers often debated whether the future is immutable.

"Does Fate or the stars or a benevolent God dictate the course of our lives?" Mr. Abercrombie asked. "Or do we pilot our own souls?"

Griffin had argued for free will, but it was a debate he would never join again.

After today, he knew the answer.

The future was fixed, whether by God or the devil or plain dumb luck. He'd tried scores of times to prevent the realization of his visions, but he'd never been able to change a single outcome.

Not once.

Fate even used his interference. It was like trying to stop the wind. Pitiless time only swept him along, no matter how he struggled against it.

He resolved not to try ever again.

CHAPTER 2

London, 1860

Lord Devonwood halted beside the hydrangea to take a longer look at the fetching young woman seated on the stone bench. *It's not every day a man finds a nymph in his garden before breakfast.*

His full given name was Griffin Titus Preston Nash, but no one had called him by anything but his title, or its diminutive "Devon" since his father had died. He'd even ceased to think of himself by any other name. However, the young woman in his garden was comely beyond the common. His blood quickened as if he were still young Griffin, as if he were not weighed down with the responsibilities of a vast estate and all the lives dependent upon him for every morsel in their mouths and each coin in their pockets.

Women usually preened like peahens when presented to Devon since he was judged to be eminently "eligible" by the matrons of the ton. This lady was preoccupied with a sketchbook and completely unaware of his presence. He could indulge in looking his fill at her unassuming beauty without concern over whether someone would take note, calculate his interest, and hope to capitalize on it.

A bachelor who wanted to remain in that happy state couldn't be too careful.

The lovely woman in his garden was an unexpected

windfall of distraction from the pounding in his temples. Devon almost blessed the grinding headache that had made him decide to take a turn in the fresh morning air before he sought his bed. He'd expected to be soothed by the scent of sweet lavender, the drowsy hum of bees in the St. John's Wort, and the patter of the fountain. The shaded alcoves of the garden behind his London town house eased his light-sensitive eyes. His quiet little Eden often relieved his suffering when he overused his "gift."

The alternative was turning to hard drink, which muddled his thinking, or opiates, which obliterated thought entirely. Devon was determined to resist those remedies as long as possible.

Fortune had been kind through the long night of gambling at his club. While he frequently lost money in the stock market, a deck of cards never lied to him. His gift of touch allowed him to make up shortfalls in the estate's balance sheet over a game of whist or poque.

Devon moved farther along the path and peered at the girl from behind the topiary. Instead of admiring the flora his gardener spent so much time pruning and fussing over, she focused on the statue of an inebriated Dionysus. Head bent, pointed pink tongue clamped between her teeth in concentration, she labored over her drawing.

Ever since it had been noised about that Queen Victoria was a dab hand at sketches and watercolors, every woman in England fancied herself an amateur artist.

But that still didn't explain the young lady's presence in his garden.

Devon moved around behind her, brushing past the roses to get a better angle from which to view her unobserved. A thorn nicked the back of his hand. He gave it a shake and brought it reflexively to his mouth to suck at the small wound while he eyed the supple line of the woman's spine. Her spreading skirts emphasized a narrow waist.

A single auburn curl had escaped her bonnet and trailed damply on her nape. Her tender skin appeared dewy and pink in the warm morning sun. He was surprised by the urge to plant a kiss on that spot, but tamped down the inclination at once.

Not that Devon was a monk. He was simply careful not to involve himself with the sort of woman who looked as if she might require a trip to the parson should a man take liberties. With her buttoned-down collar and crisply starched sleeves, this woman seemed that sort, even though the tight bodice displayed a full bosom.

But what man didn't prefer taking liberties when he could?

He moved closer so he could peer over her shoulder to see her artwork. She'd neatly captured Dionysus in every detail, even down to the arc of water spewing from the god's flaccid member into the basin of the stone fountain. Judging from the accurate rendering on the page, the lady possessed more than passing talent with a pencil.

And more than adequate understanding of male anatomy.

"You're blocking my light," she said without looking up.

Devon stepped aside so his shadow wouldn't continue to darken her page. He was treated to a clear view of her delicate profile. The slight upturn of her nose pleased him. It meant that while she was spectacularly pretty, she wasn't perfect.

Perfection was boring. And often demanding.

"The sketch doesn't seem to have suffered for my intrusion," he said. "You have an excellent drafting hand, if I may say so."

"You may." Her lips curved upward in a satisfied, feline smile over his compliment. "No harm done. I'm nearly finished as it is."

No harm done? Did she expect an apology when she

was the one trespassing in *his* garden? Her flat accent and brazen self-possession betrayed her as a Yank.

"American, are you?"

She flicked her gaze at him and rolled her large brown eyes at his grasp of the obvious. "Born and bred."

An Englishwoman would require a formal introduction before starting a conversation with a total stranger. Yanks were incredibly lax about that sort of thing. Devon settled beside her on the bench. It was his garden, after all, and his head still throbbed in time with the blood pounding through it. He ought not to stand on ceremony, especially when the lady didn't seem to mind informality.

"It's not only the accent that gives you away, you know."

"Really?" Her attention was riveted back to the page, where she added some crosshatched shading to the god's musculature. "What else makes you assume I'm an American?"

English women of his acquaintance tended to have more angular features, even bordering on coltish. The apples of this lady's cheeks were sweetly rounded, and she had that snub-nosed pertness so often found in those from across the Atlantic. With wide-set eyes, full lips, and a delicate chin, hers was a thoroughly charming, almost pixyish face, but he decided it wouldn't be politic for him to say so.

Women were unpredictable when it came to masculine opinions on their appearance. Honestly, why would his sister ask if a particular pattern in the fabric of a frock made her look plump unless she wanted an honest answer?

Devon decided to settle for something safer.

"Your choice of subject declares your nationality, for one thing. An English miss would sketch the tea roses, not a nude statue," Devon explained as he studied her work. If the image was any guide, her knowledge of the male species was detailed and unflinchingly accurate. Perhaps he'd misjudged her on the basis of her severe wardrobe. This American miss might be entirely open to his taking a few liberties.

She fixed him with a direct gaze, her widening pupils darkening her eyes to the color of rich coffee. The effect was hypnotic.

A man might lose his way in those Stygian depths.

"Choosing to draw flowers instead of this magnificent statue speaks volumes about the insipid nature of the English miss," she said with conviction.

Devon stifled a chuckle. Even though he agreed with her assessment, someone had to stand up for English womanhood. "And yet tea roses are highly regarded on this little isle."

"No doubt, but lovely as it may be, a tea rose does nothing to engage the emotions, has no intensity of feeling. There's simply no potential for the drama necessary to true art."

"No? Suppose the flowers were presented to a lady who refused them and tossed them onto the garden path," he suggested, not that he put much stock in anything as ephemeral as a feeling. "Wouldn't that mean someone's emotions were engaged?"

"Point taken, but mere flora still can't compare to the seething possibilities in that statue. I mean, just look at him." She waved a slim hand toward Dionysus. An ink smudge and a slight callus marked the longest finger of her right hand. Evidently she was as well acquainted with a writing pen as a drawing pencil. "Dionysus is a study in contrasts, sublime and corrupt, physically strong and morally weak."

Not to mention that he was completely naked. "His state of undress doesn't distress you?"

"I wouldn't dream of fitting him with a fig leaf," she said

without a trace of heightened color in her cheeks. "The beauties of the human form are not the least prurient."

Devon smiled. A woman who wasn't silly enough to be undone by the sight of a naked man. He'd lay odds she didn't feel the need to call a piano leg a "limb" either. She was a refreshing oddity. "Ah, but this Dionysus fellow isn't meant to be human, you know."

"No, but the Olympians were simply humanity writ large," she said, swiping at the deep auburn curl that had escaped her bonnet and fallen across her forehead. A few strands glinted copper amid the darker tresses. "Unless I'm mistaken, this statue is a replica of an ancient one, circa first century, judging from the attention to realism. It would be sacrilege to alter it. If the ancients had no compunction about portraying their deity in such a state, who are we to demur?"

A replica? Devon had paid the earth for the damned thing. The gong of pain sounding in his head grew louder. "What makes you think it's not an original?"

She slanted a look at him. "The marble has been distressed to give the appearance of extreme age, but I'll warrant it's not more than two or three hundred years old. Don't be dismayed. It's an excellent copy. Quite subtle. No doubt it would fool most."

It had fooled him. "So you're an expert in ancient art?"

"Hardly, but I know one who is," she said crisply, drawing her spine straight and lifting her chin. "My father is Dr. Montague Farnsworth, one of the world's foremost Egyptologists, though his knowledge of Roman and Greek cultures is extensive as well. If I know something about those subjects, it is because I have the honor of assisting him in his work."

Devon had never heard of Dr. Farnsworth, but then, his interests didn't lie in antiquities. He'd bought the statue to satisfy his mother's whim to have a classically themed garden. The countess had hoped for something like Lady Hepplewhite's collection of marble dryads.

"A veritable Grecian urn sprung to life," she'd claimed about Lady Hepplewhite's garden statuary.

Privately, Devon suspected his mother had never closely inspected an ancient urn. They were frequently peopled with figures engaged in extremely earthy endeavors, the sort the Countess of Devonwood would be certain to frown upon should any of them be reenacted in *her* garden.

He massaged his right temple in a gesture he hoped appeared thoughtful. Devon tried to hide his pain as much as possible. "So help me understand. You're a visiting antiquarian who's invaded this garden for the sake of sketching its art?"

"Nonsense. I'm merely drawing to pass the time. I'm here to meet Lord Devonwood," she said. "But apparently his lordship has been larking about London all night and hasn't found his bed yet."

After his night of gaming, Devon's pockets were lined with banknotes and IOUs. So long as he played only with those who could well afford to make good on their vowels, he suffered no pangs of conscience over the advantage his special ability gave him.

It was rarely such a benevolent gift. He reckoned the skull-splitter he experienced now more than paid for the privilege of using it.

"Out all night, eh? Larking about London?" He arched a brow at her, trying not to wince at the additional pain that slight movement caused him. "You make Lord Devonwood sound a perfect scoundrel."

"My thoughts precisely," she said with a conspiratorial grin.

"But there's probably good reason for an earl to be

abroad all night," he said, feeling he ought to defend himself, though for the life of him, he didn't know why. This girl, though very attractive, was nothing to him. "You may regret your first impression of him."

"Regret is a waste of time," she said with certainty. "First impressions are generally correct. If Lord Devonwood insists on *behaving* like a perfect scoundrel, it's more than likely that's what he *is*."

He longed to plant his lips on the dimple that marked her cheek. Then he'd show her just how a perfect scoundrel steals a real kiss. Merely thinking about it eased the ache in his head as blood rushed to another part of his body altogether.

"Tell me. Why are you here to see Lord Devonwood?"

"I'm not in the habit of discussing my personal business with strangers, but if you must know . . ." She chose that moment to flip to a fresh page in her sketchbook and accidently dropped her pencil.

In hindsight, Devon would come to realize he never should have bent to retrieve it, but his mother had tried to raise a gentleman. If the countess failed in some areas of her son's upbringing, she succeeded soundly in others. As soon as his fingers closed over the wood, the world around Devon faded to muted colors and a vision poured into him, more real than his next heartbeat.

Her breath streamed across his lips, warming as a sip of brandy. She tipped her chin up to meet his gaze, her dark eyes wide.

Devon didn't wait for another invitation. His mouth covered hers, slanting to create a firm seal. Her uniquely feminine scent tickled his nostrils. Sweet and ripe, like a peach in the sun.

He kept his eyes open as he kissed her, but hers fluttered closed. Dark lashes trembled in feathery crescents on her cheeks.

She made a small noise into his mouth, a needy sound that went straight to his groin. He pulled her flush against his body, wishing her boned corset would allow him to feel her breasts yield to the solid expanse of his chest.

The mere thought of those soft mounds roused him to aching hardness.

Hunger roared inside him, every fiber of his body vibrant with straining life. He deepened the kiss, sweeping in to explore the hot, moist cavern of her mouth. He made rough love to her with his tongue, thrusting and teasing.

She answered his invasion with her own, nipping and suckling his bottom lip, her kiss urgent and needy. She arched into him, pressing herself against his hardness.

His hands found the buttons on her bodice . . .

The pencil slipped from his fingers and the connection with his gift shattered. The vision evaporated like morning mist as his headache resumed its persistent throb. Miss Farnsworth's face came into sharp focus.

"Well, it appears neither of us can keep hold of this pencil," she said as she bent to pluck it from the clipped grass.

He reached for it as well, half-hoping for another few seconds of his vision, but he caught her hand instead. Her skin was warm and smooth and his headache suddenly lifted. The pain wasn't masked or dulled. It was completely eradicated. He held her fingers for a fraction longer than necessary, reveling in the unexpected sensation of normalcy.

"If you don't mind . . ." She gently tugged her hand away and the relentless ache slammed back into him.

The vision itself had been a welcome one for a change. He'd have liked to let the pleasant interlude spool out to its sweet conclusion.

One thing was certain though. Sometime within the next twelve hours, the farthest edge of his foreknowledge, he and Miss Farnsworth were destined to become better acquainted.

Much better acquainted.

Lord, she was sweet. Soft and pliant and responsive. The vision left him crowding his trousers.

"Why are you looking at me like that?" she asked, cocking her head at him, a hint of panic in her taut features.

He was saved from a reply when a voice called from behind him.

"Oh, there you are, Devon."

When he turned, he was surprised to see his younger brother, Theodore, coming toward him. Always the sartorial peacock, Teddy was well turned out for mid-morning. His natty hat was rakishly askew and the boots that crunched along the garden path were spit-shined to a high gloss. An older gentleman in a tweed jacket trailed in his wake. Devon rose and strode forward to meet his brother, hand extended in welcome.

"You weren't due home for another week, Ted. If you'd sent a wire, I'd have met you at the pier."

"Plans change, brother. And I'll confess to being too preoccupied to send word."

Theodore's handsome face was thinner than it had been when Devon had seen him last, but his skin was so deeply tanned, his smile was blinding. Ted's half-year tour of the major cities ringing the Mediterranean had obviously agreed with him. He pumped Devon's hand while peering around him to smile at the woman. She had risen from the bench and approached them with graceful steps.

"I say, old chap," his brother said, "you're not trying to steal my girl, are you?"

"What? No." *His girl?* Devon's gut churned furiously. "What do you mean?"

Teddy pushed past him, put his arm around Miss Farnsworth's waist, and cinched her close. "Emmaline, I'd like you to meet my curmudgeon of a big brother, Lord High and Mighty, the Earl of Devonwood. Call him Devon, if you like. We all do."

Then Teddy turned to him with a triumphant grin. "All our lives, you've been first, brother. First to ride a pony, first to go away to school, first at everything. But I always intended to be first at something. Devon, may I present to you Miss Emmaline Farnsworth?" The gaze Teddy cast toward her was filled with such adoration, it bordered on idolatry. "My fiancée."

CHAPTER 3

Devon's smile felt so brittle, he feared his face might crack.

"Theodore, please," Miss Farnsworth said, neatly extricating herself from his embrace. She hadn't blushed a bit over the naked statue, but now her face flushed crimson over Teddy's public declaration of affection.

"Oh, all right, she hasn't exactly said yes yet," Teddy admitted with a laugh. "But she's promised to consider my suit. It's only a matter of time before she succumbs to the Nash charm, and she knows it."

Less than twelve hours to be precise, but she'll be succumbing to the wrong Nash.

Devon made a bow over Miss Farnsworth's hand and tried to murmur an appropriate greeting. He must have managed something because over the roaring in his ears, he heard the low rumble of conversation continuing around him. All Devon could think was that as sure as his heart kept beating, his brother's soon-to-be fiancée was going to be sighing in someone else's arms before midnight.

His arms.

Teddy beamed at them both.

Devon felt like excrement on the bottom of a pig-farmer's boot. He was destined to kiss Miss Farnsworth thoroughly and there was no stopping it. Then he remembered that in his vision, the lady had definitely kissed him back.

His teeth clenched. What sort of woman would toy with his brother's affections by kissing someone else?

"And this, of course, is Emmaline's father, Dr. Montague Farnsworth," his brother was saying.

"Delighted, milord." The man doffed his bowler, revealing a thinning head of iron-gray hair. He peered over the tops of his half-rimmed glasses and gave Devon's hand the limp shake of an academician. "Forgive my lack of specific knowledge about the English system. I believe Devonwood is among the older peerages, is it not?"

"My brother is the fifteenth earl of the name," Teddy said. "So yes, it's rather older than dirt."

"Though not so ancient as the Egyptian dynasties I have the honor to study, milord."

The man puffed himself up like a sparrow fluffing his feathers against a breeze. Now that Devon considered it, Dr. Farnsworth really did put him in mind of a drab little bird. His gaze flicked to Emmaline.

How had this unremarkable fellow sired such a lovely creature?

"Theodore Wainwright Nash," a fluty feminine voice called from the French doors leading out to the garden. "What do you mean by coming home and running out to bedevil your brother without greeting your *maman* first?"

Their mother might only have been a countess, but she waited with empress-like dignity for her younger son to hurry to her side and offer a kiss to her expertly rouged cheek. Then Lady Devonwood swanned across the garden, clearly taking Miss Farnsworth's measure as she processed toward her.

"Welcome, my dear." As she kissed the air beside each of Emmaline's cheeks, Miss Farnsworth's face drained of all color. After the deep blush, she turned so pale, Devon wondered if the lady might swoon to the ground before her next breath, but she managed to stay upright. "So out of all the women in the world, this is the girl my son has chosen to be his bride."

The girl in question teased out a weak smile. She'd been so forthright, so quick to speak her mind with Devon before she knew who he was. The sudden change in her demeanor surprised him. It was as if she was a Drury Lane actress and had slipped into the role of shy ingénue.

"My lady," Miss Farnsworth murmured as she dropped a shallow curtsey.

"Unassuming as she is lovely," his mother said.

Teddy tossed Emmaline a roguish wink. "Unfortunately, I have to point out that she has yet to choose me back."

"But of course, she will, dearest, if that's what you want." The countess patted Teddy's cheek, then fixed Miss Farnsworth with a steely gaze. "What young lady in her right mind would refuse you?"

Miss Farnsworth's mouth twitched, but she refrained from saying anything.

Probably a wise course, Devon decided. He was the only one who could ever disagree with his mother with any hope of prevailing.

"I say, *Maman,* how did you hear about our . . . attachment, for want of a better word?" Theodore asked as he sidled up to Miss Farnsworth again, edging her father aside. "I only just now told Devon."

"You should know better than to ask that, Teddy. In a great house like this, the servants know everything. Baxter announced that you were home and informed me of your *tendresse* for the young lady in almost the same breath. I swear sometimes I think that man can read our minds." Lady Devonwood clasped her hands together and directed her attention to the Farnsworths. "But where are my manners? I'm certain our guests must be exhausted from their journey. Baxter!"

The ubiquitous butler appeared in the doorway almost immediately, a sure sign he'd been hovering just beyond the threshold. He didn't show the least sign of chagrin at having been caught eavesdropping on the family he served, but it certainly put paid to the countess's belief that he possessed the ability to divine anyone's thoughts.

Baxter kept informed the old-fashioned way. He was a world-class snoop. Devon usually didn't mind it, but now he wondered if the butler had spied Miss Farnsworth and him in conversation earlier. Baxter formed his own opinions about people, but never expressed them unless asked.

"Show Dr. Farnsworth and his charming daughter to the Blue Suite." His mother bared her bright teeth at their guests. Devon wondered if only he realized it was a cat's smile, meant to lull an unsuspecting mouse into complaisance before the kill. The countess might behave with outward decorum and welcome, but she was protective as a lioness when it came to her children. Devon was sure she was displeased over Teddy's choice.

"Devonwood House is at your disposal. Do let us know if there's anything you require." Lady Devonwood waggled her fingers at the Farnsworths in a gesture of dismissal. "If you'd be so kind as to follow Baxter . . ."

Dr. Farnsworth lingered over the countess's gloved hand as he expressed florid thanks for her hospitality. Finally, he allowed his daughter to take his arm and escort him toward the French doors. Miss Farnsworth tossed Teddy a quick smile over her shoulder before disappearing into the cool interior of the town house.

"Thank you for being so decent about putting them up. They don't know a soul in the city, and I wouldn't hear of their going to Claridges when we've plenty of room here,"

Theodore said once Emmaline and her father were out of earshot. "I know the engagement is a bit of a surprise, but you were gracious as always, *Maman*."

"You have presented us with a *fait accompli,* have you not?" their mother said. "What else could we do but welcome the girl and her father into our home?"

"I can think of any number of things," Devon said testily. "All right, Ted. What's this betrothal business all about?"

"Love, brother. It's about love."

"Don't be maudlin. The chit obviously has you dancing to her tune."

"Hmm, I wonder," the countess said as she settled onto the bench Miss Farnsworth had lately vacated. She cast a gimlet eye toward the stone Dionysus, shuddered in distaste, and turned back to her sons. "Refusing to accept his suit is an odd way of leading a man about."

Devon suppressed the urge to swear. Since he was voicing opposition, their mother was free to indulge the fantasy that she wasn't aghast at the thought of Theodore marrying a penniless nobody of a girl. Scholars like Dr. Farnsworth might be well respected, but they rarely had any money beyond parsimonious university stipends.

"On the contrary, it's the best way to snare a fellow. A "no" is like a red flag waved before a bull. Now Teddy is more determined than ever to have her." He rounded on his brother. "What do you know of her really?"

"That's enough, Devon. Honestly, Theodore is old enough to make his own choices without our prying into his privacy," their mother said sweetly. "Tell me, Teddy, how did you two lovebirds meet?"

Devon ground his teeth together. Evidently it wasn't prying if the question was asked with a meek tone and a tilt of the head.

"On shipboard, of course, between Alexandria and

Rome, so I'll admit the setting might have sped the romance along." Theodore sat beside their mother and took one of her hands. "Emmaline's father was giving a series of lectures, having lately come from a dig in the Valley of the Kings. Fascinating stuff. He found this little statue that—"

"Stop trying to change the subject," Devon said. The vision of kissing Miss Farnsworth was still so fresh in his mind, it was as if the event had already happened. "You've never made a secret of the fact that you want to marry up, Ted. Are you willing to overlook the fact that she's not only a commoner, but an American as well?"

"Whichever irks you the most holds the greatest attraction for me, brother," Teddy said with a wicked grin. "A man's opinions on such matters can change, can't they? Are you listening to yourself? You sound like the prigs you used to make fun of. Besides, I'm not the earl here. It's not as if I have to make a grand match for the good of the house and all. That's your dubious honor." Then Theodore's smile faded and was replaced with a look of genuine concern. "What's gotten into you?"

Miss Farnsworth's tongue in less than a dozen hours, Devon thought with vehemence, cramming his fists deep into his pockets.

He'd given up trying to warn others of the events his visions showed him. No one wanted a Cassandra moping about, God knew. But if he used his authority as head of the household to forbid Ted's relationship with this woman, it would only fuel his brother's determination to pursue her.

The countess patted Theodore's hand. "Not to put too fine a point on it, but Devon is making sense. I know travel is said to be broadening, but have you considered that your sensibilities might have become rather too broad, dear?"

His brother's lips tightened into a hard line.

"You could have your choice of women here in England, Teddy," she continued. "Lord Whitmore's youngest daughter has just come out. Surely you remember Lady Cressida."

"I don't want Lord Whitmore's daughter."

"Why ever not?" the countess asked, her tone still bland as porridge, as if she weren't afraid her younger son was about to make a terrible mistake for which there was no remedy that wouldn't result in scandal. "I hear Lady Cressida has grown quite lovely, and she's been hailed a very pattern sort of girl by one and all."

Calling a debutante "pattern" was their mother's finest compliment. It meant the young lady in question followed accepted protocol to the letter and never put so much as a kid-soled toe out of line.

Theodore gave their mother an exasperated kiss on the cheek, murmured something about catching up with his friends at White's, and made good his escape.

The countess sighed. Devon felt the weight of her displeasure settling on his shoulders. Since his father's death, she'd leaned heavily on him for everything. She never scolded. She had no need. One sigh was enough to curdle his guilt-ridden soul.

"I'll see about it, Mother," he said.

She smiled brightly at him. "Oh, I know you will, dear. Just as you always do."

Devon took care of everything, and in a way that kept her from knowing the burdens he bore. Thanks to his winnings from last night, the estate was solvent again, but that could change in a heartbeat.

The countess was old-fashioned enough to abhor trade, but the truth of the matter was the revenue from the estate's lands was barely enough to cover upkeep and improvements. It certainly didn't generate enough to keep his mother in the style to which she was accustomed.

Theodore wouldn't have been able to traipse about the Mediterranean for half a year on the estate's rents and their younger sister, Louisa, would have no dowry to speak of.

If Devon didn't invest, sometimes speculatively, their coffers would be bare indeed. His latest debacle was half interest in a merchant ship called the *Rebecca Goodspeed*. Unfortunately, she hadn't been heard from since she'd tangled with a storm off the Cape of Good Hope. So Devon was forced to scramble to cover the shortfall. He'd never been able to summon his gift for a peek into the future of a stock or commodity, but fortunately, cards were another matter.

Being lucky at cards was a gentlemanly virtue none could question unless they wished to meet him on a field of honor. Since Devon never palmed a card and was known to be a dead shot, it was highly doubtful such a challenge would ever come.

"Are you all right, dear?" his mother asked. "You're looking a bit pale."

He forced a smile. "I'm fine," he lied. "I just need a little sleep."

"I shouldn't wonder with the hours you keep." She made a small tsking sound, then changed the subject with her typical quicksilver style. "You know, a thought just occurred to me. Perhaps our misgivings about Miss Farnsworth are misplaced. The girl might have Teddy's best interests at heart, after all. She may have refused him because she recognizes the difference in their stations and fears they could never be truly happy because of it."

"Perhaps," Devon said, but he doubted it.

Then his mother switched opinions as she always did. She seemed incapable of settling firmly on one side of any issue. "But perhaps it doesn't signify that she is a nobody. Remember your great-grandfather married down and was deliriously happy as a result."

How could Devon forget? The woman his great-grandfather married had come from an untitled branch of the Preston family. Along with her common blood, his great-grandmother Delphinia Preston introduced the blasted gift of touch into his family's lineage.

"Maybe once we become better acquainted with Miss Farnsworth, we'll come to esteem her as Teddy has. Only . . ." She let the word hang suspended in time for a few heartbeats, signaling yet another shift in the wind. "I do wish he'd make a more conventional choice."

A "pattern" girl, in other words. Overhead, someone shoved back the heavy curtains and cranked open the multi-paned window in the Blue Suite.

Baxter would quietly have a fit. The butler was slavishly devoted to seeing that sunlight didn't damage the colors in the vibrant Turkish carpet.

Devon raised a hand to shade his eyes and looked up at the open window that framed Miss Farnsworth.

The town house was situated on a small rise. When Miss Farnsworth leaned on the sill and looked out over the brick jungle of London's chimneys and roof terraces, she could probably see all the way to St. Paul's gigantic dome. She untied the bow beneath her chin and removed her bonnet, letting it dangle by the laces as she surveyed the city.

Emmaline tipped her face to the sun's rays and her hair glistened with several shades of copper, gold, and amber. A smile of unabashed pleasure lit her features.

She was trouble, at the least. Discord, certainly. Scandal, possibly. Whatever else Emmaline Farnsworth was, "pattern" was definitely not it.

Lord Devonwood's home was designed to impress. As Baxter had led Emmaline and her father up the awe-inspiring sweep of the grand staircase, she had noted Ming vases and classically themed statuary tucked into its frequent alcoves. After the ostentatious art and the oppressive stares from the familial portraits glaring down at them on each of the landings, the Blue Suite was a welcome breath of understated elegance.

Two sumptuous bedchambers opened into a common sitting room. The walls were swathed with ornately flocked wallpaper in a shade of soothing gray, accented with bright lapis tones. The hardwood underfoot was softened by a magnificent Asiatic carpet featuring a fight between a stylized pair of mythical phoenixes, awash in blue flames.

"Oh, please don't turn up the gas lamps during the day," Emmaline said as she turned away from the panoramic view out the window. "I much prefer natural light."

"As you wish, miss," the butler replied with a purse-lipped nod. "One has taken the liberty of having your trunks delivered to each of your chambers. If you require assistance unpacking, please ring for a chambermaid or valet. The countess has ordered that servants from the house be assigned to you for the duration of your visit."

"That's most kind of her ladyship since we were unable to bring our own servants on this particular journey," Farnsworth said.

Emmaline suppressed a smirk. *Our own servants, indeed.*

"If you wish, you may join the family for luncheon at half past one in the dining room, or if you prefer, a tray will be sent up. Dinner is served at eight o'clock sharp," Baxter said frostily. "Formal dress is expected."

Emmaline had the distinct impression they'd been weighed in the butler's balance and been found wanting, but there was no fault in his behavior toward them. Just a definite chill in his demeanor. She supposed the staff at Devonwood House might well resent an upstart commoner, and an American to boot, for snaring the interest of their young master.

As soon as the butler gave them a final bow and closed the door behind himself, Farnsworth plopped into one of the heavy Tudor chairs arranged before the fireplace. A chess set squatted on the lacquered table between them.

"Well, the butler may have a broomstick up his bum, but this place simply reeks of old money," he said. "We've fallen on our feet this time and no mistake, Emma, my girl."

"Hush, Monty," she hissed as she perched on the chair opposite him. She glanced up at the portrait of a severe-looking matron hung from the picture rail above the mantel. She'd heard tell of peepholes being cut into the eyes of such paintings but these steely orbs seemed to be merely oil on canvas. "Didn't you hear what the countess said? The help knows everything in this house."

He chuckled. "In that case, you'd better call me 'father' even here in the privacy of our suite."

Emmaline snorted and picked up the black queen. The chess set was fashioned of onyx and ivory, fitted with what appeared to be small emeralds for eyes. The worth of a set like this one would keep the wolf from their door for several months. Not that she'd stoop to petty thievery.

Not yet. She replaced the queen.

"Very well, *Father.*"

She didn't share a drop of blood with Montague Farnsworth, but he'd been more a father to her than the unknown man who'd sired her. Emmaline had only a shadowy memory of her mother, a sad, thin woman with large brown eyes and what had seemed like a perpetually trembling lower lip. But she remembered with crystalline clarity the day Montague Farnsworth had claimed her at the foundlings' home.

"That one," he'd said to the head matron. "The one with the enormous eyes. She'd make someone a good daughter."

With a few strokes of a pen, she went from being plain Emma Potts, orphan, to Emmaline Farnsworth, a girl with a father and a home. He never told her why he'd chosen her or why a confirmed bachelor would bother to make room in his life for a small child, but Monty had raised her and educated her far beyond the lot of most girls. A little knowledge whetted her appetite for more. Once he taught her to read, Emmaline had devoured every book she could find.

Of course, when she grew older, Monty also trained her to use her nimble fingers to assist him in his confidence games. She became his shill for countless *pig-in-a-pokes* and *pigeon drops*. At first, the games were fun. Now, after being on the run for years, she wished they could turn to something more legitimate for their livelihood. She owed Monty so much, she rarely quarreled with him, but she felt compelled to this time.

"I don't like this job," she continued in a low tone. "It's getting out of hand. Why on earth did you give Theodore Nash permission to ask for my hand?"

"If I'd said no, the jig would've been up. He'd have gotten clean away. As it is, we're here in this lovely house. We don't have to bluff our way into a fine hotel for the duration of the job. Or sneak out when the proprietor becomes too insistent about us paying the bill. This way, we'll be able to observe the mark at close range and spring the trap when the time is right." Monty rubbed his hands together. "This is the big one. I can feel it."

Emmaline squeezed her eyes shut. Monty had been proclaiming each of his schemes the "big one" for years. So far, all they had to show for his nefarious plans were arrest warrants in several countries.

When she was younger, they'd lived a relatively quiet life in New York where Monty ran a rare book shop. On the side, he forged letters by Benjamin Franklin and

George Washington to supplement their income. But the market for old documents could bear only so many fakes before his forgery was discovered and they were forced to flee across the Atlantic.

After that, Monty made use of Emmaline's artistic talents and together they hawked sham religious relics in elaborately painted reliquaries on the Continent. If all the purported pieces of the True Cross that had passed through Monty's hands were gathered in one place, Emmaline suspected there'd be enough lumber to build a small fort.

Now ancient Egypt captured everyone's imagination and Monty stood poised to make the most of it. He had a prodigious memory, a professorial carriage, and a glib tongue. Given enough time to prepare, he could pass as an expert on any esoteric topic he chose.

"I still don't like it. Theodore seems to genuinely care for me." Emmaline crossed her arms over her chest. "It's one thing to bilk someone of his savings. A mark can only be conned if he is greedy in the first place and a man can always make more money. It's quite another thing to break someone's heart."

"Then I'll rely on you to be clever enough not to destroy the lad utterly," Monty said, surveying the room's adornments with a slightly predatory gaze. "But you must admit he didn't exaggerate his family's wealth. Young Mr. Nash has certainly got the chinks."

"No, his brother has the chinks," Emmaline corrected. "Everything Theodore has is at the earl's sufferance."

"Well, then maybe you've snagged the romantic attentions of the wrong brother."

Emmaline laughed. "I think not."

The earl had certainly seemed attracted to her in the garden before Theodore had claimed her. She'd enjoyed their verbal sparring match. With his dark good looks,

Lord Devonwood was more than easy on the eyes, but his unusual silver-gray gaze held a feral gleam at times.

She'd never been so discomfited by a man. Never been plagued with such a strange yearning as when he had held her hand for a moment. It was as though her body knew more about him than she did, and liked what it knew very much indeed. She strove not to show how he twisted her knickers, but she'd never had such a visceral reaction to any man before.

She was no pudding-headed romantic. She didn't believe in love, let alone love at first sight. As she'd grown older, Monty had encouraged her to use her attractiveness to help him manipulate the men they intended to defraud. Experience told her Lord Devonwood would be far less biddable than his younger brother, less controllable.

And far more exciting, she admitted to herself.

Theodore was rather like an overgrown puppy, affectionate but clumsy, and easily brought to heel.

Lord Devonwood was more a wolf, powerful and unpredictable. She suspected he was possessed of a savage streak if he were crossed. There had been a moment in the garden when he'd looked as if he wanted to eat her up.

Part of her suspected she might enjoy it if he did.

"Nevertheless," Monty was saying, "when the time comes to make the pitch, we ought to include Lord Devonwood in the game now that we know he holds the purse. He's the type who'll be more likely to hand over the blunt if he believes the investment is his idea rather than his younger brother's."

Emmaline nodded. Monty might chase after some wild hares from time to time, but his instincts about people were always on the nose.

He started to say something else, but was interrupted when a ragged cough wracked his frame. Monty covered his mouth with a handkerchief as the spasms continued.

Emmaline leaped up and scurried into her bedchamber to the washbasin, where she poured a glass of water for him from the ewer. When she returned, his coughing fit was winding down to shuddering heaves. He shoved his handkerchief back into his vest pocket, but not before she noticed speckles of blood on the white linen.

"Here you are, dear," she said softly as she held the glass for him to sip.

After taking a little water, he leaned back in the chair and closed his eyes.

Determination stiffened her spine. Somehow, Emmaline had to make this scheme work. He tried to hide it, but the cough was growing worse. Monty's health deteriorated almost daily.

Neither of them had ever said the word *consumption* aloud, but it didn't matter. They both were thinking it loudly enough for the hissing sibilance of the hateful disease to swirl around the room.

There was a doctor in Germany who was said to be doing amazing things for consumptives. Emma and Monty needed one last big score in order to make it possible for him to retire to that alpine sanatorium, where he might regain his health and prolong his life.

"You know, you'd make someone a wonderful daughter," Monty said as he patted her hand. The words were a tender little game they played, a reminder of his first meeting with her.

She dropped a quick kiss on his brow and fought to keep her voice from quaking with worry for him as she gave the expected answer. "And you'd make someone a good father."

CHAPTER 4

Emmaline suggested Monty take a tray in their suite for luncheon and then lie down for the rest of afternoon. She was concerned when he agreed without argument. It meant he was feeling even more poorly than she feared.

"But you'll lay the groundwork for me this afternoon if you get a chance, won't you?" he asked as she tucked the coverlet under his chin.

"Of course, I will," she assured him. An essential part of any confidence scheme was dropping subtle hints about the supposed opportunity in a way that didn't seem forced. Baiting the trap was more art than science. Emmaline had a knack for it. "I think Theodore is still off with his friends though, so it may not be possible for me to start the game."

"Not him," Monty said as his eyes closed and his chest rose and fell in a regular wheezing rhythm. "The earl. Unless he, too, is resting in the arms of Morpheus."

Her belly fizzed at the thought of the earl. "We'll see."

His lordship was probably catching up on missed sleep since he hadn't found his bed last night. Of course, that didn't mean Lord Devonwood hadn't found someone else's bed. The upper crust might be high-minded about some things, but if the members of the gentry she'd met while traveling about Europe were any guide, they were as low in their personal morals as any commoner might be.

Emma closed the door to their suite with a soft snick of the latch and made her way down the grand staircase to explore Devonwood House. She took her time, pausing before each of the portraits. She studied the faces, tracing Theodore's sandy hair through several of his progenitors, but the dominant coloring, at least in more recent paintings, seemed to be Lord Devonwood's darker hair paired with his unusual gray eyes.

She also noted the recurrence of an emerald necklace draped on the necks of several different Devonwood women, passed from mother to daughter. A portrait of the present countess boasted a long strand of beautifully matched pearls with a ruby pendant big enough to choke a horse.

Family jewels. Probably under lock and key beneath this very roof.

Emma had never stolen jewelry and suspected fencing it would be far more trouble than tricking a mark out of banknotes. But when she thought of Monty's distressed breathing after that coughing fit, she knew she was capable of attempting a burglary for his sake if necessary.

She hoped he was right about this caper being the big one. She was so tired of living out of traveling trunks and always being ready to leave in a hurry should one of their victims realize he'd been duped sooner than expected. With each turn of the seasons, Monty's face bore new lines, even aside from his growing illness. Their vagabond life had imprinted the road map of their travels on his features.

She supposed it was to be expected. He was approaching his seventieth year. Long past the time when he ought to have a regular hearth, complete with slippers and pipe, instead of their gypsy existence.

It was wearing on her soul as well. As she wandered Lord Devonwood's elegant rooms, she wondered what it must be like to have servants to shine one's shoes and mend one's socks; only to ring a bellpull to have a tray of food magically appear.

More than that, the luxury of permanence called to her. Since they'd begun traveling, she despaired of ever being able to put down roots again. To know where she'd sleep each night would be such a gift. To make a genuine friend rather than regarding every chance acquaintance as a potential mark, a blessing beyond compare.

To have a husband and children of her own.

If she accepted Theodore's suit, would she finally be able to have a proper home?

She doubted it.

Even though the countess had been kind, Emma had detected a hesitation behind her smile. And why not? The aristocracy did not suffer an invasion of the rabble gladly. There was every chance Teddy's family would cut him off if he married her. It wouldn't improve Monty's situation one jot if they suddenly had to provide a living for Theodore as well.

She wound through the dining room and a sitting room, then through a long hall tiled in deep blue squares in the style of Arabia. A fountain burbled in a sweet-smelling orangery. She peeked into a stiffly formal parlor designed for receiving callers. The rooms were all beautifully appointed in delicate French style. Genuine *objets d'art* were tastefully and sparingly displayed instead of crowding every horizontal space with endless bric-a-brac.

But all the rooms' curtains were drawn.

If she were prone to flights of fancy, she'd imagine one of Polidori's *vampyres* lurked in Devonwood House, slinking through the shadows away from direct sunlight. But when she opened the final door on the ground floor, she forgot all about *vampyres*. The chamber beyond made her breath catch.

It was a library to rival any she'd ever seen, even though it was dimly lit. As with the rest of the house, someone had drawn the shutters and set the gas sconces to flicker at their lowest level. Shelves of books stretched from the floor to the ceiling soaring twenty feet above. A wrought iron catwalk circled the room at half that height, accessible only by a small spiral staircase in one corner.

The ceiling had been painted in the rococo style, every square inch decorated with flowers and nymphs and dryads. An oval in the center was dedicated to a fresco of Cupid waking Psyche from her charmed slumber with a kiss. The simple sweetness of that captured moment, so potent with promise, made Emmaline's chest constrict with nameless longing.

She walked forward, her gaze transfixed on the ceiling. The beauty made her eyes ache.

What must it be like to be surrounded by such opulence, such incredible riches all the time?

Then a rumbling male voice came from a corner of the room, interrupting her thoughts. "Miss Farnsworth, are you having a religious experience?"

Devon had seen such openmouthed wonder only on depictions of saints in rapture. Or, now that he thought about it, on the face of a woman in the throes of sensual ecstasy.

He judged the second as far more likely in Miss Farnsworth's case. She was much too opinionated to qualify for sainthood.

After luncheon, Devon had retreated to his chamber to try to sleep away his headache, but after tossing on his bed for the better part of an hour, he finally took refuge in the dimly lit library. Baxter was sensitive enough to his moods to know when a migraine had descended and Devon must avoid bright light. Now he was seized by the wish that the heavy shutters were thrown back so he could further dazzle Miss Farnsworth with the majesty of his library.

"No, I wouldn't classify this moment as religious, milord," she said breathlessly, flicking her gaze to him before returning her stare to the ceiling. "I hope I'm not intruding."

"Would it matter to you if you were?"

Her lips turned inward for a moment and then she shot a quick grin in his direction before tipping her chin up to admire his ceiling again. "Probably not. This is far too grand a place to regret seeing, even at the risk of disturbing my host."

"And you believe regret is a waste of time. However, you are my brother's guest, not mine," Devon said, still lounging in his favorite overstuffed chair. "But as long as you're already here, I may as well welcome you to my inner sanctum."

"A lady might catch her death from the chill of your welcome." She tossed him a pointed look.

He knew he ought to stand when a lady entered a room, but whether Miss Farnsworth was, in fact, a lady was open to question. Besides, he really didn't want to be alone with her. If he was rude enough, she might leave. "Are you suggesting I should stand simply because you invaded my library without invitation?"

"No, if your manners require my prompting, the fact that you became suddenly upright would have no meaning." Her lips curled in a small grimace. "It's obvious you have little respect for me."

"As it's obvious you have little respect for my privacy," he said. "You occupied my garden earlier. Now you feel the need to skulk about my library. Turning up unexpectedly is becoming habitual for you."

"I am not skulking." Her eyes flashed and Devon decided her face flushed most becomingly when she was irritated. "Neither should my presence be unexpected. We were invited to stay in your home, milord. If you require your houseguests to remain confined to their chambers, perhaps you should bolt their doors."

"No one consulted me about your accommodations or I might have suggested it." A retort about regretting that dungeons had fallen out of fashion danced on his tongue, but he bit it back. "I had little choice in the matter."

"I find it difficult to believe you are ever without choice, your lordship."

She did a slow turn so she could take in the entire sweep of the room. Her movements were graceful and drew his eye to the supple lines and curves of her figure. He wished she weren't so comely. Maybe then he wouldn't be fighting the urge to gather her close, crowd her against the bookcase, and lift her skirts.

"Your inner sanctum, you called it," she said as she turned back to admire the contents of the bookshelves. "Are you certain you're not the one with a religious bent?"

Devon's thoughts were running more on the idolatrous side at the moment. The kiss in his vision burst back into his mind with such vibrant clarity, his body tried to persuade him that worshipping Miss Farnsworth's delectable form would indeed be a fine way to spend the afternoon. His headache dimmed a bit. He'd cut off his vision before he'd unbuttoned her bodice, but his imagination was pleased to fill in the gap.

If only his brother weren't besotted with her.

He snorted with irritation and tried to forget the thoroughly kissable Miss Farnsworth in his vision. Sensual and responsive, the miss in his fantasy bore little resemblance to the real one, who seemed more interested in the stacks of books than in him. It ought to be easy to separate the two in his mind.

Less easy for his body, evidently. He shifted in his seat and the throb at his temples resumed.

"So, you're not the religious sort," she answered for him. "But you can't deny this room inspires reverence. Yes, that's as good a way of describing it as anything."

"Reverence for what?" he asked with a huff. If he could sustain annoyance, it would be easier to resist the pull he felt toward her. "There's no cause. It's only a collection of books, after all."

"Oh, milord." She cast him a look laced with pity and shook her head. "Rich as Croesus, but totally unaware of your bounty. Your home has become so commonplace to you, you can't see how magnificent it all is."

By thunder, no man would dare speak to him so. "Use is everything, they do say. This is the manner of living to which I'm accustomed. If I fail to be overwhelmed by it daily, I do not consider it a flaw in my character."

He supposed he should be grateful. She'd effectively squashed all his lustful feelings toward her by giving him reason to stay annoyed.

"It's not just the art and architecture, though that alone would be staggering," Miss Farnsworth said. "The real treasure is all the minds converged in one place."

"Minds? What do you mean?" He wondered if the girl was a bit balmy.

"In the books, of course. The thoughts of great men, and great women, too, I hope. Why, they're fairly buzzing on the shelves." Her dark eyes snapped with genuine pleasure. "Can't you hear them?"

Minds on the bookshelves. He'd never considered his library thus, but the fanciful image made sense and in some strange way seemed to lessen the grip of his migraine. Devon smiled, despite his determination to remain irritated with her. "Now that you mention it, yes, I believe I do hear a faint hum."

"So you do possess an imagination." She strolled over to peruse the wrinkled spines in his collection. "I have hope for you, milord."

"I'm gratified to hear it." Devon's mouth twitched in amusement over her presumption this time. Women usually tripped over themselves to fawn over him. The fact that she felt no such compunction was strangely refreshing. He closed the copy of *The Mill on the Floss* he'd been attempting to read and laid it aside. It was no loss. He hadn't been able to focus on it properly for the last half hour. "Is that what attracted you to my brother? His imagination?"

Miss Farnsworth rocked on her heels, hands clasped behind her, while she studied the titles on the west wall.

"I don't believe I ought to discuss my relationship with Theodore, since it's clear you disapprove."

"Did I say so?"

"Not in so many words." She pulled a first edition Sir Walter Scott bound in Cordoban leather from the shelf and leafed through the frontispiece, examining the woodcuts of scenes from *Ivanhoe* with absorption. "You were quite amiable when we first met in your garden, but your demeanor has been noticeably cooler toward me since Theodore announced his intentions."

She was far too observant for his comfort, but at least she couldn't see the way he struggled inwardly to maintain his cool exterior.

"Perhaps I'm more concerned about your intentions toward my brother."

She peered over the top of the book at him. "Theodore and I have not known each other long. I intend to continue our association until I'm satisfied on the question of whether or not we would be well-suited."

"And it hasn't occurred to you that the brother of an earl and the daughter of a scholar might be fundamentally ill-suited for each other?"

"Simply by virtue of our births? Theodore swears it makes no difference to him, though it's obviously cause for concern to you." She replaced the Scott as carefully as if it were fashioned of glass. "I must confess, since you're Theodore's brother, I thought you might be more enlightened."

"What makes you think I'm not?" Every man of good conscience wished to be considered enlightened. Devon was a peer of the realm. Who was this backwater bluestocking to make him feel like a cretin?

"So far you've not shown a talent for thinking that differs from the accepted." She ran her fingertips over the leather-bound Dickens collection. Devon almost felt the caress along his own spine. "Though I do admire your taste in literature. Please tell me you have actually read these."

"Most of them." Devon rose and walked toward her. "Perhaps you'll allow that concern for my brother motivates me."

"Perhaps. That would be the most charitable view of your attitude toward me."

Miss Farnsworth had no idea of his true attitude toward her. Despite his determination not to, he roused to her again. Prickly and unpredictable she might be, but against his better judgment, Devon was drawn to her. Like the heliotropes in his garden that tracked the sun, he couldn't seem to look away from her.

"I'm thankful Theodore has a more open mind," she said.

Ted had always been charming, athletic and popular. Devon's brother was many things, but a deep thinker had never been one of them.

"Laying aside the question of whether or not you and my brother are well-suited," Devon said, "can you give me an example of Teddy's open-minded thought?"

She fixed him with a direct gaze and he sensed she was taking his measure in some fashion.

"Very well. Here's an example. When a discovery is made in an academic realm that upsets the previous order of thought about a subject, some scholars try to discount the new knowledge." She adopted a pedantic tone. He tried to focus on her words instead of the way her breasts rose and fell with each breath, but he wasn't entirely successful. "It means they must alter, sometimes discard completely, their previously held positions, you see. No one likes to acknowledge they've been wrong."

He'd never heard a woman speak so authoritatively. His estimate of her intelligence ticked upward by several notches. And so did his appreciation of her bosom.

"But the first time Teddy saw the Tetisheri statue, he wasn't the least concerned that it would change a number of preconceived notions," she said. "He didn't fear taking a new direction to advance our body of knowledge."

Devon scoffed and tried to steer his imagination in a new direction, away from undoing the neat row of buttons on Miss Farnsworth's bodice. "What Theodore knows about ancient history wouldn't fill a thimble."

"On the contrary, he might surprise you. He's been studying with my father every day since we met. I've never met anyone so anxious to master the finer points of Egyptology."

She pulled a copy of *Titus Andronicus* from the shelf that housed his Shakespearean collection and then leaned against the bookcase as she flipped the pages.

Probably looking for the gore-filled etchings embedded in the edition, Devon supposed.

"In fact, Teddy grasped the statue's significance almost immediately and without Father pointing it out."

"My brother has never shown the slightest interest in ancient history and even less in statuary." Unless the artwork featured a scantily clad female form. Theodore was obviously delving into ancient Egypt in an attempt to win Miss Farnsworth's favor. Devon couldn't blame him.

"Nevertheless, Theodore recognized the statue's importance." She tilted her chin up to meet his gaze. "I wonder if you would. Perhaps you should ask my father to show it to you."

"Perhaps I will." He leaned a hand against the bookshelves, pinning Miss Farnsworth against them. She held the copy of *Titus Andronicus* against her chest as if it was a shield, but she didn't try to scuttle away from him.

An eerie sense of recognition descended upon him. Devon suddenly realized that he and Miss Farnsworth were positioned exactly as they'd been at the beginning of his vision. Close, so close he could smell her sweet, peachy scent.

He felt a tug toward her, but resisted. Teddy would never forgive him.

She looked up at him, her eyes enormous. "What about you, your lordship? Are you the type to bow to convention or would you take bold action whether it's approved by the world or not?"

Yes, blast it all, he was very likely to take action. And kissing his brother's almost fiancée would most definitely not be approved.

Unless . . .

Unless he did it to *save* his brother from a woman who was undoubtedly wrong for him. It could be argued in that case that Devon had Theodore's best interests at heart. That motivation would cast his actions in a very different light.

Miss Farnsworth tilted her head slightly. Her warm, sweet breath streamed across his lips.

"Damnation," he murmured and covered her mouth with his.

CHAPTER 5

Oh, no! Emmaline thought as the earl bent to kiss her. She ought not to have goaded the man, but honestly, he was so blasted pompous and remote, she couldn't resist needling him. Evidently, he found her argumentative behavior attractive for some odd reason. Now there was no way to escape his attentions gracefully.

Then, as he slanted his mouth over hers, she wasn't sure she wanted to escape.

His mouth fitted to hers perfectly, moving, seeking. His tongue traced the seam of her lips and, God help her, they parted enough to grant him entrance. He invaded her mouth and a low fire flared to life in her belly. A deep throb began in her lady parts, but the ache was far from unpleasant. Her knees went wobbly.

Oh, for pity's sake. Pull yourself together, Emma! Is there anything more trite than weak knees?

Anyone would think her a pudding-headed debutante, the way she sagged against him, but she couldn't seem to help herself. His kiss was a drugging elixir and she wasn't ready to stop imbibing yet.

The copy of *Titus Andronicus* slipped unheeded to the floor. She grasped both his lapels and hung on for dear life.

Lord Devonwood's hands found her waist and pulled

her flush against his body. Beneath the superfine of his waistcoat and the lawn of his shirt, the earl's corded muscles didn't have an ounce of give in them. If she struggled to free herself, she'd be on the losing side of the contest.

But she didn't exactly *want* to free herself.

This wasn't her first kiss. She'd received amorous attention from a number of gallants during her travels, but their stolen kisses were meaningless and quick and even more swiftly forgotten. Theodore had kissed her on three separate occasions, but she'd been careful to keep a firm rein on the situation each time.

Now she couldn't delude herself. Emmaline was wholly out of her depth. Lord Devonwood was not some swain who could be put off with a coquette's arts, even if she possessed any. For the first time in an amorous situation, she was not in control.

Judging from the low groan the earl made into her mouth, he wasn't either.

He needed something from her and her body wept to give it to him. Emma heard herself moan, and she began kissing him back with a fierceness that surprised her. She nipped at his lower lip. She suckled his tongue.

Good heavens! I'm kissing a man I dare not call by his Christian name. Why, I don't even know his proper name, in point of fact!

The realization shamed her, but did nothing to quench the sense of longing.

Lord Devonwood ground his body against hers till her back pressed the uneven spines of the books. His hard maleness rocked against her belly. Even through the layers of her skirt and crinoline, the contact was both alarming and arousing. Moist warmth pooled between her thighs.

Emmaline broke off the kiss and wrapped her arms around his neck, feeling a little like a drowning victim trying to climb atop her rescuer.

Or was Lord Devonwood the undertow trying to drag her down?

His long fingers found the buttons marching down the front of her bodice. Her nipples perked to hard awareness.

And so did her reason.

He was trying to ruin her. He intended to drive a wedge between her and Theodore. Worse, he'd ruin the scheme she and Monty were running. They'd be out on the street with Monty's hacking cough growing worse every day before she could say *Titus Andronicus* three times fast.

She pressed against his chest, but he didn't release her. She tried to speak into his mouth, but even to her own ears, her vocalizations sounded more like passionate babble than protestations.

Finally Emmaline did the only thing she could think of. She brought up her knee into Lord Devonwood's groin as sharply as her skirts allowed.

Pain exploded in his ballocks, followed by debilitating nausea. Devon released her with an oath and bent double, clutching his belly. She tried to dart away, but he grasped her forearm before she could escape.

"Why did you do that?" he said between gasps.

"Why did you kiss me?" she returned tartly.

"Damned if I know." It had seemed the right thing to do at the time. If he exposed Miss Farnsworth as a lightskirt who'd submit to anyone's caress, Theodore might be furious at first, but in time he'd come to thank Devon for saving him from a life-altering mistake.

How could he have suspected she'd try to unman him for daring to kiss her and prove him wrong, destroying his plan utterly?

Along with his balls.

"You're hurting my arm, milord." Her voice quavered. She wasn't nearly as calm as she pretended to be. "Of course, since you made advances to me, it's obvious you don't mind wounding your brother. I suppose it's of little consequence to you if you injure me."

"I've never hurt a woman in my life." He released his grip and, to her credit, she didn't bolt. Devon forced himself upright, swallowing back the aching misery between his legs. Surprisingly enough, his headache was gone, but he'd willingly wish it back for the off-chance that he'd still be able to father children someday. He stifled a groan. "Let me assure you, Miss Farnsworth, you're in far less danger from me than I obviously am from you."

"But you *kissed* me."

"And you *liked* it."

Her mouth opened and closed a few times as she tried several retorts on her tongue and discarded them unspoken. Finally one corner of her mouth turned up. "Yes, I suppose I did."

"You have an odd way of showing it." Devon winced as another twinge of discomfort coursed through his groin. At least she was honest. A woman who could admit to enjoying physical pleasure was an oddity in a land where brides were admonished to grip the bed frame securely on their wedding night and "think of England."

"I apologize for having discomfited you," she said. "But you surprised me, milord."

"The feeling is mutual." Few men had ever blindsided him so. Certainly no woman.

"However, we ought not wonder at the fact that we enjoyed the kiss," she said. "You're a man and I'm a woman. It's human nature to take pleasure in such things."

"Indeed." Amazingly enough, his traitorous cock stiffened at her words despite his still aching balls.

"However, it is of no significance. While we humans share animal passions, unlike lower creatures, we do not have to be governed by them," she said, careful to keep beyond his reach. Her breathing was shallow and hitched uncertainly at times. "As soon as I collected my wits, I realized that however much I enjoyed your kiss, it was wrong, in the worst possible way. And it had to be stopped."

"Also in the worst possible way," he grumbled.

She crossed her arms over her chest. He knew she was continuing to talk because her lips moved and he heard the flatly accented sound of her Yankee voice, but no meaning registered in his brain.

Devon was distracted by the top two buttons of her bodice. They were still unhooked and the white expanse of her throat beckoned so loudly that her words faded to unintelligible noise. Despite everything, Devon's mouth watered to suckle that tender skin, to make her cry out his name, to make her ache so that she wouldn't fight him, wouldn't order him to stop. Instead she'd beg him *not* to . . .

". . . and so it makes no sense whatever to burden Theodore with this," she was saying.

He refocused on her words in time to realize she wasn't going to tell his brother that he'd kissed her. He had to admit that was damned decent. The true account would only make Devon look like a scoundrel for trying to encroach on his brother's would-be fiancée.

"From the time we passed Gibraltar, all I heard from Theodore was how wonderful his brother Devon was and how he couldn't wait to see you again," she said. "It would devastate him to hear of this."

"Agreed," Devon said, shoving his hands into his pockets to disguise his semi-roused state. "Of course, you realize why I kissed you, don't you?"

"I don't believe that reason has changed much since our first parents were driven from Eden."

He shook his head. "The only reason I kissed you was to test your regard for my brother."

Her mouth formed a silent "oh." The skin of her neck flushed to the peachy color of the tea roses in his garden. Then the blush rushed upward to paint her cheeks with a most beguiling stain.

"It didn't feel like a test," she said, one hand straying to stroke her kiss-swollen bottom lip.

The simple gesture rendered Devon rock hard again. He looked away. "Well, it was."

"Then since I rejected your advances, I assume I passed," she said after a few heartbeats. "I have no wish to hurt your brother."

"Which is not to say you love him."

The words had tumbled out of Devon's mouth before he could stop them. He was not one for sentiment. The idea that Miss Farnsworth had fallen in love with his brother after such a short acquaintance sounded ridiculously soppy, even to his own ears. He had no idea why he'd even brought it up.

"No, it isn't," she said without a flinch. "I have not claimed to love Theodore."

It was difficult to catch a person up if they wouldn't indulge in a self-serving lie. Whatever else she might be guilty of, Emmaline Farnsworth seemed devoted to baldly telling the truth.

"However, whether or not I love your brother is an intensely personal matter and not a topic of discussion I ought to pursue with you, milord." She dropped a shallow curtsey. "If you don't mind, I'll be on my way now."

She turned and headed toward the door.

"Without anything to read?" he called after her. Wasn't that why she'd invaded his library in the first place? He waved a hand toward the Shakespeare she'd left on the floor. "What about *Titus Andronicus*?"

"I've read it," she said. "Too violent for my taste."

"I find that difficult to believe from a woman who's just done her best to geld me."

She flashed him a grimace and slipped out the door. Devon stood perfectly still until the swish of her kid soles on the marble floors faded completely.

He expected his headache to descend once more. He had no idea why it had miraculously disappeared. It usually took all of a day to recover from a full-blown migraine after spending the night using his gift, but from the first moment his lips had touched Miss Farnsworth's, his head had felt perfectly fine.

He wished he could say the same for his balls.

So, Emmaline Farnsworth wasn't the light-heeled chit he took her for. She was honest. Painfully honest about both her reaction to his kiss and her relationship with his brother. Devon couldn't find reason to fault her.

He ought to have been satisfied, except for the niggling worry that there was something else afoot, something besides a misalliance in the making in Miss Farnsworth's attachment to his brother. Instead his gut roiled in a jumbled mess. Something was very wrong here. There was nothing specific he could point to, but he'd learned to trust his instinct in such matters.

He'd watch the American lady and her father like a mastiff guarding the estate grounds.

Devon started to bend down to pick up the discarded *Titus Andronicus,* but stopped himself before his fingertips brushed the tome. The last time he'd retrieved something Emmaline had dropped, he'd seen himself kissing her.

What if the next vision showed him shagging her silly?

While his body applauded this line of thinking, his head rejected it as disloyal to Teddy in the extreme. Even if Emmaline would let him take her to bed, how could it be worth betraying his brother?

Devon swallowed down the tightness in his throat.

She was so soft and sweet, a disreputable part of him thought she'd definitely be worth it.

He might have been able to rationalize kissing the girl to save his brother from her. Swiving her was another thing altogether.

He strode from the room, leaving Shakespeare on the floor. Baxter would pick it up later. Devon couldn't chance it. He didn't want to know.

If he was destined to defile his brother's fiancée, he preferred to let the fact that he was a Judas come to him as a surprise.

"You're certain the old man still has it?" The gentleman raised the pint to his lips and sipped the sour ale, pinky out, dainty as a doily.

Thomas O'Malley suppressed a grunt of disgust. Whatever contempt he might feel for his employer, it wouldn't do to openly disrespect the man who paid the bills.

The jacket his lordship sported was shiny in spots with wear. O'Malley suspected he'd dressed carefully, probably borrowing threadbare clothing from his valet in order to blend in with the working-class pub patrons. His true breeding, however, showed in every foppishly aristocratic movement.

"O' course, Farnsworth still has it." Thomas O'Malley tossed back half of his pint and then swiped his mouth with a grimy sleeve. No fancy-arsed manners for the likes of him. "I tailed him from the ship straight to Devonwood House, didn't I? He ain't put his nose out of doors since."

"I don't know why you couldn't have relieved him of the item while you were still shipboard."

"With him and his daughter traveling first class courtesy

of the earl's brother and me stuck in steerage? Not bloody likely," O'Malley said. "They don't let us salt-of-the-earth types mingle with the hoity-toity so free, ye know."

His lordship's aquiline nose crinkled a bit as if he wished such stringent rules applied everywhere. Between rancid wool and the unwashed bodies beneath it, even O'Malley had to admit a number of the pub's patrons were pretty ripe.

"Beastly rotten luck that chap in Cairo made such a mistake in the first place."

"Never ye fear, milord. He paid for it." O'Malley had seen to that, strangling the skinny Egyptian with his beefy bare hands. How the poor bloke had confused an American for the Irishman he was expecting still had O'Malley scratching his head.

This was supposed to be such a simple job. He only had to travel to Cairo, go to a certain shop in the bazaar, and pick up the item for His Nibs. Whatever the blasted thing was, it had already been paid for, but the item wasn't the sort of article a body put in a crate and shipped in some rat-infested ship's hold. It required hand delivery, his lordship had said. But when O'Malley had arrived in Cairo, the bloody thing was already gone—given by mistake to that Farnsworth fellow. Now, his lordship wasn't making so free with the ready coin till O'Malley corrected the error.

"Whist, don't ye be frettin' yourself, your lordship," O'Malley said. It was unfair that he should be blamed for something which was clearly no fault of his, but them what got the chinks got to make the rules. "I'll have the item for ye before ye know it."

The gentleman's fingers closed over O'Malley's wrist in a surprisingly painful grip. "Do not presume to tell me what to do."

"No, no, o' course not." O'Malley's fingers curled inward from the pressure being exerted on his wrist. The bones ground together beneath his tough skin with a series of soft clicks. Agony made him clench his teeth. He had no idea the gentleman was so strong. "I think—"

"I'm not paying you to think," his lordship snapped. "You have no idea what you're dealing with. You're not equipped for thinking. I pay you to obey me."

He released O'Malley's wrist and turned his attention back to his pint as if nothing had happened. O'Malley narrowly resisted the urge to cradle his injured paw.

"What d'ye want me to do, then?"

"First, hope that Farnsworth is as blithely ignorant of what he has as you are of what you've lost," his lordship said. "Now that the American has come under the Earl of Devonwood's protection, our course is more difficult, but not impossible. I want you to simply watch for now."

"Watch?"

"Keep track of Farnsworth's comings and goings. Find out what social events Lord Devonwood and any of his party will be attending," the gentleman explained with an annoyed scowl. "I'd hoped not to involve myself in this, but there seems to be no help for it."

His lordship's eyes had gone quite as dark and hard as obsidian. For the first time, O'Malley realized that beneath the silks and jewels the gentleman usually wore, he was a man to be reckoned with.

And feared.

O'Malley gulped. "And when we see the main chance to retrieve the item—"

"Then I may allow you to earn your over-large retainer, Mr. O'Malley." His lordship stood and looked down his noble nose at him. The chill in his eyes froze O'Malley's soul. "If by that time you've proven to me you are still worth my trouble, of course. Pray for your sake that you do."

CHAPTER 6

Emmaline strongly contemplated begging off on supper that night.

It wasn't because she didn't have an appropriate gown. Her cream and rose tulle was exceptionally fine and its bodice fitted her like a second skin. Even that crusty butler Baxter wouldn't be able to fault it. The gown had cost the earth, but Monty claimed it was worth the investment. She might have worn it to dine with a duke and not have been out of place.

Of course, the décolletage was a bit more daring than she wished, but Monty insisted that a woman could provide an excellent distraction when needed merely by displaying that she was a woman. It would be a sin not to take advantage of the fact.

It wasn't because she didn't want to see Theodore after the debacle in the library. She missed his uncomplicated presence. She was beginning to need his unfailing adoration as much as an opium fiend craves her next draught of laudanum. It bolstered her confidence to have a man she could bring so neatly in line with her wishes with so little effort.

Nor was it because she had given up on Monty's plan. The bones of the game were sound and there was no time like the present to sow the seeds. She suspected Monty might need her during the meal if the opportunity arose to drop a few well-placed hooks. It would be a shame to waste a captive audience because she . . . well, she might as well admit it.

She was afraid.

She drew a deep breath as Monty escorted her down the long hall toward the formal dining room. *Afraid.* Her belly contorted like a Chinese acrobat.

There was no doubt about it. She'd rarely experienced this gut-wrenching sensation, but she recognized it for what it was. Fear.

The clack of Monty's heels on marble echoed against the walls as they processed to the dining room. The sound seemed to repeat "a-FRAID, a-FRAID" with a heavy soled accent on the second syllable. Emma couldn't escape the sensation that she was marching to her doom.

How could she bear being in the same room with that scoundrel Lord Devonwood?

Or maybe she was the scoundrel. It was hard to have any moral certitude when one lived as she and Monty did. After the way her body had responded to the earl's advances, she felt doubly false in her role as the professor's blue-stockinged daughter. Surely like Hester Prynne, a scarlet "A" would materialize on her breast and everyone would know her body had nearly capsized the wobbly boat of her faux respectability. Not to mention the way she'd endangered the success of Monty's plan.

And over nothing more than an ill-considered kiss.

Even though he'd agreed not to mention the unfortunate interlude in the library to his brother, she had no way of knowing whether the earl would keep their tawdry little secret.

She didn't love Theodore. But even though she was set on making off with some of his money, she liked him immensely. If she focused solely on absconding with a good deal of cash, perhaps she wouldn't have to see hurt on his boyishly handsome features. Some betrayals cut far deeper than being taken by a pair of confidence professionals.

"There you are, darling." Teddy caught up with Emmaline and her father as they entered the elegant dining room.

He pressed an ardent kiss on her gloved knuckles. Judging from his clear-eyed gaze, it was safe to assume his brother had not spoken to him. He turned her hand over and kissed the center of her palm.

"Teddy, please," she murmured. "Not in public."

Open displays of affection made her feel naked somehow, as if her reactions might be gauged by others for depth of feeling. Since her depth with Theodore was only about an inch, it was scrutiny she didn't welcome.

Good thing no one had been about to observe her moaning like a ten-penny whore in the earl's arms that afternoon.

Except the earl, of course.

She swept the room with her gaze. Monty had abandoned her to lean an elbow on the sideboard and was doing his best to charm the countess and a young lady whom Emmaline didn't recognize. Lady Devonwood's elegant cheekbones were echoed in the girl's face, but her luxuriant blond curls and vivid eyes were a departure from the original. Obviously this was Theodore's younger sister.

Lord Devonwood was nowhere to be seen.

Was it possible he was afraid to see her, too?

Not likely. But before Emma could decide to hope so, the girl left Monty and her mother's company and scampered over to Theodore with her arms spread wide.

"Oh, Teddy," the girl exclaimed. "You weren't due home till next week. It's only dumb luck I came back to town early. Oh, I can't believe you're finally home."

He scooped her into his arms and twirled her around twice. "And I can't believe it's you, Louisa. Where's the little girl I left six months ago?"

"I grew up," she said, her eyes bright as bluebells in May, her golden ringlets shining. "Something I hear you're trying to do now, too. Come now. Don't be shy, brother. Introduce me to your bride."

Emmaline knew she ought to explain to Louisa that she really wasn't engaged to be married to Theodore, but she bit back the words. They were both so obviously enjoying their reunion, she didn't want to ruin the moment.

Louisa kissed the air by both her cheeks in the French fashion. "I've always wanted a sister, Emmaline," she whispered confidingly. "You have no idea the trials I've been through growing up with two brothers. This is going to be such fun!"

Emma's smile was fragile. Before when she and Monty worked a mark, she'd been able to keep a professional distance. She took comfort in the fact that it was impossible to con an honest person. All their games worked only if the mark was greedy for financial gain or selfishly had to have something no one else could have.

Adding a sham engagement to the mix of subterfuge was full of potential complications beyond simply her relationship with Theodore.

When she looked into Louisa's eyes, all she saw was yet another person who'd be hurt when their scheme was discovered. Then Monty excused himself suddenly and headed for the hallway, covering his mouth with his handkerchief to muffle his cough. Emma's spine straightened. Pity for a mark was a weakness, a luxury only the affluent could afford.

She was willing to bet Louisa Nash had never wanted for anything in her life. Emma would have traded her left arm for even one brother and all Louisa could do was complain about having two, even if she was speaking in jest. A little hurt might do her a world of good.

"Have you any brothers, Miss Farnsworth?" Louisa asked.

"No," she said with a shake of her head. "But I'll be happy to help you even the odds against yours." The first step in the long confidence game was establishing trust. She smiled at Louisa. "Please, call me Emmaline."

Eight o'clock, the hallowed time to begin the evening meal, came and went without Lord Devonwood deigning to appear. Finally at half past, the countess ordered Baxter to serve the soup course and the party assembled around the long table glittering with Reed & Barton silver and Limoges china.

Louisa regaled them with tales of the ton and the slightly naughty goings-on among the Upper Ten Thousand. She'd just returned from a house party at the country home of His Grace, the Duke of Kent, where no fewer than three couples had announced their engagements by the end of the fortnight.

"Honestly," Louisa said with an expressive roll of her eyes, "the way couples were pairing off, you'd have thought it was time to board the Ark." She sighed dramatically.

"And what of you, my dear?" Monty asked. "Has some beau caught your fancy?"

"Not yet, professor." Louisa dimpled prettily at him. "But I'm in no hurry. This is only my first Season. You see, until I settle on one fellow, I can flirt to my heart's delight with all of them. An engaged lady doesn't have nearly as much fun."

"Louisa, please," the countess said, her lips drawn into a prim line. "Dr. Farnsworth will think you shockingly fast."

"Nonsense, my dear lady." Monty leaned across the table and gave Teddy's sister an avuncular pat on the hand. "She's perfectly delightful."

"But she's likely to taint Emmaline with her unladylike ideas," Theodore complained.

"Oh, that's right. I keep forgetting dear Teddy is engaged," Louisa said. "Pay no attention to me, Emmaline. I'm sure you have more excitement as a betrothed lady than you know what to do with."

If being kissed into incoherence by Theodore's brother qualified as excitement, Emmaline was forced to agree.

"We're not quite engaged yet, sister," he said with a wink to Emma. He caught her hand under the table and squeezed. "But I'm working on it."

"Careful, Miss Farnsworth," Lord Devonwood's voice came from behind her. "If Teddy claims to be working, lightning strikes will no doubt commence shortly. You'd do well to move down a chair or two."

He took his place at the head of the long table without a word of apology for his tardiness. The countess, however, apologized for starting the meal without him.

Devon waved off her words and signaled for the footman to fill his soup bowl. The servants nearly stumbled over each other in an effort to see that his wine goblet was brimming with a golden Reinish vintage and that his napkin was arranged just so over his impeccable finery.

The rest of the party had polished off their lamb and were ready for dessert. However, it was obvious they'd simply have to sit there digesting and sipping the burgundy that had accompanied the meat entrée, while Lord Devonwood ate his leisurely way through the five courses they'd just finished.

How the world adjusts itself to please an earl with no effort on his part at all, Emma thought.

And yet his lordship had the temerity to berate his

brother for not working. Emmaline's enterprising soul rankled at the way Lord Devonwood felt himself above honest labor or even common courtesy for those who engaged in it.

"Actually, your lordship, Theodore worked very hard indeed while he was in Egypt," she said with a surreptitious glance in Devon's direction. The earl was definitely wearing his station, resplendent in a cloth of gold waistcoat and elegantly tied cravat starched to perfection. But even without the trappings of his title, the man himself was enough to make her insides caper about like a troop of drunken faeries in the garden, not quite balanced on the daisy stems.

"It's true," Teddy said with a laugh. "At the dig outside of Thebes, I developed a genuine blister."

"A blister! Don't be gauche, Theodore." The countess frowned at him.

"Sorry, *Maman*. But you can't imagine what fun it was to muck about in the dirt and hope to turn up something astonishing."

The earl's spoonful of white soup halted halfway to his mouth. "And did you turn up something astonishing?"

Ted caught Emma's hand and brought it quickly to his lips for a kiss. "Not until I boarded the *British Star* and met Emmaline."

"Well put, Teddy. You'll win her yet." Louisa beamed at her brother's gallantry.

Emma's cheeks heated as she disengaged her hand from Theodore's grasp. She didn't feel astonishing. She felt lower than shoe leather. Even though Theodore showered her with compliments, she'd caught herself reliving that blasted kiss with his brother in the library more times than Egypt had dynasties.

Since Egypt had poked its way into her mind, it was

high time she made use of it. "Actually, I think Theodore is referring to the Tetisheri statue and the academic work he did on that piece."

"No, I'm not." He tossed her a hopeful grin. "I was talking about you and you know it."

"Theodore, please," she murmured. It was bad enough that he was determined to court her. It was unconscionable that it should all play out before his family. The public nature of his coming humiliation would be all the more painful.

"Don't be modest, Miss Farnsworth. It doesn't become you." Lord Devonwood signaled for the footman to remove his soup, waved off the fish course, and accepted the meat instead. He speared a glistening bite of lamb with mint relish. "Your intended and I had a chance to become better acquainted in the library this afternoon, Ted, and I must agree with your assessment. Miss Farnsworth certainly astonished me."

He popped the meat into his mouth with a wicked grin.

"My lord, you exaggerate." Now the drunken faeries in her belly threatened to escape in a panicked rout. Would he actually expose her for a wanton between the lamb and the crème brûlée? "His lordship was kind enough to show me his library. I was quite taken with it."

"Quite taken," he repeated as he skewered her with a look. Heat sizzled beneath the words.

If she hadn't stopped him when she did, he'd have been perfectly capable of taking her there on the venerable marble floor of the library with the ghosts of Sir Walter Scott, Dickens, and Shakespeare cheering them on.

"Yes," Lord Devonwood continued, "I was quite impressed with her taste . . ."

Memory of the citrusy freshness of his mouth returned to taunt her. Emmaline stared at her empty plate. It seemed the only safe course, but silence hung suspended over the table like a strand of bubbles waiting to burst. She was forced to look down the long table at the earl.

". . . in literature," he finally finished. "Ask her how she feels about *Titus Andronicus* sometime."

He would have to remind her how Shakespeare had slipped from between them moments before her knee connected with his nether parts. She jerked her gaze from him, sure her cheeks were giving her unmaidenly thoughts away with another infernal blush.

Monty caught her eye and cocked a questioning brow, but Emmaline gave him an almost imperceptible shake of her head. She ought to have warned Monty of this potential complication, but she couldn't bring herself to tell him she'd kissed the earl or worse, that she'd enjoyed it like a common strumpet.

"Yes, indeed, Teddy," the earl said. "Your Miss Farnsworth is absolutely astonishing."

"You see." Theodore turned to her with a soppy grin on his face. "I told you my family would love you, too."

"What's this business about the statue Miss Farnsworth mentioned, Theodore?" the countess asked, signaling an abrupt change of topic. "I've never known you to be interested in art, dear."

"Well, it's not exactly art," Theodore said. "It's an artifact. It'll revolutionize the study of the ancients and our understanding of them if we can only convince others of the import of the piece. I wonder if you'd mind showing it to my family, Dr. Farnsworth."

"Certainly, my boy." Monty stood and bowed to the countess. "If you'll excuse me for a moment, milady."

Emma dabbed her lips with her napkin to hide her smile. They couldn't have planned matters more neatly. She hoped Monty restrained himself from taking the stairs two at a time in his zeal to retrieve the statue and return quickly.

A clever trickster could maneuver the conversation in a way that benefitted him, but patience was always best. The hook went in deeper and without causing alarm if the mark asked for more of his own volition.

"Keep your seat, Farnsworth," Lord Devonwood said. "We haven't had dessert yet. We've only just begun to recover from our astonishment over your daughter. I'm not certain we can bear much more amazement. Surely whatever wonderment this statue represents will keep till we've digested our crème brûlée."

CHAPTER 7

Devon knew he was being churlish, but he couldn't seem to help himself. Emmaline Farnsworth turned the color of a ripe peach with guilt every time she glanced his way. Her bare shoulders and exquisitely displayed bosom in that cream-colored gown threatened his self-control so thoroughly, the only way he could keep a handle on the situation was to exercise his control over others.

Otherwise he might give in and announce to the world and his brother that he'd kissed her. More than that, he'd made her moan. Of course, she'd launched a serious attempt at maiming him for life after that delicious moment, but for an indecent interval before, she'd been as lost in lust as he.

He ought to have let Emmaline's father go retrieve whatever it was that Teddy was so excited about. Perhaps it would've distracted him from the sweet hollow between his brother's almost fiancée's breasts.

Devon was no stranger to a woman's charms. It was no surprise that he'd enjoyed kissing her, but it astounded him that he couldn't stop thinking about it. The warm sanctuary of her mouth, the honeyed sweetness under her tongue, the way she'd suckled his—he couldn't shake the dark and delectable sensations she stirred in him.

Then there was the fact that her kiss had driven away his beastly headache. Nothing had ever touched his malady like that before.

He drained his wineglass and upon a mere flick of his gaze, the footman refilled it without being told. Maybe getting roaring drunk would drown out the siren call of Miss Farnsworth's dangerous allure.

Dessert came, but the crusty sweet wasn't nearly as luscious as the memory of her lips. Still, Devon bolted it down, sheered every last bit of the crème brûlée from the delicate china with a loud scrape. Then he licked the spoon clean. His mother shook her head at him, but said nothing.

What could she say? He was the earl, the peer. A country that tolerated mad kings had no trouble accepting eccentricities in its gentry. If he wanted to stand on his head in the middle of the table, no one would tell him it wasn't perfectly appropriate.

"Well, let's see this wonder you're so enamored with, Ted." Devon rose from his place without first making sure the rest of the party had finished their desserts. He strode down the length of the table and offered Emmaline his arm. "While her father collects the artifact, I'll show Miss Farnsworth around the orangery. We'll join you in the parlor in a bit."

Sometimes, it was very good to be a titled lord.

She rose to her feet and took his arm. What else could she do?

At least he wasn't standing on his head.

Without bothering to see how the rest of the party paired off to adjourn to the parlor, he whisked Miss Farnsworth out the door and down the hall toward the fragrant orangery.

"In most civilized countries, it is customary to remain

at table until everyone is finished dining," she said once they were out of earshot of the others. "That was more than a little rude, don't you think?"

"No one else complained."

"How would they dare? Your mother feels it necessary to apologize to you even when the error is yours. Your sister would be grateful as a basset if you'd only notice her once, and Theodore worships the air you breathe. You're either unaware or unconcerned that you're behaving boorishly and no one has the courage to tell you."

Oh, that's right. Yanks don't put up with kings, mad or otherwise, do they?

"No one except you, Miss Farnsworth."

She kept her voice pleasantly low and musical, as if she weren't berating him. Should the rest of the party chance to overhear, they'd never suspect from her tone that she was verbally flaying him alive.

"Why do you torment your family so?" she said, increasing the pressure of her fingertips on his arm to punctuate her words. "You've been an insufferable bully all evening."

"How kind of you to notice." For the life of him, he couldn't remember the last time anyone had taken him to task over anything. It felt strangely comforting, nearly as comforting as the slight weight of her fingertips on his sleeve. As an earl, he was a man without limits. Even his tutors had stopped chiding him once he came into the title. Short of doing murder, Devon could get away with anything. "I was doing my best to irritate you mostly."

"You succeeded, but I'm not the only one who notices your brusqueness," Emmaline said. "Just because no one else brings you to account, it doesn't mean that your family doesn't suffer from the things you do."

She had no idea the things he did to ensure his family's comfort. "Believe me, my days are thoroughly occupied with making certain my family does *not* suffer."

"Do you think Theodore is blithe about the way you spirited me out of the room?"

Devon shrugged. "Teddy is anxious for me to approve of you. I expect he's pleased I've condescended to show you some attention."

She actually snorted. "My heart will continue to beat without your *condescension*. Pray, do not trouble yourself on my account, milord."

"It's very little trouble. I wouldn't do it if it were otherwise."

"Oh, that's right. You abhor labor of any kind."

Devon had no problem with work. In truth, he worked unceasingly to keep his very leaky estate afloat, but it wouldn't do to be seen to be laboring. While Polite Society was harsh toward its impoverished nobles, it set strict limits on how wealth might be acceptably achieved. Devon would happily tell the ton to go chase itself, but he knew the good opinion of that world mattered to his mother. Without continued success in his myriad investments and occasional winnings at the gaming tables, he might be forced to petition the House of Lords to break the estate's entail and sell off a portion of his sprawling property.

Only last year, his friend Lord Northrop had gone crawling to that august body begging to be allowed to part with some of his land in order to prop up his decaying estate. The marquess had tired of dealing with the incessant water damage from the faulty roof, the moldering tapestries of his country seat and his tenants' constant complaints over lack of maintenance to their cottages.

Of course, the fact that Northrop gambled to excess and overspent on his high-flying mistress might have been his main trouble, but there was no denying it was deucedly expensive to keep up the style expected of a landed noble.

No Earl of Devonwood had ever yielded a foot of earth. He was determined not to be the first.

"Actually, Miss Farnsworth, you might want to refrain from scolding me because in a few moments I'll be taking your advice."

That brought her up short for half a step, but then she continued by his side. "How so?"

"You pointed out to me this afternoon that my home abounds in beauties to which I've become inured. Since I suspect you are the sort who relishes being proved correct, I thought you might enjoy accompanying me as I rediscover the delights of my orangery."

He pushed open the door leading to the enclosed garden and the fresh breath of citrus, gardenias, and oleander rushed into his nostrils. The south-facing room was lined with Palladian windows and during his grandfather's tenure as the earl, the slate roof had been replaced with glazed glass to further extend the artificial growing season. Now it exposed the black vault of the night sky and hazy stars winking above them, barely visible in the low flicker of the gas wall sconces.

"Of course, the orangery at Devonwood Park is much larger." It needed to be in order to service his rambling country estate. "But this little jewel box of a room is truly lovely, isn't it?" he said with fresh appreciation for something he'd almost forgotten he possessed. " 'A thing of beauty—' "

" 'Is a joy forever,' " she finished for him, unconcerned over interrupting a peer of the realm. She left his side to advance into the sweet-smelling bower, paused by the fountain, and smiled over her bare shoulder at him. "So you have read a bit from your library. I adore Keats, too."

Surprisingly enough, he didn't mind that she'd interrupted him. *Must be the novelty of anyone daring to do it.*

"Along with poetry, I also enjoy a spot of botany. I recognize most of the plants here," she said, "but what is that creeper in the corner along the brick there?"

"Ficus pumila." The scientific name bubbled to the surface of his consciousness. It was one of the myriad facts he'd squirreled away during his interminable studies with his tutors before he went away to Oxford. Yet another speck of minutiae he'd never expected to need once he came into his title. Now, because of the way her brows arched in surprise, he was glad to be able to call up the information. "It's a sort of climbing fig."

It had, in fact, climbed around the arch of one of the Palladian windows.

"It does seem to be taking over," she said. "Does it bear fruit?"

"No, it can be pollinated only by a certain species of Asian wasp."

"So there can be no growth without the risk of a few stings," she said.

His mother wouldn't welcome the introduction of winged six-legged beasties into their home, even in the interests of horticulture. "Who wants to deal with that?"

She frowned at him. "Someone who likes figs. I doubt it's occurred to you that all growth involves pain of some sort. You really don't allow yourself to be inconvenienced in the slightest, do you?

"I beg to differ. I suffered quite a sting in my library just this afternoon."

She had the grace to look chagrined. "About that . . . I hope you haven't sustained any . . . lasting damage."

The becoming blush spread over her exposed skin again, like a maple tree erupting in the flame of autumn. Lord, he loved it when she changed colors.

"I'm truly sorry, your lordship."

He almost asked if she'd like to kiss it to make it better, but decided he wasn't nearly drunk enough to get away with that level of lewdness. Still the thought of her mouth on him made his cock swell and ache pleasantly.

"Don't think on it again." If her knee to his groin was the price for being able to kiss her thoroughly, he considered it a bargain in hindsight. Especially since for some unknown reason, the kiss had completely banished his migraine. "However, I want you to know I don't normally force myself on women who don't welcome my attentions."

"Then why did you kiss me in the first place?"

I saw myself kissing you in a vision and couldn't resist the pull of destiny.

No, he couldn't divulge his foresight to her. The last person he'd taken into his confidence about his gift of touch was a professor at university whom he'd tried to warn about eating an apple too quickly. In Devon's vision, the man died clutching his throat and thrashing on the floor. The professor began enquiring about the process of how one might quietly have a nobleman committed to Bedlam. Only the fact that Devon's vision came to pass within the usual twelve hours ensured his continued freedom.

"Who knows why a man feels his kiss will be welcomed by a woman? Courtship is a dance, a ritual, if you will. Signals are given and received," Devon said. "Obviously, I must have misinterpreted yours."

"I'm gratified to hear you say so. I certainly didn't intentionally encourage your advances."

Her hand crept to her cheek. She brushed back a tendril that had escaped her chignon, tucking it behind the shell of her ear, unaware he found that nervous gesture utterly adorable.

"I want to assure you, milord," she said in clipped tones, "that I do not make a habit of kissing men whose Christian names I don't even know."

She fixed her gaze on the creeping fig as if unable to meet his eyes.

"It's Griffin," he said suddenly. He couldn't remember the last time he'd heard it used. "My name is Griffin Titus Preston Nash."

"Griffin." Her lips curved in a smile. "A mythological beast. I should have guessed."

A gryphon had the head and wings of an eagle and the body of a lion. With his confounded gift of touch and the future pressing in on him uninvited at any moment, he often felt less than human.

"I suppose you think it fitting that I should be named for a monster," he said.

"Oh, no, not a monster. A gryphon is a majestic creature, a protector and guardian of the things it holds precious." She bent to sniff a budding camellia.

He plucked it off and gave it to her. If she had any idea what happened to her décolletage when she tipped forward like that . . . He was able to catch a fleeting glimpse of the slightly darker skin of her areolae around her nipples. If she knew, she wouldn't do it.

Or maybe she would, if she were trying to send him a furtive signal . . .

"With a name like Griffin, I shouldn't wonder that you've appointed yourself your brother's keeper." She held the camellia to her nose, closed her eyes, and inhaled. A smile burst over her face like sunrise cresting over Snowdon. "They mate for life, you know."

"Who does?"

"Gryphons. I read a medieval treatise on them once." The way she peered at him over the waxy petals of the flower reminded him of how she'd peeked over the top of *Titus Andronicus*. She sighed. "They are elegant and noble creatures. Even if one member of a mated pair dies, the other will not seek a new mate, but will grieve over its loss till it joins its true love in death."

"Gryphons are mythological, remember."

"I know, but it's a charming thought in any case," she said. "Fidelity is something to be prized."

So was loyalty to a brother, but Devon still felt an undeniable pull toward Miss Farnsworth.

"I'm no coquette, Lord Devonwood, no debutante out to snag a husband. More of my life has been spent in lecture halls and on archaeological digs than in ballrooms. I speak Italian and French, but have no idea how to use the language of the fan. I'm not adept at this sort of game. I hadn't considered that there are ways a woman might encourage a man without meaning to," she said. "Just so there's no mistake in the future, would you mind telling me why you thought I wanted you to kiss me this afternoon?"

"Well, first there's your directness," he said. "Your frankness of expression invites a man to be straightforward about his wishes right back."

"That hardly seems fair." She twirled the camellia stem between her fingers, making the blossom spill fresh scent between them. "You mean a woman must parse her words and discuss only safe topics like the weather lest she seem to be encouraging a man's advance?"

"I don't make the rules."

"And don't play by them either, I'll wager," she said with a knowing grin.

"You have me there." Devon cocked his head in a self-deprecating gesture a certain widowed viscountess had once assured him was most charming. He might have saved himself the trouble. Miss Farnsworth edged away, not seeming the least charmed.

"Very well. I shall confine myself to meteorological observations in your presence." She straightened to her full, if inconsiderable, height and looked up at him. "Spring has already been quite sultry. As I'm unaccustomed to English weather, perhaps you could enlighten me. Do you think the summer will be sweltering?"

"Ah, Miss Farnsworth, you've erred once again," The orangery was humid enough to suggest a tropical Eden. A flash image of Emmaline Farnsworth, in glorious peach-toned nakedness, blushing as Eve never did, scrolled across his mind's eye. Everything about this woman conspired to make him feel achingly male. "When you speak of anything as sultry, a man's thoughts turn immediately to sweat-dampened sheets and bodies without clothing writhing upon them."

Her dark eyes flared wide. "Not a gentleman's thoughts surely."

"All men's thoughts. Ditch-digger or duke. Trust me in this."

"So a woman is unable to speak her mind on anything without danger of misunderstanding?"

"It pains me to admit it, but beneath our civilized trappings, all men are dogs." Devon shrugged. "It's the nature of the beast."

"Very well. I shall embrace silence when I am in your company." Her generous lips clamped shut.

"I'm not sure that's the best course either. Silence begs to be filled and not necessarily by speech." He moved closer to her but this time she didn't edge away. Her peach scent tantalized him over the citrusy fragrance of the orangery. "We all surround ourselves with a bit of unoccupied room. If a man encroaches on a woman's space and she doesn't offer to correct him, he can't be blamed for feeling a tacit welcome."

"So that which is not expressly forbidden is assumed to be accepted?"

She still didn't step back, didn't shy away.

He braced a hand on the palm tree trunk over her shoulder and leaned toward her. "Yes."

"I see." She worried her lower lip a bit, long enough to make him wish he could suckle it as well. "So you think because I don't run from you like a scared rabbit, I want you to kiss me again."

"The thought has occurred to me."

"Don't entertain it. As you pointed out, I'm a very direct person," she said, focusing her gaze somewhere between his chin and sternum with only occasional nervous flicks upward to meet his eyes. "Rest assured. If I wanted a kiss from you, I would initiate one myself."

"I doubt that." He laughed. "What a terrified little bunny you are. Look at yourself. You're frozen like a coney with a hound sniffing nearby. Too addlepated to even look me in the eye, let alone kiss me."

"Don't be so sure." She glared up at him, annoyance glittering in her dark eyes now.

"I'm rarely wrong about this sort of thing."

"You are this time. Consider me an exception to the rule." She reached up, cupped both his cheeks, and kissed him right on the mouth.

Chapter 8

Emma intended to give him a resounding smack, a mere exclamation point of a kiss, simply to emphasize her words. But his mouth was so beguiling, so firm and warm, she found herself lingering like an unfinished sentence, dangling midair in search of a rational conclusion. His arms circled round her with a rightness that belied the wrongness of the kiss.

He'd goaded her to this, as surely as a lamb driven to market.

And she'd allowed him to.

Whatever is not expressly forbidden is assumed to be accepted. She hadn't forbidden him. Worse, she hadn't forbidden herself.

His masculine scent, rich with bergamot and sandalwood, tangled up with the perfume of the orangery. It was a gentle assault on her senses, but it bore down with unrelenting persistence, like the trickle of water that will eventually hollow out solid rock.

His mouth moved surely on hers, tempting her to tarry in the sweet wickedness of this moment.

Even though she knew everything about this kiss, this moment, this man, was wrong, she couldn't pull herself away from the torrent of sensation. His lips on hers stirred up an inner storm. It was like heat lightning sparking across a summer sky, crackling with both potent energy and potential disaster.

Oh, Lord, not another inappropriate thought about the weather.

It brought back his comment about sweat-dampened sheets and bare bodies. Coupled with Devon's kiss, the mental image made her feel achy and swollen.

Needy.

Ready to writhe on a sweat-dampened sheet.

Emmaline had always been a very private person. The idea of being that close to another human being with nothing to shelter behind was daunting. She was aware of the mechanics of sexual congress. She knew what transpired between a man and a woman, knew what would be expected of her should she ever become a wife, but until she'd kissed Griffin Titus Preston Nash, Lord Devonwood, she'd never understood how a woman might *want* to engage in such intimacies.

How would it feel to be all tangled up with this man, slick and wanting? Bare of soul as well as body?

It would be wicked and wanton and wonderful all at once. She was hollow with longing.

Her insides clenched as his tongue swept into her mouth in a soft, moist parody of how their bodies might join in other ways. That other connection, the sinful one that was topmost in her mind, would not be soft like his kiss. It would not be sweet.

It would be a possession. A claiming. A rutting, swiving, shagging, fu—

No. She'd heard those coarse words plenty of times. Her father's fellow confidence artists were not known for delicacy of speech except when it suited their schemes. But she'd never said those words. Never even thought them.

Till now.

Now they were all she could think. The aching hollow

inside her longed to be filled. She imagined how it would be, stretched out with Devon on those sweat-soaked sheets.

In. Out. Hard. Bruising, even.

Her body didn't seem to mind this mental ravishment. In fact, it cheered this line of thought by weeping fresh moisture and speeding up the drumbeat of urgency that pounded between her thighs.

Devon released her mouth and began to kiss his way down her throat to her bared décolletage. Her nipples hardened painfully, throbbing for his touch. If his uneven breathing was any measure, he wanted her as badly as she craved him.

His need touched her in a deep sheltered place and made her chest constrict. She ran her hand through his dark hair, reveling in the newfound sense of feminine control she felt as he worshiped the exposed parts of her breasts.

Control, Monty always preached. *Control of the mark. Control of the information. Control of every aspect of the situation spells the difference between the success and failure of the long confidence game.*

It was his primary rule. Her heady illusion of control over the earl was just that. Illusion. She was playing with forces beyond her experience.

And she was further jeopardizing Monty's chances in the big game with each passing moment she spent in this lovely, filthy diversion with Theodore's brother. If her waywardness led to their being thrown to the streets, what would become of Monty then?

Devon's hand slid into her bodice, claiming a breast. Desire seared from her nipple to her womb in a lightning flash of wanting.

"Griffin," she whimpered. "Please."

"Of course, I'll please you. Anything you want," he

murmured into the hollow of her décolletage. He lifted her breast, exposing a nipple above the cream and rose bodice, and flicked it with his tongue.

Oh, God.

How to stop. How to end this delicious torment.

She didn't think she had the strength.

He took the taut peak into his mouth and she thought she might turn into a puddle on the orangery floor.

Hoping to gain resolve, she tried to recall Theodore's face. Even though she'd spent almost every waking moment with him for the last three months, his features were hazy or at best mere shadows of Griffin's sharper ones.

With supreme effort, she called up Monty in her mind. She couldn't disappoint him like this. He needed her to keep her head, to think strategically, and not get swept up in wanton dalliance.

"Griffin," she said again, barely aware her lips were moving.

"Hmmm?" He kissed his way back up to her mouth while his finger and thumb continued to torment her.

She pressed a hand over her breast to still its silent pleading. Lord Devonwood's lips were but a finger-width's from hers. His face seemed different.

Sensual. Vulnerable. As if he'd shed his title and was simply a hungry man like any other, intent on working his way under her skirt.

But no matter who he seemed to be, it didn't change who she was. Or what she had to do.

"Stop," she pleaded.

He kissed her again and her insides continued to melt. She'd had no idea she could ache so.

"Please," she moaned into his mouth.

He stopped and looked down at her, still rolling her nipple between his thumb and forefinger. Every fiber of her being was intent on his wicked byplay. Who'd have suspected the needs of that tiny bit of flesh could so consume her?

"You're quite certain that's what you want?" he asked.

"No," she admitted, "but we must."

He still didn't release her, didn't decrease the gentle pressure on her nipple. She slid her hand between her exposed skin and his damnably talented fingers, to shield herself from his touch.

"I beg you." She wished he knew what it cost her to whisper those words.

Devon straightened to his full height and looked down at her, something like anger glinting in his burnished pewter eyes. He gave a shuddering snort of frustration as he took a half step away from her.

"Well, this is an improvement over a knee to the groin," he said with a sardonic smile. "But only by the slimmest of margins. Perhaps next time we should fit you with a bell. Like a pugilist who's had enough, you can ring to signal when the round has ended."

She shoved her tender breast back into the bodice, biting her lower lip against her body's riotous protest. She definitely hadn't had enough.

"That would presume you know how to fight fair, and we both know that's not the case," she accused.

"How so? Whatever the rules are, they don't seem to apply to us," he said, his tone still husky with lust. "And if there are any, you set them for this little interlude yourself when you kissed me, so you can't rightly complain. You don't seem a stickler for fairness. I'll set the rules next time."

How could she admit her own body had turned against her, causing her to trample every rule she'd ever embraced? "There will be no 'next time.'"

"I wouldn't be so sure," he grumbled under his breath. "We've been alone exactly three times and you've been in my arms for two of them. At least, tell me you're not still considering my brother."

"You know I haven't accepted Theodore's suit and . . ." Her mouth fell open. "That's why you made sure this would happen again. You don't care a thing about kissing me. Your only interest is in seeing Teddy and I go separate ways."

"Yes, er, no. That's not why I kissed you. Christ, you make me sound like a monster, ravishing my brother's intended solely for the sake of controlling him. And for the record, *you* kissed *me* this time!" He paced the small space, nervous energy crackling off him like static electricity. "I want only the best for him. If that turns out to be you, Miss Farnsworth, so be it. Whatever you may think, I do care about Teddy."

"As do I." Emmaline folded her hands before herself, fig-leaf fashion. They were trembling and she didn't want him to see. The earl was a powerful man. No doubt he wouldn't be moved by weakness. It would only encourage him to press her for further indiscretions. She had to be strong. "I don't want to hurt him. If Theodore and I part ways, I don't want it to be because of a scandal between you and me."

He stopped pacing. "I don't want that either."

She drew courage from their shared affection for Teddy. Surely Devon wouldn't want to injure him with the unsavory little truth that they couldn't seem to keep their hands off each other if they were left alone for longer than a few minutes. "We must simply make sure we aren't presented with an opportunity for foolishness again."

"It didn't feel foolish to me," he admitted.

She squeezed her eyes shut. No, foolish was the wrong word. It felt wonderful . . . exhilarating . . . strangely right. But of course it couldn't be, could it? That was her body reasoning, not her head. Certainly not her heart. "I mean we must try not to be alone with each other."

"That will be easier said than done."

"Not if we both commit to it." Her heartbeat pounded in her ears, in her chest, and lower down where the wicked ache still throbbed. "I don't know what else to do. In all honesty, Lord Devonwood, this sort of thing has never happened to me before."

One of his brows arched in surprise. After their shared passion, she almost wouldn't blame him for not believing her a virgin.

"Oh, I rather think we're past the Lord Devonwood stage, don't you?" He fixed her with a pointed gaze.

At least he didn't doubt her innocence aloud. She could've kissed him again.

"I liked when you called me Griffin," he said.

"Yes, well . . ." She liked calling him that. It suited him far better than Devon. "But using your Christian name implies the sort of intimacy we've agreed is not in Theodore's best interests."

"What about *our* best interests?"

In that one word she saw a logical way out of her quagmire. Cynical, but logical.

"Our? There is no 'our,' no 'us.' You were upset enough that my name might be linked with your brother's, and he's not a true titled lord. As I understand your system, he's actually as common as I. But you, you're not a man who can ignore such things, milord. You're a . . . an embodiment of an estate, for pity's sake. There's no way you'd ally your earldom with an American commoner. You and I both know there can never be anything between us other than a liaison that involves a wink and a nod." She lifted her chin. "I may not be a titled lady, but I'll be no man's mistress."

Why should she when Theodore offered her marriage? His suit glittered with more hope now that she considered it afresh. Her chest brimmed with equal parts affection for Teddy and loathing for herself. True, he had never made her knickers twitch like his brother's mere presence did, but Theodore had also never tried to seduce her into wantonness either.

He *respected* her.

More than she respected herself, evidently.

What had she been thinking when she'd kissed Lord Devonwood? If she were being truthful with herself, she'd admit she hadn't been thinking. She had simply acted on instinct, and that was not the best course. Hadn't Monty told her about strange little Scandinavian rodents called lemmings that hurled themselves into the sea for no apparent reason? She'd kissed Theodore's brother on the same sort of self-destructive impulse.

She hadn't expected he would kiss her back with such devastating disregard for sense, too.

Emmaline cleared her throat. "Now, milord, if you'll please convey my regrets to the rest of the party in the parlor, I think it's high time I retired for the evening."

She dipped in a shallow curtsey and started past him. He caught her by the elbow.

"No, you don't. You're not getting off that easy. If I have to face Teddy with the scent of you still in my nostrils, you have to be there, too," he said harshly. "Call it a condition for not going to my brother immediately with word of our indiscretions."

"You would hurt him like that?"

"Better a nick now than a dagger thrust later." He offered her his arm, his glare daring her to take it.

She narrowed her eyes at him. He liked walking the edge of a parapet and wouldn't be happy unless she tottered on the ledge beside him.

"Very well, milord." She rested her trembling fingertips on his forearm, dismayed over the way his heat radiated through the fabric of his jacket. "But do not ask me to visit any other part of your home with you alone again. I don't care how public the invitation. I don't care if my refusal embarrasses you, I will still refuse."

"Duly noted," he said as he covered her fingers with his for a searing moment. Then he removed his hand and led her from the orangery with a step full of purpose. "And if you're waiting for such an invitation, I advise you not to hold your breath."

The sensual tension between them was so potent, Devon felt it humming in the air about them. The raging need was still there, seething beneath the surface of their even gaits and perfect grooming. They walked in silence toward the parlor, but he could hear her occasional hitched breath. It made his own catch in his throat.

She didn't dare be alone with him. She was afraid of him, for God's sake.

It confirmed what he'd always suspected.

He *was* a monster.

He'd long recognized that his unusual gift of touch imparted a sort of "otherness" to him that could be sensed even if one knew nothing of his ability. He doubted anyone could point to a specific reason why being around him made people uneasy. No one could say definitively, "*This* is why Lord Devonwood is different from the rest of us." It was simply the sort of thing that raised the hair on the back of one's neck for no apparent cause, left a vague uneasiness in the belly, and made a person shift subtly away from the source of difference.

Even his closest friends, whom he could count on the fingers of one hand, would charitably name him "a hard man to know."

Theodore's voice wafted toward them from beyond the open parlor door, his tone excited. Teddy was always one for great passions—French paintings and German composers, the latest medical advances, and new cartography from the South Pacific. His knowledge of arcane subjects was broad as the ocean, but shallow as a puddle. He never stuck with anything long enough to get bored. The long string of his past fixations would stretch from London Bridge to the Cliffs of Dover.

This Egyptian phase was only the latest.

Perhaps the woman on Devon's arm was also a passing fancy. Maybe he worried for nothing. Emmaline Farnsworth might have no greater tenure in his brother's attention than that canal-widening project Teddy had thought would make them a fortune. By the time Theodore had lost interest in it, Devon had already invested heavily on the strength of his brother's enthusiasm. The family might have seen a devastating loss had Devon not guessed correctly that the rail system would eclipse canals for transporting goods. Fortunately, he moved his holdings to railway stocks before the market turned on the canal company.

All their lives, Devon had cleaned up after Teddy, making sure he didn't suffer for his fecklessness. It was what an older brother was expected to do, especially once their father had died. He was six years Ted's senior. There was enough difference between them that fourteen-year-old Devon must have seemed like a man already grown to Teddy when they'd buried their father and Devon had ascended to the earldom.

Or maybe it was only the weight of his guilt over their father's death that made him seem so much older.

Devon slanted a gaze at the woman on his arm. Emmaline Farnsworth was just another of Theodore's canal certificates. The sooner Devon moved her out of the family portfolio, the better.

"I tell you, the Tetisheri statue will revolutionize the way we view Egypt," Theodore pontificated to his mother and sister as Devon entered the parlor with Miss Farnsworth on his arm. "It's nothing short of a sea change in the body of knowledge on the subject."

On the low table from which his mother usually served tea stood an object about twelve inches high. It was draped with a square of black silk, as if it was a new work of art about to be unveiled before an adoring public.

"Ah, Devon, there you are." Ted waved a hand toward the covered object. "Will you do the honors?"

Devon supposed he should be grateful his brother was so wrapped up in his new amusement that he couldn't be bothered to notice his intended was pale as parchment. It wouldn't do to allow Teddy time to detect that something was amiss. Without thinking, Devon strode forward, reached out, and grasped the black silk.

Everything went suddenly hazy, as if watered gauze had been drawn across his vision.

Devon advanced toward a phantom table where a tall wicker basket stood. A musty, withering scent filled the room with an unwholesome tang.

His hand sank into the basket's narrow opening, but he drew it back sharply when he heard the hiss. Coiled in the bottom of the basket was a black asp, its scales glittering like polished jet. The serpent reared its triangular head and flicked a bifurcated tongue, tasting the air. Its lidless eye fixed on Devon.

Death was hungry for its next meal.

Devon dropped the silk and the vision melted away, like steam evaporating from a mirror. He was back in the familiar parlor with his family and the Farnsworths with neither a bit of wicker nor a single reptile in sight. His mother and sister "ooh-ed" and "ah-ed" over the artwork he'd exposed, but he didn't want to even glance at the Tetisheri statue.

The stench of evil surrounding it was too strong.

Chapter 9

Devon blinked hard, wondering if the flash vision had lasted long enough for anyone to notice. Aside from Emmaline, who'd gravitated toward the fireplace and seemed to be fascinated by the tips of her own shoes, almost everyone's attention was riveted on the Tetisheri statue. Only his mother, the lone other member of his immediate family who was occasionally afflicted with the gift of touch, cast him a questioning look.

He'd been *Sent* an odd vision. Usually his glimpses of the future were much more concrete. He'd even class them as hideously vivid in detail. Since he couldn't imagine any situation in which he'd be called upon to reach into a basket that held an actual snake, this vision had the illusory feel of an allegory. It was a mere impression, not a factual representation, of what was to come.

The realization that he'd likely not be confronted by an asp in the next twelve hours gave him no comfort. In fact, given the hazy nature of the vision, he doubted the twelve-hour rule applied. The danger of which he'd been warned was likely of an extended duration. The moldering scent of a crypt still lingered in his nostrils.

"What did I tell you?" Ted enthused. "Isn't the statue amazing?"

Devon forced himself to look at the cursed thing. At

first glance the carving seemed typical of Egyptian art. The granite sculpture rested on a basalt base, the darker stone emphasizing the lighter coloration of the schist. The work depicted a young woman seated on a throne wearing a braided wig and serpent crown. Her arms were crossed over bared breasts and in her clenched fists she held the crook and flail that bespoke royal rule.

Devon wasn't an aficionado of Egyptian relics, but he'd visited the British Museum often enough to be aware of some of the conventions of the ancient culture's art. He didn't see anything out of the ordinary in the work until he observed her features closely.

Devon snorted in surprise. "She's as European as a Botticelli angel."

"Exactly!" Teddy slapped him on the back. "No flies on my brother, eh? I told you he'd see it straight away."

Devon frowned at him. "All I can see is this must be a forgery of some sort. That girl is no more Egyptian than our Louisa."

"I confess I thought so myself, milord," Dr. Farnsworth said, "At first. But then I began working on the hieroglyphs along the base. They are absolutely genuine."

"Based on what?"

"In this endeavor, I confess to standing on the shoulders of giants. It's been more than sixty years since the discovery of the Rosetta Stone first unlocked the key to this ancient tongue and I relied heavily on an English translation of the work of Antoine-Jean Letronne." Dr. Farnsworth smiled at Theodore. "However, may I add that your brother has been instrumental in assisting me with the translation?"

"Oh, I wouldn't say that," Teddy said with a self-deprecating smile. "Dr. Farnsworth does the work. I merely take notes most of the time."

"Nonsense, my boy." Farnsworth patted Devon's brother on the back. "You're invaluable."

Devon squinted at the squiggles and abstract beasts parading across the base of the statue. "What does the inscription say?"

"Translating hieroglyphs is not an exact science, you understand. However, we are confident we have settled on a fair approximation of the original for the front section of the base. We continue to work on the rest." Dr. Farnsworth adjusted his spectacles so they perched on the end of his nose and then ran a finger over the markings along the front. "Tetisheri, beloved of Isis and Anubis. Pharaoh of the Upper and Lower Kingdoms of the Nile."

"I thought "pharaoh" was the designation for a male ruler," Devon said with a skeptical scowl.

"Normally, yes, but there is precedent for a female pharaoh in Egypt. Remember Cleopatra. She reigned without benefit of a permanent male consort. If you'll kindly direct your attention to this portion of the work . . ." Farnsworth pointed to the statue's chin. "There's a rough patch just there in the granite, if you'd care to feel it."

Devon shook his head. Touching the silk that had covered the benighted thing was bad enough.

"At any rate, it suggests the statue once sported a false beard—an affectation common for female rulers of the Double Kingdom," Dr. Farnsworth explained.

"But why does she look so . . . un-Egyptian?" Louisa asked, leaning forward to peer at the statue intently. "Give her a bonnet and a parasol and your Tetisheri would be perfectly at home strolling in Hyde Park."

"And she'd turn more than a few heads," Ted said. "But the more interesting question is how she arrived in Egypt. We have a theory on that. Dr. Farnsworth, if you'd care to do the honors?"

"You can explain it as well as I," the old man said with a beneficent wave of his hand. He beamed at Theodore with the self-satisfied glow of a professorial soul basking in the accomplishment of his protégé. "Go on, lad."

"We know that Egypt was overrun from time to time by other population groups. For example, about the era of the thirteenth dynasty, the Hyksos came down out of Syria with their chariots and conquered the Lower Nile and its rich Delta." Ted spoke with confidence, but Devon noticed he tucked his hands in his pockets to keep from gesticulating nervously. It was an old trick their tutor had taught him. "The Egyptians had never seen a horse before that time so the Asiatic chariots made quite an impression."

"Never seen a horse?" Louisa said with a giggle. "Can you imagine it?"

"Don't laugh," Theodore said. "I bet you've never seen a camel."

Louisa pulled a face at him. "But at least I know they exist," she grumbled.

"At any rate," Ted said, determined to soldier on despite his sister's interruptions, "the Egyptians must have thought horses were demons of some sort because the Theban royal court fled up the Nile and lived as exiles for years while the Hyksos intruders occupied their homeland."

"Glad to see you've decided to get serious about studying history, Ted," Devon said, impressed that his dilettante brother actually seemed to have learned something.

He noticed that Emmaline had settled into one of the wing chairs flanking the fireplace, positioning herself as far as possible from the rest of the group without actually leaving the room. She stared into the cold hearth without the slightest hint of interest in Teddy's exposition. Well, she'd presumably heard this story before, he supposed.

Or perhaps she was more troubled over that kiss in the orangery than he thought. Devon tried to put the lush softness of her lips out of his mind and concentrate on his brother's new scholastic interest instead.

It was an uphill battle.

"What does the Hyksos invasion have to do with this statue?" Devon asked.

"It establishes a precedent for what we believe this statue proves," Theodore said. "The Tetisheri statue indicates that at some time in the distant past, a *European* group swept down into Egypt, much as the Syrians did. Moreover"—he paused to emphasize his next words—"they stayed to rule."

Dr. Farnsworth clapped softly. "Well done, Theodore. I want you by my side when I present a paper before the Society of Antiquaries on Tetisheri. In fact, I believe you should receive equal recognition for the find."

"Speaking of that," Devon said, "just where did you find it?"

"Therein lies the problem," Dr. Farnsworth said. "Emmaline and I were strolling through a Cairo bazaar one day. If you've never been to one, I can only tell you, you have missed quite an experience. The smell of the spices alone is enough to fill a man's head and—"

"Father," Emmaline said from her self-imposed exile without a glance in his direction, "you're rambling."

"Ah, yes, well, a turbaned fellow there stopped us as we passed his stall and declared he had something for us. That's a frequent opening gambit for a pretty hard sales pitch, but he disappeared behind a curtain and returned with the statue wrapped in cloth. Very excited he was, and adamant that we should take it." Dr. Farnsworth leaned toward Devon's mother in a confiding manner. "Most insistent, I tell you. He wouldn't even accept payment, if you can believe it. He said he'd been expecting me and knew I was the one who should take the statue to where it belongs."

"My, that seems very mysterious," the countess said, fanning herself in excitement.

"Mysterious and in some ways, unfortunate," Dr. Farnsworth said with a deep sigh. "Since the statue wasn't discovered in a documented dig, its provenance is difficult. Moreover, it begs a number of tantalizing questions."

"Such as?" Devon asked.

"Artifacts like this routinely find their way out of the desert and into the bazaars. This is probably a funerary statue for Tetisheri," Theodore said. "The question is where is the rest of it? Where is her tomb? Someone must know where it is. If we could find that, we'd find the record of so much lost history."

"And I suppose you have no idea where to begin that search," Devon said.

If they did, the possible return on investment would be enormous. Back in 1799, when Napoleon's forces commandeered the Rosetta Stone, scholars made much over the chance to decipher hieroglyphs. Earliest known bits of Egyptian culture were excavated and carted off to the Continent by the French forces, along with gushing reports of the splendor of tomb finds and tales of vast riches buried in the sand.

But the Egyptian desert was an exceedingly large haystack and the tomb of a previously unknown female pharaoh who looked strangely European was an exceptionally small needle.

"Actually," Dr. Farnsworth said, "we may be making some progress on that front. As I said before, we've only translated one side of the base. The others may well give us the clues we need in order to mount an expedition."

Devon studied the statue's enigmatic smile. Tetisheri

seemed to be privy to a secret joke. "Other than this statue, has any mention of this unknown queen been found on other ancient markers?"

Farnsworth blinked at him in surprise.

"Unfortunately, no, though your lordship is correct in assuming there ought to be. I applaud your comprehension of such arcane knowledge." The quick frown that pressed his bottle-brush eyebrows together seemed to indicate the opposite. "Tetisheri *should* be listed on other stellae alongside previous and subsequent rulers, but the fact that she has not been discovered there is not, in itself, informative. It was not unknown for names to be expunged from such lists as the rulers fell out of favor with those who came after."

"History is always written by the conquerors, you know," Teddy said.

"No doubt the Theban court regained its ascendancy later and may have been the reason for her eradication from other monuments," Dr. Farnsworth said. "Even so, it seems we have a genuine mystery on our hands. One that begs to be unraveled by an expedition."

"Mounting an expedition is highly speculative," Devon said.

"But it would be a quest for knowledge," Theodore countered. "Even if we failed, we wouldn't lose anything but time."

"And someone's money," Devon said. While the potential payoff for such a gamble could mean great riches, the chances of success were slim. Even given the availability of cheap labor, an archaeological dig would be a logistical nightmare. Travel, equipment, bribes to the local officials for the necessary permits, food for the army of workers—a man could become deluged in debt quicker than the Nile flooded each year.

"That's why I wouldn't dream of seeking investors until we have something more concrete to go on," Dr. Farnsworth said, removing his spectacles and cleaning them on his handkerchief. His face was surprisingly pale for someone who'd supposedly been on site in the Egyptian desert. "To do otherwise would be tantamount to . . . well, to fraud."

The old man gave a devout shiver of distaste. Devon wondered how Farnsworth's complexion could have remained so pasty when he'd arguably spent a good deal of time under the desert sun. It made Devon doubly suspicious of the professor and his highly questionable "find."

"We'll keep working on it, though I wish you had better help than me." Theodore slapped his thigh as an inspiration struck. "Perhaps there's someone from the Society of Antiquaries who knows about hieroglyphs and could help us with the rest of the translation."

"A suggestion worthy of consideration," Dr. Farnsworth said, "but I regret to point out that inquiries such as this are often fraught with layers of professional jealousy and bickering. Even among the very learned, the worst of human nature is likely to rear its ugly head. No, Theodore, we'd do well to keep the statue and our findings about it a secret until we feel confident enough to publish them."

"Would a month be enough time?" Devon's mother wondered. "By then we'll have moved out of the city to Devonwood Park for the summer and could host a large party of guests to view the statue and hear your paper."

Dr. Farnsworth cast a quick glance at his daughter, but Emmaline was still seemingly entranced by the cold fireplace. "Yes, milady," he said. "We might very well have what we need by that time."

"How lovely. It's settled then." Lady Devonwood clasped her be-ringed hands together in delight over the prospect of hosting a large gathering. "I'll start working on the guest list tomorrow and—"

Dr. Farnsworth erupted in a deep hacking cough. Emmaline stirred herself from her place by the fire and hurried to his side.

"Father, are you all right?"

Farnsworth nodded, unable to speak between coughs. Emmaline said their hurried good nights as she shepherded him to the door. The old man muttered halfhearted protests, but allowed himself to be led away, supported by his daughter's arm around his waist.

Theodore hurried after them to offer his help, solicitous as a family beagle.

After seeing the coughing fit, Devon realized Dr. Farnsworth's pallid skin was probably due to illness and in no way detracted from his account of the Tetisheri statue. He shook his head at the way he'd suspected the professor of chicanery. He was in serious danger of becoming a skeptic.

"Let me know if I can help you with the guest list, *Maman,*" Louisa said as she excused herself with a yawn. "There are several charming fellows I'd like to see in Devonwood Park."

"Don't trouble yourself about that. The party will be sprinkled with your gallants," his mother said. "After all, it's your brother's responsibility to make sure you marry well. Where better for you to make your choice than at a house party?"

"Who said anything about choosing?" Louisa said. If Beelzebub had a daughter, she couldn't have managed a more impish grin. "I don't want to marry one of them. I only want to play with *all* of them."

She kissed her mother's cheek and flounced from the room, her broad skirt swaying saucily.

Devon frowned after her. His normally tranquil family life was becoming more chaotic by the moment. He was unexpectedly attracted to the woman his brother wanted.

His brother was turning into a lap dog without any will of his own. And their baby sister was well on her way to becoming a flirt of monumental proportions.

"Good night, *Maman,*" Devon said, as he gave his mother a dutiful peck on the cheek.

"Do not think you'll get away that easily, young man. I saw your face after you lifted that bit of black silk. You had a vision." She grasped his hand and pulled him down onto the settee beside her. "Now what was it?"

"Nothing," he said, dragging a hand over his face. He didn't want to tell his mother about the eerie sense of doom the image of the asp had left him with. "It was nothing. A flash Sight only. No true message. Once I realized the cloth was *Sending,* I dropped it."

That was true enough. His last vision was like nothing he'd ever experienced. It was like trying to peer through isinglass or interpret the shadowy remnants of a dream. He was certain the snake wasn't real.

But Devon was convinced the danger was.

"No vision. No headache. Truly." He had to distract her from this topic. No good could come from sharing his disturbing *Sending*. "Nothing for you to worry about."

"Then tell me, what on earth were you doing with your brother's fiancée so long in the orangery?"

His mother's new subject of conversation was not an improvement over the old one.

"I wasn't doing anything with her, and she's not his fiancée." *Yet.* "We know next to nothing about her. I was hoping to remedy that."

"Hmmm." Lady Devonwood leaned back and cast an appraising gaze at him. He'd seen the same look in her eye the last time she'd considered acquiring a new stallion for their herd in the country. The horse had already thrown a couple riders. She had to weigh whether the beast was already too riddled with vice for subsequent training to make a difference. In the end, she'd bought him, but no one other than Devon could ride him. "And what did you learn about Miss Farnsworth?"

That she kisses like Aphrodite reborn. And if I don't get her out of Theodore's life quickly, our family may never recover. Of course, he couldn't tell his mother any of that. "She enjoys Keats and a spot of botany."

"Hmmm," his mother said again. "What a pity the girl doesn't wear spectacles like her father. I suspect I could get a good *Sending* out of that sort of glass."

Despite her glowing praise for the ability that marked them as unique, Devon's mother hadn't willingly sought out an opportunity to use her gift of touch in years. Hers was a weaker gift than Devon's. It was limited to discernment of a person's past through contact with any glass object they'd handled, but using her abilities still carried a stiff price for Lady Devonwood. The last time she'd purposefully touched a glass object, the ensuing headache had left her bedridden for a week.

"No, *Maman,* I don't want you to subject yourself to that," Devon said. "We'll learn more of Miss Farnsworth in the days to come without resorting to Preston witchery."

"It's not witchery. It's simply something we're born with. Would you call it witchery had you been left-handed or redheaded? No." She gave her head an emphatic shake. "I'll not have you denigrating Great-Grandmere Delphinia's legacy to the lineage that way. Besides, according to all the family stories, it was love at first sight between her and your great-grandsire and—"

"Love at first sight," Devon grumbled. "Yet more proof of witchery."

"Bite your tongue, son. Love, however it arrives, is not something to be mocked."

He knew his parents' marriage had not been a love

match, at least, not at first. His mother often likened them to a pair of frogs set in a pot to boil. Their affection warmed so slowly, she only realized at his passing how deeply she'd come to love Devon's taciturn father. His father had loved her just as intensely, even though he'd found it difficult to express.

His mother rested a gentle hand on his forearm. "I only tell you these things because I want you to be proud of who you are, Devon, where you've come from and what you can do."

"There's the rub, isn't it? There's not much I can do with my prescience." He leaned forward, elbows balanced on his knees, and sighed. "What good is it if I can see the future but am powerless to change it?"

"Devon, stop blaming yourself." She palmed his cheeks and turned his face toward her so she could press her lips to his forehead. "I certainly don't blame you. You did all you could."

She rose and bade him good night, leaving him to stare at the strange statue alone.

Her words were cold comfort. Even if she didn't hold him responsible, that didn't change a thing.

His father was still dead.

Chapter 10

"Now, children, stop fussing," Monty said as Theodore and Emmaline helped him up the long staircase. She was surprised to notice how loosely his jacket draped around his frame. He'd lost more weight than she'd suspected, leaving him frail, his bones bird-thin. Another spasm of coughing shook his body. He pulled out his handkerchief again to cover his mouth, but wasn't quite quick enough.

Theodore stared at the faint pinkish tinge at the corner of Monty's mouth and then met Emma's gaze in wordless sympathy. He left Emmaline in the sitting room of the Blue Suite, hustled her father into his chamber, and rang for the valet, Fritz, who appeared almost instantly.

Emmaline was prepared to help Monty, but the valet wouldn't hear of it. He promised to take special care of "the good Dr. Farnsworth," and disappeared into Monty's room.

"Fritz will get him ready for bed, and if I know our Fritzi, he'll see that your father has a hot toddy to bundle him off to sleep as well," Teddy said, his tone brittle with forced normalcy.

Emmaline heard Monty's voice through the closed door, rasping after his fit. She still detected his usual lilt of jocularity as he spoke with the man who assisted him into his nightshirt.

"Tell Mr. Fritz to be sure to mix in extra honey and lemon," Emmaline said. Her father wasn't fond of the peaty, smoky flavor of scotch without plenty of other mitigating ingredients. Still, a toddy might be just the thing to quiet his cough and help Monty sleep.

"Travel is exhausting and we've been on the move for months now. That's all it is," Teddy said. "With a proper bed, I'm sure the professor will be right as rain in no—"

"No, he won't." She'd been lying to herself for a while now. Tonight, she finally had to face facts. Emmaline sank into one of the Tudor chairs and let her tears come. Her shoulders shook.

She'd tried to fool herself into thinking Monty's ailment was temporary, but she'd never heard of anyone who suffered from consumption getting better. Even if they were successful with this confidence scheme and managed to raise the ridiculous sum of money demanded by the Görbersdorf sanatorium, there was no guarantee of a cure at that German mountain retreat.

Theodore knelt beside her chair and took her hand. "Do you want me to summon a physician?"

She shook her head. "We both know what this is. All a doctor will do is bleed him and purge him. It'll only make him weaker."

It was hard to imagine her life without Monty and his outlandish schemes twirling at its center. The small scared child who still lived inside her shivered. With Monty gone, she'd go back to being plain Emma Potts, alone, cast adrift in the world.

"Don't be afraid, Emmaline," Theodore said softly.

His words startled her. She hadn't thought him able to divine her emotions so accurately.

"You have me now." He pressed a kiss to her knuckles.

Her breath caught at the shining goodness of his heart. Not for the first time, she wished there was something real, something true about her courtship with Theodore.

Maybe she could will it to be so.

She leaned down and cupped his chin to tip his face up to hers, inviting him to kiss her. She needed him to kiss her. Needed it to be more searingly real than his brother's kiss in the orangery.

Theodore's mouth closed over hers for a few heartbeats.

It was pleasant. A gesture full of comfort. Sweet enough to melt the heart.

But Teddy's kiss didn't make her toes curl in the slightest.

Why couldn't she love this kind man? Theodore's soul might glint with shining whiteness, but hers was black as a Stygian stream. She drew back. "You'd better go."

"I wish I didn't have to. I wish we were already married so I could stay with you."

"Theodore, please, that's inappropriate." She bit her lower lip. "I haven't even said yes yet."

"Why don't you?" He plopped down on the floor beside her chair and rested his head against her knee. "You know how I love you, Em. What's stopping you?"

Yesterday she'd have told herself it was because she was a confidence huckster and he was her mark. She needed to maintain professional distance. But what if she convinced Monty to abandon the game? Maybe then she could accept Theodore's proposal.

Emmaline had picked up the *pigeon drop* in no time. Would love be so difficult a game to learn?

She stroked his thick blond hair, feeling very tender. Teddy was sincere and attentive. He made her feel like a princess every time he looked at her.

So what if his kisses were as exciting as a second cousin's?

Of course, Emmaline didn't have any second cousins so far as she knew, but she imagined kissing one would feel exactly like kissing Theodore. Plenty of women made do with the merely pleasant and were grateful to have found it in a husband.

Emmaline might have been one of them if she hadn't kissed Lord Devonwood. Twice.

Monty's renewed cough in the next room made her lift her head. Just like that, she knew she was deluding herself when she imagined that anything deeper might grow between her and Theodore. Even if she weren't confused by her body's response to Lord Devonwood, there was still the fact that for the sake of his health, Monty needed this confidence game to succeed. That sanatorium in the Alps was his only hope.

Which meant she was better off without permanent entanglements with either of the brothers. It made no sense to become attached to someone she had to swindle.

"I must go." She rose and headed for Monty's chamber. "Father needs me."

Chapter 11

Emmaline didn't say no this time.

Her breasts fit Devon's hands perfectly. Soft and silky, with hard tips the color of peach pits that fairly burned into his palms. The wonderful thing about that cream and rose gown was the neckline was cut low enough that her breasts practically tumbled out of their own accord, though it had been his pleasure to ease them free. The stiff bodice provided an admirable shelf for her luscious bosom now that he'd liberated her breasts from their whalebone constraints.

He stepped back to admire his handiwork. Emmaline looked up at him, her eyes enormous, her face taut with need. Her breasts rose and fell in time with her short jerky breaths.

He could happily watch them for hours.

"Griffin, please," she said. She made a desperate little noise in the back of her throat as he bent to circle her nipples with his tongue. The fact that she wanted him nearly made him lose control and spill his seed in his trousers like a callow youth.

He'd always known there was a caged beast within him. Now the chain he kept on it snapped. He turned her around with no gentleness at all and made short work of the lacing at her spine. Then he clawed through the similar fastenings of her corset and released her. He grasped the neckline of her undergarment and ripped the cotton all-in-one beneath the corset. He bared her back all the way down to the sweet cleft of her bum.

He yanked the gown lower, taking the crinoline with it, ripping the sheer cotton between the wires of the hooped cage that enclosed her lower half. She didn't complain.

He made a mental note to buy her a new wardrobe later, one that was designed to be removed with less effort. Of course, he could always just lift her skirt, but he burned to see all of her.

She stepped out of the ruins of her gown, her back still to him, wearing only her gartered stockings and neat cream-colored slippers. She lifted her arms and pulled the pins from her coiffure, shaking out her long locks. Gleaming with inner fire, her hair draped her shoulders like an autumn mantle.

But lovely as the shining locks were, his attention was riveted below the curve of her waist.

He didn't think he'd ever seen anything more erotic than her heart-shaped bum above those neatly tied bows on the backs of her thighs.

He sank his teeth into her shoulder as his hands palmed the globes of her buttocks, lifting and teasing. He didn't break her skin, but he marked her all the same. She was his. She groaned in pleasurable agony and leaned back into him. She arched her spine, pressing her bum against his hardened groin.

He thought about bending her double and taking her from behind with her fingers splayed on the cool slate squares of the orangery floor.

No, if his goal was to convince his brother Emmaline was wrong for him, it wouldn't do to ravish her here in the solitude and sweetness of his interior garden. Better for him to carry her naked through the house so all could see the American miss for what she was.

He scooped her up and started for the door. She draped her arms around his neck and leaned her head on his shoulder.

"I've wanted you since the first time I saw you," she murmured.

So confiding. So trusting.

He wanted her, too. And now he'd have her. Protecting his brother from her was just an added bonus.

"I just didn't know how to tell Teddy." She took one of his earlobes between her lips and sucked hard.

His eyes threatened to roll back in his head and he stopped before he reached the door.

What if he didn't want to protect Ted? What if he wanted her for himself?

He pinned her against the smooth stone wall of the orangery. After a few moments of fumbling, he freed his cock from his trousers. She hitched a leg over his hip and he slid into her, a warm, wet homecoming.

For a moment, he found himself wishing there was more to this joining than animal passion. He was surprised and a little shaken by the longing in his chest. A pleasurable release was all he'd come to expect from such an encounter.

Why hope for more?

But part of him still wondered if it was possible that in taking him into her body, she could also take in his soul. Might it be that she knew him? And despite what she'd seen inside him, still accepted every bit.

Then their mouths met in a kiss that stole the breath from his lungs.

Like a succubus, she drained every bit of moisture and wind, every bit of his life from him, but he didn't care. Devon strained against her, plunging in with abandon while she urged him on with nearly incoherent little commands.

"Deeper . . . yes, there . . . oh, that."

Devon's world spiraled down to the ethereal physics of heat and friction. To the wonder of her dark, wet cavern and the pressure of seed rising in his shaft.

"Devon, you bloody bastard!"

As his body erupted in shuddering spasms, he turned to see his brother standing in the orangery doorframe.

Murder glinted in Teddy's usually mild eyes.

Devon jerked himself awake. Daylight streamed in narrow slats through the shutters over his windows. His body continued to pump the last bit of his nocturnal emission onto his own belly.

"Damnation," he muttered.

He removed his nightshirt and used it to clean himself, feeling even dirtier when he was done. He drew on a black silk banyan and rang for a bath to be drawn, hoping that would remove the musky tang of his dream from his mind.

Emmaline Farnsworth had been as good as her word. In the weeks that followed the tumultuous day of their arrival, she'd been careful never to be alone with Devon again. He saw her only each evening at the supper table and once at breakfast when he'd been foolish enough to rise early to join the family for buttered eggs and kippers.

Fritz bustled around the suite, setting up and filling the copper hip bath in the adjoining private dressing room. Devon's bedchamber faced the front of the house, but the dressing room looked out over his walled garden. He parted the heavy curtains and looked down at the Dionysus statue.

She was there again. After breaking her fast each morning, Emmaline had taken to spending time in the shady retreat. Continuing to draw the drunken god, he supposed. She was always bent over her sketchbook.

Devon watched her from his window above, tormenting himself with the line of her spine and the way her hair curled in tiny tendrils along her nape. He could almost taste the salty sweetness of the skin along her hairline.

"Your bath is ready, milord."

Devon dismissed his valet with a silent wave. He didn't trust his voice not to be inappropriately passion-rough.

As Devon removed his banyan and settled into the tepid

water, he reminded himself that he had not experienced a vision. Nothing was written in stone. Just because he dreamed of rutting Miss Farnsworth six ways from Sunday, it did not signify that sexual congress between them was inevitable.

It was only a dream.

Part of him didn't seem convinced. Up it rose like a tower between his legs.

He took it roughly in his hand.

"It was only a dream," he repeated as his strokes fell into a frenetic, almost punishing, rhythm. "Only a dream."

CHAPTER 12

When Devon finally made it downstairs after his ablutions, he was met at the foot of the steps by his butler.

"Good morning, your lordship. One trusts you slept well." It was Baxter's standard morning greeting and did not require a response. The butler held a silver salver before him with a single card on it.

"Despite the earliness of the hour, Lord Northrop has come calling. He awaits your pleasure in the parlor," Baxter said with an irritated sniff.

Devon suspected it upset his butler's agenda when members of the aristocracy forgot the accepted hours for receiving guests and appeared willy-nilly at inopportune times.

"Shall one inform him that you are not at home?"

Baxter wasn't proposing he tell a lie. Such a thing would be as far removed from that worthy servant's righteous imagination as the outrageous idea of sitting down in his employers' presence. "Not at home" might well mean "not receiving guests at this time" for any number of reasons, even if one was on the premises.

Or more sinisterly, it might signify "not at home" to the specific visitor. That carried almost as sharp a sting as a direct cut.

The convention was understood by all.

All but Northrop. If Lionel Norris, Marquess of Northrop, was told such a thing, he would roar through the house in any case in search of Devon. Northrop had no patience for anyone else's schedule. Devon's mercurial friend cared only that his own be disrupted as little as possible.

"No, I'll see him," Devon said. He hoped his friend wasn't in search of another loan. Northrop was always light in the pockets and just as perpetually forgetful about repaying his debts.

He had been his frequent companion since their days at Oxford together. Northrop didn't come into his title until much later, long after he had passed the age of majority. But when they were boys together, he understood how the weight of the peerage acquired early bore down on Devon and did his best to lighten matters. Even if their interests had diverged spectacularly since their school days, they still had a solid past as the foundation of their friendship. Loyalty was something upon which no man could put a price.

And Northrop was nothing if not doggedly faithful.

To his friends, at least. Devon knew better than to inquire too closely on that subject with respect to Northrop's mistresses.

Devon found him sprawling on one of Lady Devonwood's favorite wing chairs, a thigh slung over its brocade-covered arm. Northrop's booted foot tapped out the rhythm of a tune only he could hear. His chin rested in his palm in an air of total boredom. His jacket and waistcoat were cut in the first stare of fashion, but the elegant fabric was so wrinkled it was obvious he'd passed the night in them. The top two buttons of Northrop's shirt were undone. His collar was missing a stud, sticking out on one side at an odd angle.

A shock of dark hair fell over his forehead, nearly obscuring eyes that were blue as the surf off Brighton on a summer's day. Northrop didn't twitch so much as an eyelash when Devon entered with Baxter in his wake.

"Hullo, Dev," Northrop slurred. "You're unusually late to rise."

"And you're unusually early to call."

"Not me. Haven't been to bed yet. Why don't you keep a dram of whisky in this blasted parlor?" Northrop shot an evil glare at Baxter. The whites of his eyes were shot through with tiny ribbons of red. He'd either been drinking all night or someone's finger had poked him soundly in both sockets. "All that one would offer me is tea."

He shuddered as if Baxter had suggested he drink hemlock.

Devon glanced at the ormolu clock on the mantel. Only half past ten. When Northrop was this deeply in his cups it was very hard to fish him out of them. Best thing to do was see him safely under the table with more spirits and let him sleep it off.

"Fetch some whisky, Baxter." Devon turned back to his friend and took the other wing chair. "To what are we drinking this fine morning?"

"To heaven. To hell. To how many angels can dance on the bloody head of a bloody pin. What do I care?"

"Good." Devon hitched a leg over the arm of the chair in conscious imitation of the marquess. Later he'd move his leg back down and Northrop would probably follow suit. He often used this technique to settle his friend. "I thought we might be drinking to your health and I'd hate to waste the whisky. Seems to me that's a lost cause."

Northrop cast him a withering glance.

Baxter returned with two tumblers of amber liquid and served both gentlemen. Devon made to clink rims with Northrop, but his friend tipped up his glass and drained the contents in one swallow without waiting for a toast. Baxter raised his brows wordlessly and sidled from the room.

"You're vexed over something," Devon guessed.

Northrop lifted his empty glass in an equally empty toast. "High marks to you, Griffin. You were always the brightest of the three of us."

He referred to the trio of friends who styled themselves the "Fallen Angels." Devon, Lord Northrop, and Lord Kingsley had formed the unholy trinity while they were at Oxford. Tales of their bad behavior set the bar quite high for would-be scoundrels who hoped to follow their example. Devon and Kingsley had grown up since then. The jury was still out on Northrop.

Devon let his leg slide off the arm of the chair and sat upright.

"A regular Lucifer the Light-bearer in the flesh, that's you." Northrop eyed his glass as if considering whether or not to lick its sides for the last of the whisky, then laughed, raucously and belatedly, at his own wit. He slid his leg off the arm of the chair and let his boot hit the parlor floor with a resounding thud. "Of course, I'm vexed. I had to hear about it at White's, for God's sake, instead of from you. How could you keep this opportunity from me when you know damned well it could be the answer to all my money woes?"

Better stewardship would be the answer for his friend's money woes, but Devon knew better than to suggest it. Northrop might not mind taking loans, but he was adamant about not taking advice.

"What the devil are you talking about?" Devon asked.

"That bleeding statue, of course, the Titty-sharing thing-gummy. What did you think?" The tumbler slipped from Northrop's fingers and shattered on the polished hardwood. "Sorry about that. Deucedly clumsy of me."

Devon waved away his apology. What was Sheridan crystal among friends? "How did you happen to hear about the Tetisheri statue?"

"I told you. I was at White's and who should be there but your brother with an older gent. Thick as thieves, the pair of them, huddled over a thick journal, nattering away at something in a secretive manner." Northrop leaned back into the tufted wing chair. "Well, nothing draws a crowd like a secret, you know."

He looked hopefully at Devon's whisky glass, but Devon didn't see the need to ring for another one for his friend, even though he was certain Baxter lurked just on the other side of the doorjamb. If Northrop was already unable to keep a tumbler in his grasp, he'd be safely snoring soon.

"At any rate," Northrop went on since no more whisky seemed to be in the offing, "pretty soon someone asks Theodore what's the meaning of all those odd little squiggles and drawings in his book. Frankly, I suspected they had a stash of French postcards hidden in there, myself."

Trust Northrop to hope for pictures of women in lewd positions and indecent states of undress. Northrop changed mistresses more often than some men changed their socks.

"Imagine my surprise when I find out there's a treasure to tempt Midas hidden in the Egyptian sands. And it seems our Teddy's got hold of the map, as it were." Northrop pressed a fist to his breastbone to stifle a belch. He was less than successful. "Then I learn your brother's all set to mount an expedition to recover the hoard."

So much for keeping the statue a secret till Dr. Farnsworth was ready to present his scholarly paper on the subject at his mother's house party.

"Trust me, the investigation is still in the preliminary stages," Devon said. "No one should be contemplating an expedition yet."

"Well, they are, and it was damned bad form of you not to let your friends sign on with the first subscription of investors."

"Investors?"

"Yes, the way fellows were clamoring to be allowed to buy into the enterprise, I wouldn't be surprised if Teddy's already incorporated the damned thing and sold stock certificates. I certainly would have," Northrop said, his speech as thick as his tongue. "I'd expect Theodore not to come to me with it. But you, Dev, what are you thinking to keep such a thing from your friends? If we split the expedition between you and me and Kingsley, we'll be rich as Croesus when all's said and done. Now, whatever they find, it's likely to be divided so many ways, the riches will be like a trickle of water when it ought to have been a flood." He shook his head. "Badly done, old son. Badly done."

"First of all," Devon said testily, "you haven't any money to invest."

"I would if you loaned it to me."

"Not a farthing." Devon rose and pulled his friend to his feet. "Come, Northrop. Be serious. Do you really think I'd keep you from something I thought had a Chinaman's chance of success? You're drunk and you're rambling. Let's take a turn around the garden to clear your head and I'll send you home in my barouche."

Devon's chest constricted at the thought of running into Emmaline in the garden after his erotic dream and just as deeply erotic bath. All he wanted was a few moments with her to prove to himself he wasn't a mindless, rutting beast, but she'd been adroit at avoiding him.

Devon was counting on the fact that he had Lord Northrop with him to keep Emmaline from bolting when she saw him approach. He understood why she took pains to steer clear of private speech with him, but he chafed at not being able to talk with her at all. With his slightly tipsy friend in tow, Devon could force a conversation without seeming boorish.

"I guess you're right. I do need some sleep," Northrop said with a sigh, the wind spilling from his sails now that the hope of a quick, easy fortune had been squashed. "Damned if I'm not supposed to be at Lord Whitmore's this evening for yet another tedious debutante ball."

Devon frowned. "I think my family is committed to that occasion as well."

"Then I'm sorry I roused you out of bed early. We'll both need our rest to be ready for that. A fellow has to stay on his toes at those pesky things, lest he be entrapped by an enterprising miss."

"I hate to break it to you, but most marriage-minded mammas have already warned their daughters off as far as you're concerned," Devon said as they walked companionably down the corridor. "You rarely have two coins to rub together. Your estate is mortgaged to the rafters and you're like a hound to the scent for anything in skirts. You are, in a word, *ineligible,* despite your title."

Northrop's grin stretched pleasantly across his handsome face. "What makes you think I haven't worked damned hard to be accorded that status?"

"In that case, my congratulations," Devon said. "But don't worry. I doubt you're destined for perpetual bachelorhood. Perhaps a wealthy industrialist's daughter with creaky knees and a case of the squints will want her papa to buy her a title one day."

"Bite your tongue. A bundle of cash wrapped in a plain wife is not part of my plan. But it may well come to that if I don't figure out how to stop the estate from leaking funds like a sieve." Northrop shuddered at the thought, then sighed expressively. "Still, I am in the middle of my thirty-first year without a wife or child—that I know of, in any case—and, well, hang it all, a man begins to wonder sometimes what a little domesticity might be like."

Devon figured that was the whisky talking. His friend had never shown the least interest in a permanent relationship with a woman before.

Northrop stopped beneath a painting of a young lady in a fetching yellow gown from an earlier century when it was no sin for the daring décolletage to proclaim her femininity, nearly to the nipples. "A singularly handsome woman that," Northrop said as he admired the portrait, with special attention to her bosom. "Both of them."

"Careful. That's my great-grandmother Delphinia. It's said my grandsire forsook a very profitable match with the daughter of a duke for the chance to marry that singularly handsome commoner. She had no fortune, nothing to commend her." Except a bit of otherworldly ability Devon heartily wished had skipped over him in the Preston side of his lineage. In most grand homes, a maternal great-grandmother's portrait would have been relegated to a distant chamber in an unused wing while patriarchal ancestors graced the public rooms. But Lady Devonwood was proud of Delphinia and the gift of touch she'd brought to the family. If only Devon didn't find the ability more a curse than a gift he might agree with her. "It was love at first sight apparently."

"With magnificent breasts like that, I shouldn't wonder." Northrop scoffed. "Still, one ought to call things what they are. *Lust* at first sight is more likely."

"Good, so you don't believe in it either," Devon said.

"Oh, I believe in it. Every time I take up with a new mistress, I believe in love at first sight most sincerely," Northrop said. "But then the notion wears off after a fortnight. Without fail. One could practically set one's chronometer by it."

A fortnight. It had been more than that since Emmaline

Farnsworth had burst into his life and captured his thoughts in almost every idle moment. If Northrop was right, Devon shouldn't still be mooning around over her like a lovesick calf. Perhaps he simply required more time. Maybe he need wait only another week or so and her allure would begin to pale.

When Devon and his friend pushed through the French doors leading out to the garden, Northrop stopped short on the crunching gravel.

"Hallo. What manner of angels are these who've fallen from heaven? They want a bit of corrupting, I'll wager." Northrop's eyes darkened with interest as he gazed at the two women seated near the Dionysus statue. Louisa had joined Emmaline in the bright mid-morning. "Yet another thing you've been keeping from me."

"That's Theodore's fiancée," Devon said. Emmaline and Teddy still weren't officially engaged, but Northrop didn't need to know that. "Behave yourself."

The women laughed over something on Emmaline's sketchbook, Louisa's silvery peal and Emma's melodious lower tones harmonizing in the fresh morning air.

"Teddy's captured that blond goddess?" Northrop shook his head in wonderment.

"No, the other one."

"The redhead, you mean? Yes, she is lovely. I can certainly see why Teddy's smitten."

Teddy wasn't the only one. Devon's fixation on Emmaline Farnsworth was fast becoming an obsession.

"But any lady over one and twenty is a bit long in the tooth for my taste," Northrop said. "Who's the blonde?"

Devon's blood heated. "That's my sister."

"That's little Louisa? Oh, you poor man. You'll wear yourself sick trying to beat the wolves away from that door," Northrop said. "Why, she was still in leading strings when you came into your title. To think I used to tug her pigtails and dandle her on my knee. Damned if that doesn't still sound like good sport. Believe I'll just nip over and reintroduce myself, shall I?"

"Not if you value your manhood, friend," Devon said sternly. "Meddling with my sister is a two ball offense, I assure you."

Northrop laughed. "Who says I want to meddle with her? I just want to renew our acquaintance." He glanced down at his less than impeccable appearance. "But perhaps you're right. There'll be time enough for that at Lord Whitmore's this evening. Be kind enough to ask your sister to save a waltz for me. There's a good chap."

"Not a chance." Devon led him to the stable and ordered his groom to take Lord Northrop home.

"Just a dance, Dev," Northrop said in the same wheedling tone he used when he tried to borrow money he had no intention of repaying. "Surely you don't think me so mean a fellow that I'd despoil a friend's sister, do you?"

"Ask Louisa yourself, if you want to waltz with her," he said with gruffness as Northrop climbed into the elegant equipage with less stumbling than Devon expected. Northrop's speech had stopped slurring, too.

Perhaps Northrop wasn't as drunk as he'd seemed, but why would he fain inebriation?

"If you venture more than tripping the light fantastic with Louisa, remember what I said." Devon made a snipping motion with his fingers. "Two balls."

Chapter 13

"A man is here to see you, milord. A Mr. O'Malley," Lord Kingsley's butler Farley said, stressing the Irish surname with noticeable repugnance. "He did not present a card. Shall I tell him you will not receive him?"

He frowned. The last time he'd met with the Irishman, he'd been unrecognizable in shabby attire at a disreputable pub. He'd warned O'Malley not to show his face in Mayfair and most specifically not to call openly at his home. If his underling disobeyed a direct order, it meant something important must have transpired.

"No, Farley, show him in. But when he leaves, make sure he uses the kitchen door."

"As to that, at least Mr. O'Malley knew he would err sadly should one of his ilk darken your front doorstep. He presented himself to Cook in the back alleyway before he asked to be received."

Farley turned on his heel to retrieve O'Malley from wherever he'd been left cooling his heels. He was probably languishing in the scullery, seated on a high stool before the piles of root vegetables waiting to be scrubbed and peeled for the evening meal. Or perhaps he was situated beneath the pheasants Cook had left hanging in the larder till they were nearly rancid in order to tenderize the meat. Such slights would serve to show O'Malley his place and were bound to appeal to Farley's extreme sense of decorum.

Sometimes Kingsley thought Farley had an even higher sense of his employer's worth than he did himself. And that was saying something.

He returned his attention to the book he'd been studying. It was an obscure tome, a grimoire of sorts, dealing with the ancient cult of the Egyptian afterlife. The text was an exhaustive translation of the *Book of Anubis,* a collection of wisdom from the keeper of the dead.

He narrowed his eyes and tried to concentrate. He'd never been a scholar, not even when he had studied law at Oxford to appease his father.

Wouldn't the old man be surprised to see me studying this hard?

So would the other two "Fallen Angels."

His father had insisted he study law so he'd be adept when it came time to take his place in the House of Lords. Instead of wasting his time on arcane bits of common law, he'd discovered a passion for the occult.

According to the preface, the original manuscript was one of the few scrolls saved from the catastrophic fire that destroyed the library of Alexandria. The translator, who boasted advanced degrees in several dead languages, claimed to have discovered the manuscript in an old monastery high in the Alps. The text provided the secret incantations and spells necessary to insure a superior afterlife.

In Kingsley's opinion, this world was infinitely preferable to the next. An afterlife was all well and good, but given a choice, he would take this life, thank you very much.

He simply needed a good deal more power and money, and buckets more time to enjoy wielding them.

Fortunately, there was one potion in the book that promised to deliver all the time he wanted.

The Flail of Anubis.

The spell had a fanciful name, but he considered it fitting. The jackal-headed god of death was often depicted holding a flail, an agricultural tool that resembled a crop-sized whip, and a shepherd's crook. Taken together, they symbolized kingship.

Kingsley didn't aspire to that. He had no wish to tend a flock of stupid people. Caring for the whiny, incessant needs of others held no allure. It reminded him of the constant complaints of his estate's few tenants. But the power represented by the flail appealed to him immensely.

According to the grimoire, the real flail of Anubis wasn't an actual whip or even a threshing tool. It was a potion of such immense power, the one who brewed and used it daily would be gifted with preternatural long life—hundreds of years, quite possibly millennia depending on how much of the active ingredient one had—with no diminution of intellectual or physical prowess.

It would also render the bearer impossible to resist. With a word, he could sway a hearer to take any action he wished. Once he'd brewed and drunk the potion, if he ordered his butler to run into the street before a team of runaway horses, the power of this suggestion would mean faithful Farley would find himself unable to disobey. Even if it was obvious his obedience would result in a very unpleasant death. The grimoire was specific on this point.

Kingsley had already tried some of the lesser spells in the grimoire and found they worked very well indeed. The strengthening potion, for example, had given him a grip that made larger men flinch. He saw no reason to doubt that the incantation and potion for the Flail of Anubis would be any less effective.

But what good were spells if one didn't have the proper ingredients to brew them? Unless O'Malley retrieved the

Tetisheri statue, he didn't see how he'd ever come by the elusive grains necessary to complete the potion.

The text was very specific. There was no substitute for the required grain. Even though the receipt for the potion called for only a pinch of the active ingredient, it was that which gave the spell its power.

According to the text, the ancient rye needed had been found during Alexander's time. It had been ground to a fine powder. Then the grain was secreted inside a hollowed-out female statue with the stylized beauty of a Greek goddess disguised as an Egyptian queen.

It had seemed the pinnacle of good fortune when word of the Tetisheri statue had come to him through his long-tentacled network of occult-minded folk. Its unique properties, the European appearance of the statue dressed in Egyptian garb, fit the description in the text exactly.

When the statue, for which he had *already paid,* wound up in the hands of an American, he'd nearly had an apoplectic fit. How could this Dr. Farnsworth, who didn't have a clue of its true significance, surface with his Tetisheri when it should have been delivered into Mr. O'Malley's grimy paws?

"Your lordship," the man with the aforementioned paws said at the open doorway.

Kingsley motioned for him to enter. O'Malley doffed his disreputable cap and twisted it nervously.

"If it so pleases you, sir, I know I wasn't to come here, but—"

"You're right. It does not please me."

"Be that as it may, milord, I thought an exception might be made once you'd heard my news."

Silence stretched between them. A bead of perspiration slid down O'Malley's cheek, though the day wasn't especially warm for June.

"While one of us is still young, Mr. O'Malley."

"Right. As you know, I've been keeping me eye on the folk at Lord Devonwood's house."

"Don't tell me what I know. Tell me what I don't know." Lord, the man was an idiot. Perhaps when it came time to test the efficacy of the Flail of Anubis potion, O'Malley would be the one galloping headlong before a runaway team.

"It's come to me notice that all the fine folk at Devonwood House are going to be gone this evening."

Again, it was something he already knew. After all, he too was expected at Lord Whitmore's ball, but he wondered about O'Malley's sources. "How did you come by this knowledge?"

"The scullery maid there at Devonwood House, sir. She . . . she talks in her sleep sometimes."

Tupping a slattern for information. Well, he expected no better of O'Malley. Serve the man right if he got himself a good dose of the French pox along with his pillow talk.

"And what's more, the help's bein' given the night off to boot," O'Malley said. "There'll be nary a soul about this evening, so I was thinkin'—"

"Something you've been warned not to attempt." A little spite would serve to keep O'Malley on his toes. Nevertheless, Kingsley hadn't known about the Devonwood House help being absent this evening, so the Irishman was proving his usefulness. "In this case, however, I believe you may have stumbled upon an actual idea. You will avail yourself of this opportunity to enter Devonwood House and remove the statue from the premises by whatever means necessary."

"I'm not exactly sure where they're keeping it," O'Malley admitted.

Scullery maids rarely ventured beyond the lower realms

of any great house. Would that O'Malley had set his sights a little higher and lifted the skirts of the upstairs maid.

"Guests at Devonwood House are always quartered in the Blue Suite." He ought to know. He'd slept there often enough over the years. Taking a sheet of foolscap from his desk drawer, he sketched a quick floor plan of the third level of the town house. "It is logical to assume that Dr. Farnsworth keeps the statue close by him."

But since the American could have no idea of the piece's true significance, he probably didn't have it under lock and key.

Once the statue fell into Kingsley's hands, he'd see it enjoyed more protection than the Crown jewels. After all, once the magical grain stored inside Tetisheri was gone, there'd be no more to be had.

Ever.

"I tell you, my dear, I see this little plan of ours unfolding so neatly, it's almost as if the game's running itself," Monty said, smoothing his waxed mustache with the back of his hand. "You should have heard them at White's. A whisper campaign has been launched on our behalf by the nattering wags of London and now half the ton seems to be lining up, clamoring to invest in our expedition."

Emmaline heard him wheeze a bit when he drew a deep breath. He'd not had another coughing attack since that horrendous one that had driven him from the dining room on the night of their arrival. Theodore had given him a bottle of Glenlivet to keep in his bedchamber and since he frequently called for lemon and sugar to be brought up, Emmaline suspected Monty was self-medicating with regularity. If the additional spirits kept him from hacking out his lights, she wouldn't scold.

She caught him stealing a glimpse of himself reflected in the window glass. He turned sideways to examine his reed-thin physique and straightened his posture. She smiled. No matter what their age, all men were peacocks at heart.

"Yes, indeed," he went on. "I'm almost of a mind to form a corporation and sell shares."

Emmaline's heart lifted. It might mean they didn't need to bilk Theodore.

Or his brother.

"Everyone's doing it. Why, the other day I saw a notice for –and I am not exaggerating—a corporation formed 'for the undertaking of a great enterprise, but no one to know what it is.'" Monty chuckled. "We may have wasted our time in the confidence game, Emma, m'love. The stock market is where the real dupes can be had."

"But isn't there more risk of prison with stock fraud?" she asked as she turned around to allow him to fasten the choker of fresh water pearls at her throat.

"There is that," he admitted. "A solitary person who's been swindled is reluctant to own up to it. They'd rather suffer the loss in private than be known for a fool in public. But when a whole gaggle of folks are taken in by fraudulent stock certificates, they feel safety in numbers when it comes to unmasking their foolishness and greed."

Emma's heart sank. "Then we proceed as planned."

"And on schedule." Monty pressed a quick kiss on her forehead and ran an appraising gaze over her. "My God, you're growing lovelier by the day. I shouldn't wonder that you'll find yourself besieged by admirers this night. If you weren't the sensible sort, I'd be quaking in my boots for you."

Emmaline didn't feel sensible. Any woman who let one brother court her while she pined for the other one's kisses was *not* sensible. By night in her bed, she relived those wicked moments in the orangery with Devon. The mere thought of his mouth at her breast was enough to prick her nipples to hard awareness and cause moist warmth to heat her inner parts.

Distressingly, it wasn't just her body that wept for him. She longed for him in a dozen other ways. She ached to hear him laugh. He did it so seldom, but the few times she'd heard it, the sound threatened to break her heart with borrowed joy.

She yearned to talk with him about the books in his library, to ask him about his boyhood, to plumb the depths of his fine mind. He was like the library in so many ways—a treasure trove of secrets and adventures waiting to be discovered if she was brave enough to dare the scowl he wore to warn others away.

It made no sense for her to moon around after this man. She really didn't know enough about him for that. But she wanted to know him.

Wanted it with a desperation bordering on sickness.

She'd been levelheaded enough to keep out of Lord Devonwood's path for the past fortnight or so, but it wasn't easy. How did one avoid a thunderstorm? Who could outrun a flood? A chance meeting with the lord of the house in a secluded corner was a disaster waiting to happen.

Emma didn't need a disaster. She needed a miracle. She needed enough money to see Monty admitted for treatment at the Görbersdorf sanatorium before a wet fall came and swept summer clean away. Her father's breathing had been better in the hot dry heat of Egypt, but based on the way his illness had progressed in London's damp summer, she doubted he'd survive another winter in northern climes without life-saving treatment.

"It's just that beauty, not unlike a mark, often forgets caution," Monty said, chucking her under the chin. "I'm glad you haven't let some gentleman make a fool of you."

It was the closest he'd ever come to giving her a lecture on morality. Monty wasn't the pontificating sort. When the time came for her to learn what passed between a man and a woman, he'd given her a medical treatise on the subject and told her to use her imagination.

He hadn't needed to tell her that chastity was her best option. She was smart enough to figure out it was the only winning card she held.

"Don't you worry about me," she told him as he escorted her out the door of their suite. The rest of the party was probably waiting for them below. "My father raised no fool."

As they reached the lowest landing, she saw that only Lord Devonwood stood in the center of the marble foyer. She'd never seen him less than well turned out, but this night he fairly gleamed with sartorial splendor.

However, his allure went far deeper than a tailor's art. There was something about the man himself, beneath the trappings of an earldom, a certain elegant aggression in his stance that made Emmaline's breath catch and her heart do a shuddering little jig.

Why couldn't it do that when she looked at Theodore?

He glowered down at his pocket watch for a moment. Then he tucked it away, the gold chain and fob glittering against the superfine of his jacket. Her father's clacking footfalls on the stairs made him look up.

If Lord Devonwood had intended to chide her for tardiness, the reproof died on his lips.

In the time it took to flick an eyelash, Emmaline saw raw desire flare in his eyes. Then just as quickly, the earl schooled his face into a bland mask. She wondered if her own features telegraphed the unsettling flutter of her insides as clearly as his heat-filled glance.

"Good evening, professor. Miss Farnsworth, if I may." He held out her short silk cape and waited for her to turn around so he could drape it most correctly over her shoulders. By the time she'd completed her turn, he'd shepherded her father out the door ahead of them and waited to offer her his arm.

It would be churlish not to take it after he'd comported himself like such a gentleman.

He bowed when she rested her gloved fingertips on his forearm. "That violet gown is most becoming, Miss Farnsworth."

"Thank you, milord." How should she return the compliment? *You make my pantaloons twist, too, milord* would be honest, at least.

"I find the current trend in women's fashions both fascinating and mystifying," he said as they strolled out the broad double doors toward the barouche that waited on the street. The countess, Louisa, and Theodore were already in the equipage and her father was being helped in by one of the Devonwood House footmen. "Louisa is constantly complaining about how tightly she has to be laced in order to fit into the narrow waist of her gowns. It almost seems as if modistes are determined not to use an inch more fabric than necessary on the top half of a woman's ensemble, but when it comes to the skirt, they've gone a bit balmy. I believe my mother said her gown's skirt measures fifty-eight inches across. I'm sure my sister's is that wide as well."

"I wouldn't doubt it." Her own crinoline also pushed the farthest limits of fashion, but she had no idea why such details should matter to Lord Devonwood.

By the time they reached the barouche, her father and Theodore were embroiled in a debate over whether the cartouche on the right side of the Tetisheri statue ought to be translated as "eternal" or "lasting."

Emmaline realized immediately why Lord Devonwood was taken with fashion all of a sudden. The women's skirts filled the carriage, so there was no room for another passenger.

"Ah," Lord Devonwood said with a hint of a smile. "There's insufficient room for Miss Farnsworth and me. We'll catch a hansom and join you at Lord Whitmore's."

Before anyone could object, he closed the door and slapped the side of the barouche with the flat of his hand to signal the driver to move along.

Whether she liked it or not, Emmaline would have to be alone with the earl for the length of a cab ride to Lord Whitmore's town house. Unfortunately, a wicked part of her would like it very much.

Very much indeed.

CHAPTER 14

"You arranged matters to ensure this would happen," she accused.

"It is not my fault women dress in such outlandish costumes that a carriage which should have easily held six will only accommodate four." He gestured to the cab that was stopped at the end of the block and the equipage started toward them.

She was right, of course. He'd made sure his mother and sister were ready before Emmaline by giving them an earlier departure time. He hoped she wouldn't guess he'd also arranged for the hansom to be available at his signal.

"One could as easily believe that you finessed a way not to ride in the barouche by virtue of being the last woman to descend this evening," he said.

"You know better than that." Her dark eyes snapped at him. She'd been resolute in her determination not to be caught alone with him.

"I suppose I do." He wasn't proud of stooping to trickery in order to be with her, but the need to have her to himself was smothering. Like having an anvil on his chest. Even though she frowned like a stern governess, he breathed easier just being with her. It made no sense to his mind that merely being in her presence should have that effect on him, but there was no denying it simply *was*. "You've made your aversion to my company quite plain."

"It's not that." Her lips turned inward for a moment as if she wished to shush herself. Then she met his gaze steadily. "It's my lack of aversion to your company that is the problem."

Emmaline didn't despise him, then. Like a batsman who'd just struck the winning run, something inside him leaped up in victory. When he offered her his hand as the hansom rattled to a stop before them, she slipped her gloved one into it and allowed him to assist her into the cab.

"You have no cause for alarm now, my dear Miss Farnsworth. As you can see, we'll be chaperoned by London itself in this open equipage."

There was still plenty of foot traffic even though the gas lamps were being lit along the thoroughfare. Night was drawing around them, but technically they'd still be in the public eye. He'd considered hiring an enclosed carriage to take them to Whitmore's, but figured it would be more temptation than he could resist. He told himself he wanted only to talk with her, to reassure her that he was not the sort of monster who would try to seduce his brother's intended.

The fact that he'd like nothing better than to shag her senseless was beside the point.

As the cab rattled along, she fidgeted with her fan, opening and closing it for no apparent reason.

"You're nervous about this evening," he guessed.

"Wouldn't you be?" She sighed. "I wish Theodore hadn't made his intentions toward me so very public. These are his friends, his people, I'll be meeting tonight. I'm sure they'll be wondering what he sees in me."

"I don't think that will come into question at all," Devon said. "You're bright and attractive and—"

"Dowerless and common," she interrupted.

"You know you really shouldn't do that."

She rolled her luminous eyes at him. "What? Interrupt an earl when he's trying to whitewash a problem?"

"No, interrupt a man when he's trying to give you a compliment."

She cast her gaze downward, her dark lashes quivering on her cheeks. "You were attempting to be nice and I failed to note it. My apologies."

"It wasn't an attempt," he said with irritation. "I *was* being nice."

"Yes, milord."

"Griffin," he corrected. He ached to hear her say his name.

"Griffin," she whispered.

It was barely audible over the steady clop of the horse's hooves and the clatter of wheels on cobbles, but she'd said it nonetheless.

Now if he could only get her to think of him as "Griffin" instead of "Lord Devonwood."

"You're right, of course," he said. "You will be the subject of scrutiny tonight. And the ton will be collectively wondering why you haven't snapped up one of its most eligible bachelors. The worst of the gossips will probably assume money is the issue. They'll believe you hesitate because you fear the family will cut Theodore off if he marries you."

"Teddy and I have never discussed that," she said, smoothing nonexistent wrinkles from her skirt in order to avoid meeting his eyes. He wished she'd look at him again.

Maybe she'd really see him if she did.

"Then it will be of no consequence to you either way if my brother suddenly finds himself without means." Devon didn't know why he'd said that. He'd never cut his brother off, no matter what Theodore did.

"But it may matter to Teddy," she said. "He values your good opinion more than his stipend. Cutting him off from *you* would hurt him more than stopping his allowance."

Guilt was an unwelcome bastard. Devon shoved it aside. He would feel guilty later, when he wasn't with her. Now he simply wanted to bask in her presence, to let her low voice wash over him like warm rain, to fall headlong into her coffee-colored eyes. He'd trade his soul to the devil if he could simply feel normal all the time, as he did when he was around Emmaline Farnsworth.

"There may even be a few less than charitable tongue-waggers who claim you haven't accepted Theodore because you're angling for someone else."

Damned if I'm not as hopeful as a spotty-faced boy.

"Who would that be, milord?"

He snorted. Not only had she smacked him down, he was back to "milord" again after having tasted the joy of being "Griffin" for a moment.

Then one of the hansom wheels dipped into a pothole and her fan flew out of her hand. Instinctively, he reached for it to keep it from falling from the carriage. The moment his fingers closed over the ivory handle, he realized he ought to have donned his gloves. He'd kept them in his pocket so he could enjoy the unfettered pleasure of touching Emmaline as he helped her descend from the cab once they reached their destination.

It was a huge mistake.

The world went soft and hazy as a sharper reality scrolled over his vision. He could still see the London neighborhood they traveled through—there was the tailor's shop, the baker, the pungent fishmonger—but they were shadowy images, fleeting scents, faded sounds, mere reflections. The *Sending* from Emmaline's fan appeared in stark relief, dark across the indistinct backdrop of reality.

It was the only true thing in his world at the moment.

Devon heard the door creak but didn't turn to see who'd entered the room. It was too dark to see properly, but that only served to put his other senses on high alert. He knew who was there in any case. A slight peach fragrance announced her arrival, but it was shrouded with a heavier scent, a spicy floral.

He still knew it was she.

Soft footfalls told him Emmaline was approaching the bed. She hesitated. Every fiber in his body screamed with excited awareness, but he forced himself to breathe as if he still slept.

She lifted a corner of the sheet, the soft rustle of bed linens unnaturally loud to his ears. Then the mattress dipped slightly as she slipped in beside him.

He still didn't move. He didn't dare for fear the vision would take a disastrous turn and she'd run screaming from him.

Her hand, hesitant and cool, brushed his shoulder. Then her palm smoothed down his spine. She moved closer and curved herself around him, tucking herself against his backside and pressing her cheek between his shoulder blades.

Her breasts were soft against his bare back. Only her thin nightshift separated them.

He breathed a silent thanks to whatever God might listen to an undeserving wretch's prayer. Against all expectation, she'd come to him.

It was a minor miracle.

He resisted moving, lest he break the spell. But when she reached around and let her fingertips flutter over his belly, he couldn't remain immobile another second.

He rolled over and pinned her to the feather tick.

Emmaline made a soft sound, as if she'd started to say something, but his mouth covered hers.

What did they need with words? She was there in his bed of her own volition. Words would only muddy the waters. There was no purer communication than the warm glide of skin on skin, the tattoo of two hearts falling into the same rhythm, the mystery of a shared breath.

While he kissed her, he shifted to one side so he could pull up her nightgown. She trembled when his fingertips brushed over her knees and past her thighs. He toyed with the curls between her legs. Griffin swallowed her small sound of need as he gently parted her intimate folds. She was warm, feverish almost, in her most secret parts.

He feared he might have rushed matters, but he needn't have worried. She was already wet. Slippery and slick and swollen with wanting. When he touched her, a shudder of desire rippled over him in tandem with her shiver of delight. She arched into his hand, her softness molding to his palm.

He'd never felt so wanted.

Griffin settled his hips between her legs and while he tongued her mouth, he pushed into her wetness. A slow, deliberate claiming.

He was stopped by the barrier of her purity.

He hadn't expected her to be a virgin. She didn't kiss like one. She certainly didn't spread her legs and hook her ankles at the small of his back like one.

But she was.

He withdrew slightly and then pushed himself home in a single rending thrust. She went rigid beneath him. There was no going back now, but he wasn't sure she wanted him to go forward. He held still, barely daring to breathe.

He wished there was more light. She was only a dark shadow beneath him. He wished she could see how much this incredible gift meant to him.

"No more pain now," he whispered and kissed her neck.

"My lord," she said softly. "Are you quite all right? You've gone so pale."

How could she see him if it was still too dark for him to see her clearly?

"Please, milord. What's wrong? Cabbie, stop the hansom!" she called out.

Suddenly Emmaline's face came into sharp focus and the *Sending* faded as she took her fan from his hand.

CHAPTER 15

Lord Devonwood didn't blink. He barely breathed. His face had blanched to the color of white marble and a large vein stood out on his forehead. He was still blessed with buckets of masculine beauty, but he was also clearly in agony for some unknown reason. Panic swirled in Emmaline's gut.

"Griffin, what's wrong?" She gripped his forearm, as much to steady herself as to give him comfort.

His eyelids closed slowly, his thick lashes settling like curtains being lowered. Then, as if recovering from a mesmerist's trick, he gave himself a slight shake and drew a deep breath. His pupils were so enlarged, his usually pale eyes were nearly black, the irises reduced to slender gray rings. His features were drawn taut, the skin scraped thin over his angular bones.

He smiled at her.

A strangely knowing smile. Then he looked away.

"I'm fine," he said gruffly, then raised his voice to the cabbie. "Drive on."

"You most certainly are not fine. I've never seen anything like that. One moment you were talking and then suddenly it was as if you . . . weren't here. I mean, of course, you were still physically here, but your mind seemed to have taken itself on holiday."

She knew she was babbling, but couldn't help it. He'd scared her. Badly. Her nerves were frayed enough dealing with Monty's illness. She didn't think she could bear learning that Griffin suffered from some malady, too.

"'No more pain now,' you said. Were you . . . are you in discomfort?"

He pulled a pair of kidskin gloves from his pocket and jerked them on. "No, I'm perfectly well. Amazingly well, actually."

His color returned to normal and tension drained out of his features. The vein on his forehead disappeared. Even his eyes regained their silver-gray intensity. If she were the fanciful sort, she'd almost believe she'd imagined the event.

But Emmaline was nothing if not a realist. Griffin had definitely been in the throes of some sort of apoplexy. "Surely there will be a physician in attendance at Lord Whitmore's. We'll have him take a look at you."

"We will not," he said with vehemence; then he softened his tone. "Trust me. It's nothing a physician can help. I insist you respect my wishes."

"Then you've had"—she tried to think of what to call it that wouldn't upset him further—"*episodes* like this before?"

He nodded.

"Do you know what it is?"

"Miss Farnsworth, every person on earth holds at least one secret close to their chest. I'll wager you have yours. Would you be willing to share the deepest knot in your soul in exchange for mine?"

He had her there. Everything about her had to remain an enigma. She was a huckster. A fugitive, even. She might be tempted to swap secrets with Devon. She was burning with curiosity, but she couldn't very well admit she was a thorough fraud without jeopardizing Monty as well.

When she didn't answer immediately, he went on. "No? Well, that's all right. I'll learn all your secrets soon enough, I imagine."

She hoped not. If he learned the truth, she and Monty would have to take to their heels.

"But I will make you a promise," he said as the cab slowed before a magnificent edifice. Light blazed in every window of the four-story town house. "I will tell you my secret. Tomorrow. You'll need to know it then."

He alighted from the hansom and paid the driver. Then he handed Emmaline down, holding her fingertips a fraction longer than necessary.

Why would she need to know something later that he wasn't willing to tell her now? Curiosity threatened to turn her inside out. "Why tomorrow?"

His lips twitched in a half-smile. "Let's get through the next twelve hours, shall we? I've a feeling everything will be much clearer in the morning."

Euphoria flooded Devon's mind as surely as if he were an opium eater. Even though he'd just had a long, detailed vision, he suffered not the slightest twinge of the debilitating headache that ought to have accompanied it. At Emmaline's touch, his pain retreated, like mist before the morning sun.

For whatever reason, she made his gift bearable. Emmaline removed the curse of his prescience with her slightest caress. She was his cure.

And his sickness, he realized, as Theodore hurried toward them. Dr. Farnsworth was already squiring his mother and sister toward Lord Whitmore's open front door. Of course, Teddy would want to collect Emmaline.

The same Emmaline who would climb into Devon's bed this very night.

The *Sending* was unequivocal. Theodore might escort her

to Whitmore's ball, but later tonight, Devon would take her maidenhead. Normally, he writhed under the threat of what was to come, but there was no avoiding the future rushing toward him. For the first time in ages, he felt no desire to try.

"There you are, love," Teddy said as he offered Emmaline his arm. "I'm sorry for the mix-up. Your father and I were jawing about the statue and you know how we are. I hadn't even realized there wasn't room for you till Dev closed the carriage door. Thanks for bringing her along so quickly, brother."

He flicked a grin at Devon before turning his attention back to Emmaline.

"Now don't fret a bit, dearest," Ted said. "Everyone is going to love you as much as I do. I'll see to it that you have a wonderful time tonight."

"Me, too," Devon murmured once they were out of earshot. The first time a woman shared a bed with a man should be magical. He'd make sure it was for Emmaline.

Then Teddy's laughter floated back to Devon and he and Emmaline approached the open doors. Guilt tried to dig in its talons, but Devon shrugged it off.

How could this be his fault? Emmaline was going to come to him of her own free will. Myriad details from his last *Sending*—her needy sighs, the softness of her breasts against his back, her slick readiness—rushed back into him, leaving him hard with anticipation. A man couldn't help it if a woman climbed into his bed.

Could he?

Yes, damnation, he could. He'd protected Teddy since their father's death. He must at least *try* to protect him now. Somehow, even if it meant he had to leave his own house and sleep somewhere else, Devon had to find a way to keep this vision from coming to pass.

It wasn't that he didn't want Emmaline, especially now

that he was certain there was something unique about her that kept the aftereffects of his gift in check. That alone made a connection with her seem "meant" somehow. If his gift had done nothing else, it had made him a believer in Fate. He still hadn't settled the question of whose hand might be behind those preordained events, but his abortive attempts to change outcomes in the past had convinced him of the futility of struggling against the future.

Beyond the obvious metaphysical connection between him and the American miss, the state of his trousers made it abundantly clear how badly he wanted Emmaline simply for herself.

But he wanted not to betray his brother almost as badly.

He looked up at Lord Whitmore's door in time to see a liveried servant usher Theodore and Emmaline inside.

The best people arrived fashionably late. No one would take it ill if Devon took a turn around the block so his body could settle before he entered Lord Whitmore's resplendent home. He strode quickly through the immaculate neighborhood. The street twisted around on itself and made for a long circuitous walk, a vicious circle that mirrored his dilemma.

No matter how far he went, eventually he'd end up back where he started. No matter how briskly he walked, he realized one trip around the block would not be sufficient for his body to forget the vision. No matter what he did, Emmaline Farnsworth was going to slide between his sheets later that night and he was going to sink into her sweet flesh.

Theodore shepherded Emmaline around the elegantly appointed rooms, introducing her to barons, viscountesses, members of parliament, and one slightly inebriated marquess. After meeting so many people, Emmaline had no hope of keeping all their names straight, let alone their titles. To confuse matters further, given the slightest encouragement, most of them launched into a recitation of their illustrious relations as well.

Emmaline danced the Grand March with Teddy, then followed it with the first waltz. There were easily twenty or more couples crowding the dance floor, so she was grateful Teddy was a graceful dancer who knew how to maneuver in tight spaces. She was conscious, in the same manner that wary woodland creatures note the presence of predators, of the number of eyes on her and Theodore as they glided around the room.

Each time a matron brought her fan to her lips and leaned toward the woman next to her, Emma was sure she was the topic of conversation. She was being measured in the balance of London Society and probably found sadly insufficient.

Her next partner for the polka, a short, round, and rather talkative Sir Somebody-or-other, was less gifted in his feet than his tongue. By the time the music ended, Emma felt she'd taken an unfortunate ride on a bouncing ball.

Even if she was the subject of speculation and gossip, this occasion shouldn't be so difficult. She'd managed to finesse her way through a dinner with a Grand Duke once when she and Monty were in Paris. They made off with a king's ransom for one of her fake reliquaries at the conclusion of that particular last supper.

But she hadn't had a carriage ride with Griffin Titus Preston Nash before that dinner either.

The man addled her. He made her feel prickly all over, slightly achy, as if she had the beginnings of a fever. She caught herself watching him from the corner of her eye to make sure he was all right. He showed no ill effects from that awful fit whatsoever.

She was very nearly worrying herself sick over him and

there he was, tripping the light fantastic with a Miss Von Schreppenheim from Leipzig. The wretch had the gall to wink at Emmaline as he and his dance partner stepped lively to the mazurka.

Worry was replaced by something dangerously close to jealousy.

"Pardon me, Lady Bentley." She turned to the turbaned lady Theodore had left her with while he collected his dance partner for the gavotte. Her own dance card was empty for the next two musical selections. "Could you please direct me to the lady's retiring room?"

Lady Bentley did better than that. She escorted her there, saying, "A young lady ought not leave the hall alone, you know. Could lead to all sorts of unwholesome speculation about whom she might meet in an inappropriate circumstance."

Lady Bentley inquired gently after Emmaline's familial relations in New York as she showed her to the room reserved for ladies who needed to loosen their laces or remove pinching slippers for a bit. Since Emmaline had no relations to speak of, in New York or elsewhere, it was a decidedly one-sided conversation.

"Oh, dear." Lady Bentley lifted her head when a new musical piece began. "There's the quadrille. I promised it to Lord Harrow."

"By all means, go," Emmaline said. "I shall only be a moment. And if we're close enough to hear the quadrille, we're not so far removed from the main party either."

"Well, I daresay it'll be all right then." The worthy matron bustled away, as flushed with excitement over the prospect of a dance as a debutante.

The room was deserted, which wasn't surprising since the evening was still young. A porcelain chamber pot had been thoughtfully placed behind a chinoiserie screen. Before Emmaline could settle her broad skirt over it, she heard the rustle of silk on the other side of the screen. She couldn't bring herself to relieve her bladder with someone there, but felt equally shy about making a sudden appearance from behind the screen.

So she kept silent and the speakers on the other side of the hand-painted silk resumed a giggling conversation. Then the giggling stopped.

"This American girl, is he truly serious about her, do you think?"

Emmaline's ears pricked. The speaker could be referring only to her.

"I believe he is," came the second voice. Emmaline recognized this one as Louisa. "Don't let the Yankee accent fool you. She's really quite nice once you get to know her."

Seems I have her fooled. Emma resisted the urge to sigh. If things were different, Louisa might truly have been her friend. Her sister, even, if Emmaline could accept Theodore's proposal.

Being a scoundrel was a lonely business.

A small sob escaped from one of the girls on the other side of the screen.

"Oh, Cressida, darling," Louisa said. "Whatever is the matter?"

"I'm sorry, dear. It's only that I've had my heart set on your brother for just ages. Ever since you and I went off to school together, in fact." Lady Cressida paused to sniff and then blew her nose loudly. "I know Teddy always thought of me as a child. Seven years difference in our ages was a lifetime when I was in pinafores, but it's truly nothing now. I so hoped things would be different tonight, that he'd finally see me with fresh eyes."

Emmaline stooped to peer through a slit in the screen where one of the silk panels was attached to the carved wood. Lady Cressida, Lord Whitmore's daughter, was lovely, a pink and cream confection topped off with golden curls. Her little bow of a mouth was a much coveted feature.

Emma knew her own lips spread too broadly across her face for fashion and her hair was too nearly a garish red to turn many masculine heads. She wondered how Theodore could have passed over this girl on his way to her.

"Oh, Cressie, don't take on so. Truth to tell, Teddy's become a frightful bore. I don't know why you'd fancy him. All he talks about is that Egyptian statue he and Dr. Farnsworth are working on. You really don't want him. Truly, you don't," Louisa said with a wicked grin. "Not when there are so many other eligible men."

"You only say that because he's your brother. Theodore is the finest of men."

Emmaline was forced to agree. Teddy certainly deserved better than she was giving him.

"Lady Bentley had it on the best authority that Miss Farnsworth hasn't even a proper dowry to speak of," Lady Cressida went on.

Emmaline's brows arched in surprise. Lady Bentley had been so pleasant to her face, so solicitous when enquiring about her family, when all the while she'd already begun spreading rumors about her. The fact that the gossip was true didn't negate the sting.

"She even hinted that Lord Devonwood might cut Theodore off if he goes ahead with this misalliance," Cressida said.

"That's ridiculous. Dev may not approve, but he's devoted to Teddy," Louisa said staunchly. "And he certainly hasn't threatened Teddy with a reduction of funds . . . that I know of."

Emmaline's belly churned. Now that she thought about it, Devon had almost promised to do that very thing while they rode to Lord Whitmore's together. She was used to scrabbling for a living with Monty, flush one day, stomach knocking on her backbone the next, but Theodore wasn't. He'd feel the pinch sharply and, being raised a gentleman, would resent having to descend to trade, or worse, to Emma's brand of skullduggery in order to make ends meet.

"I confess I was hoping you'd tell me Miss Farnsworth is a disagreeable sort who'll run him off in a month," Lady Cressida said with a charming whimper. She even cried prettily. "Do you think me terrible?"

"Of course not."

There was a whisper of fabric and the friends shared a quick hug. Loneliness stabbed at Emma's chest. She had no extended family, no friends. All she really had was Monty. And she wouldn't have him much longer if they couldn't make this scheme work.

"Since Teddy's all but taken, why don't you set your cap for Devon?" Louisa suggested. "Heaven knows he needs to take a wife sooner rather than later."

"Lord Devonwood?" Cressida sounded shocked. "He's a handsome man, of course, and considered no end of a catch, but he's so dark and stern. Surely he'd be a difficult husband." She paused to sigh dramatically. "But Theodore is all that is lightness and amiability."

"You could be Lady Devonwood, a countess," Louisa argued. "That counts for something. With Teddy, you'd just be Mrs. Nash."

"You know I've never been one to measure a man by his title."

Spoken like a woman who was born with a "Lady" already attached to her name, Emma though uncharitably.

"All I really want, Louisa, is a home and children and a husband who cares for me."

The same longing made Emma's chest constrict. Against her better judgment, she found herself liking Louisa's friend.

"Frankly," Cressida said, "Lord Devonwood terrifies me."

Emmaline felt a strong kinship with her. She feared Devon, too, but not for the same reason. She was afraid he'd unmask her. Hadn't he said he'd know her secrets soon enough?

And she both feared and enjoyed the sensations he sent rippling over her with no more than a look.

The ladies clucked over their appearance for a few more minutes until the strains of a waltz permeated the retiring room.

"Oh! Oh!" Cressida said, puffing like a little steam engine. "That's my waltz with your brother."

"Don't sound so distressed," Louisa said. "Devon doesn't bite."

"No, not Lord Devonwood. It's Theodore for this dance." She consulted her gilded card. "Yes, there it is, the second waltz. I know you'll think me horribly fast, but if that Miss Farnsworth hasn't the sense to snap Theodore up, I'm going to do my best to charm him away from her. All's fair, you know."

Lady Cressida hurried from the room with Louisa at her heels.

Emmaline sighed. Cressida had a daisy-fresh prettiness about her. She was well-born and no doubt well-dowered. Her money and position would stand Theodore in good stead after Emmaline and her father finished snookering him out of an astounding amount of cash. Teddy really couldn't do better than Lady Cressida.

Emmaline almost wished her luck.

Chapter 16

"I'll say this much for them," Lord Northrop said, scowling into his cup of weak punch. "They may not have a brain among the lot of them, but this year's crop of debutantes is blessed with an abundance of beauty. Take Devonwood's sister there."

"You'd better not," Devon said darkly and sipped his punch.

There was only the slightest whiff of alcohol in the drinks. Lady Whitmore was a notorious teetotaler. Even the dash of spirits had probably been introduced to the punch without her knowledge. Given Northrop's proclivity for excess, the tame punch was probably for the best. Devon and his two friends refilled their etched crystal cups.

Make that one of my friends, he amended in silence. Bernard Seyton, Lord Kingsley, was the third pillar of the unholy triumvirate known as the Fallen Angels from Oxford. So far, Kingsley hadn't overstepped with Louisa so he was still technically in Devon's good graces, but that could change in a heartbeat. Northrop's appraising gaze swept over her again, dancing on Devon's last nerve.

Who knew having a marriageable sister could be such a burden?

"You can't fault the man's eyes," Kingsley said, laying a

conciliatory hand on Devon's shoulder. "Seems your sister has turned into quite a tempting armful when you weren't looking. Worse luck for you, old chap."

"It's one thing to beat off the rakes out there. I expect that," Devon said. "I didn't think I'd have to threaten to thrash my friends over her. Isn't there supposed to be honor among thieves?"

"Now, Dev, you know we Fallen Angels never stooped to thievery. If we gathered a few maidenheads along the way, it was because they were freely offered, not stolen," Northrop said, draining his punch cup and setting it on the beeswax polished mantel instead of a servant's empty tray. "Speaking of things stolen, what's the status of that statue business? I know you think I was drunk the other day, but I haven't forgotten about it. Finding a fortune in the desert is a bit akin to stealing it, isn't it?"

"Ted and the professor are still working out their translation of the hieroglyphs. You'll learn more at the house party, though it promises to be dull. They've been preparing 'a paper' on it," Devon said gruffly. "I seem to recall someone put your name on the guest list, but for the life of me, I'm not sure why."

Northrop's wicked smile stretched across his face. "Ah, yes, I was invited for a 'fortnight of frivolity at Devonwood Park.' If you didn't see to it I received an invitation, I wonder who did." His gaze shot to his dance card and then back to Louisa. "And now I believe I've a lady to collect for the waltz, if you'll excuse me."

He gave them a mocking bow and headed straight for Devon's sister.

Devon took a step forward, but Kingsley stopped him with a hand to his forearm. "Don't object. It only encourages him."

"You're right," Devon acknowledged. When Louisa rapped Northrop with her fan before she allowed him to escort her to the dance floor, he felt marginally better. Northrop must have said something inappropriate and his sister was smart enough not to countenance any nonsense. "The best way to make certain Northrop ever does anything has always been to tell him he can't, or better still, he mustn't."

Would Lionel Norris react to a rap with a fan like a bull to a red flag? Devon wished for the millionth time that his father was still alive. Seeing Louisa safely wed was a heavy responsibility.

"Ow!" Northrop said, rubbing the spot on his shoulder where Louisa's fan had stung him. "There's no need for violence."

"That was a mere love tap to remind you not to overstep the bounds of propriety, Lord Northrop." Louisa laughed musically. "If you wish to see real violence, perhaps I should pull your hair as you used to pull mine when I was child."

"For that infraction I'll apologize all day," Northrop said as he led Louisa onto the dance floor. "I was an ass when I was younger."

"Only then?" She arched a knowing brow at him.

He snorted. Usually, he avoided clever women, but when they looked like Devon's sister, he couldn't help being drawn in. The gown she wore was cut low enough to bare the rounded tops of her breasts. Her skin was milk-white and was probably softer than fine satin. He wondered about the color of her nipples. Would they be pale pink or peachy or—

Louisa rapped his shoulder smartly again.

"Ow! What was that for?" he demanded in a furious whisper without breaking their dance hold.

"Because of the way you're looking at me."

Surely she couldn't divine his thoughts. If so, the girl

was both more dangerous and more interesting than he'd first supposed. "And how was I looking at you?"

"As if my face was a foot lower than it is."

Northrop smiled. "My dear Louisa, if you don't wish a man to admire your bosom, you ought not display it to such advantage."

She lifted her palm from its position on his shoulder to deliver another ringing blow, but he caught her wrist this time. "Pummeling one's admirers is not the done thing, you know."

"You were ogling, not admiring."

"Semantics. And rest assured I have the utmost admiration for you. All of you," Northrop said. When the tension went out of her wrist, he replaced her hand on his shoulder and continued to twirl around the room with her. "Now, I'll concede I bring out the worst in you. Because of that, I'll not hold your assault on my person against you, if you'll concede that a man cannot be held accountable for his thoughts provided he hasn't acted upon them."

She sniffed and studiously looked away from him. After a few more turns around the room, her gaze drifted back to his face.

"What sort of actions?" she asked.

He choked back his surprise. "That, my dear, is a trick question. If I answer truthfully, your fan is bound to attack me once again."

"I promise not to hit you," she said with an expressive roll of her eyes. "Now what sort of actions?"

"To be honest, then, I was contemplating how I might remove enough of your clothing to determine the color of your nipples."

Her eyes flared in surprise, but she kept her word not to give him a rap of reproof. "Why should the color of my . . . Why does that matter to you?"

"In truth, the answer to that burning question is not as important to me as the method of discovery."

"And how did you think you could accomplish that?"

"By seducing you into accompanying me to a private place, of course," he leaned down and whispered into her ear. "Then I'd kiss you into a condition of acquiescence and peel away the layers from your bodice till you were reduced to a natural state."

He still didn't know the color of her nipples but the rest of her flushed a becomingly rosy hue.

"Seems like a good deal of trouble just to determine what color . . ." Her whisper faded as she struggled to complete her thought.

"Oh, that wouldn't be the end of the matter." Northrop tugged her closer to him so he wouldn't be overheard. "You see, that small part of a woman's body is very sensitive to touch. I'd tease and stroke and—well, there are a number of other things I'd do that might shock you now, but I promise you'd experience delight such as you've never known. And with no danger to your purity," he added, remembering Devon's promise to make meddling with his sister a two ball offense.

She lowered her gaze to his chest, considering his words. "There's no way to slip away from the crowd here," she said softly. "Will you be attending the house party at Devonwood Park?"

"I assure you, milady, my acceptance will be returned tomorrow," Northrop said, wondering if his breeches would hold the strain. He'd ached just thinking about diddling her breasts. Now that she'd all but promised to allow it, he was near to bursting. "After your sweet words of hope, nothing will keep me from it."

CHAPTER 17

"Northrop must be behaving himself. Louisa has stopped giving him raps with her fan, but I'm afraid Northrop has always been a contrarian," Kingsley said. "Back to that statue . . . I've sent your lady mother my intention to attend the house party, but I wonder if you ought to rethink having it at all."

"Why is that?"

"Well, for one thing, I know you don't credit such things," Kingsley said, watching the dancers with the same sharp-eyed attentiveness a hawk gives a clutch of field mice, "but I've heard from reliable sources that a number of those Egyptian gewgaws are . . ."

"Are what?"

"No, forget it. You'll think me a fool."

"Never. Among the three of us, Northrop has that title sewed up without contest," Devon said. "Now what have you heard?"

"Well, from what I gather, Egyptian artifacts often come with curses attached." Kingsley narrowed his eyes at him. "By Jove, you're not laughing."

If Kingsley had seen Devon's vision, he wouldn't laugh either. The image of the wicker basket and the asp rose sharp and fresh in his mind. A vague sense of dread settled over him. A curse, eh? He could well believe it.

"With any luck, we'll be rid of the thing soon," Devon said.

"Oh?" Kingsley sipped his punch. "Then you do believe there's something to the whole curse business."

"No." Even if he did, it wasn't something he was prepared to admit. "But I do believe in business. Dr. Farnsworth may be learned, but he has no means of support that I've been able to discover." Devon had tasked his man of affairs with making discreet inquiries about Farnsworth the day he and Emmaline had arrived. So far, Mr. Bollinger couldn't find much information about the professor or the small college in the Catskills of New York from which he was purportedly on sabbatical. "I think the good professor could be persuaded to part with the statue for the right price."

"Indeed?" Kingsley eyed his dance card, then the room. "Hang it all, I'm paired with Lady Bentley and there she is over by the longcase clock in the corner, scouring the room for me. My toes will never be the same. *Morituri te salutamus*." He gave a fist to the chest salute and stalked toward his dance partner with the same grim determination as a gladiator entering the Roman Circus.

Devon glanced at his own card and smiled. Emmaline was seated by herself near an arched door. She considered it surreptitiously as if contemplating making her escape. He wasn't about to let that happen. He walked around the perimeter of the room and bowed when he stopped before her.

"Shall I have the pleasure of this dance, Miss Farnsworth?"

She blinked up at him, her cheeks blooming with color. He'd never observed her blushing with anyone else and the realization pleased him enormously.

"You're not my scheduled partner. I'm supposed to waltz with a Viscount Edmondstone. Do you know him?"

Devon suppressed a grin. "I do. Very well, in fact."

"Do you see him?" she asked.

He made a great show of looking around the room. "No. I cannot see Viscount Edmondstone, but I suspect he'll be along shortly. Until such time, I'll keep you company."

"I do not require a keeper, milord."

"Perhaps not, but gentlemen are expected to look after ladies at a gathering such as this."

Without waiting for permission, he sat down beside her, curbing the impulse to take her hand. He ached to touch her, but knew it was out of the question unless they were dancing. Still, it was almost enough that his thigh rested close to hers, despite the layers of her skirts and petticoats separating them.

After the *Sending* in the hansom, he didn't trust himself to have actual contact with her. While he welcomed more of that particular vision, he didn't want anyone else to catch him entranced.

"We wouldn't want folk to consider you a wallflower, would we?" he said.

"Wallflower might be the kindest word circulating about me this night."

She laced her fingers on her lap, gripping tight enough that Griffin imagined her knuckles were white beneath her silk gloves. How ironic that being close to her gave him rest from the worst part of his gift, while it was obvious she was agitated by his presence.

"If I had wagered, I would have bet you are not the sort who cares what others say."

"I don't." She straightened her spine. "But I do care what they say about Theodore."

He arched a brow in question.

"They say you'll cut him off if he marries me."

"Who is *they,* if I may ask?"

She didn't answer, but her eyes followed Lady Bentley and poor Kingsley around the room for a bit.

"Ah, that *they*. No matter," Devon said. He'd been on the receiving end of Lady Bentley's acerbic tongue more than once. "When an inveterate gossip does not know something for a fact, she liberally spreads icing on a rumor and offers it up instead. People are always ready to partake of her dainty dish until they find themselves the main course at one of her feasts. Pay her no mind."

Her chin quivered. "She doesn't bother me."

"How charmingly you lie, Miss Farnsworth."

She rewarded him with a glare.

"Smile," Devon advised. "This is your first outing in London society. You must be seen to be enjoying yourself. Our Theodore certainly is."

Ted waltzed by with Lady Cressida in his arms. Ballroom etiquette required a dancing couple to merely smile in silence, but those two were obviously enjoying a whispered conversation as they dipped and twirled around the room.

"He's a fine dancer," she said. "But he won't be able to do much of it if his allowance is cut off and he's forced into trade of some sort. Of course, as an American, I see no shame in working for a living, but I know it's different for the English."

"Let me set your mind at ease on that point. Nothing Theodore does will make him less my brother. Less my responsibility," Devon said. "If and when he marries, he and I will discuss what his needs might be and what duties he'll be willing to assume in connection with the estate so his allowance may be increased in order to meet them."

"That's . . . very generous of you, milord."

"I sense I've surprised you."

"You have," she said. "I owe you an apology. I suspected your disapproval of me would lead you to punish Theodore."

Disapproval was the least of what Devon felt for her.

"Not at all. I rather like the fact that you are in my debt, Miss Farnsworth." He smiled at her smugly. He couldn't help himself. "For two things, actually."

"In your debt?" Her brows knitted in a frown. "How do you mean?"

"First, by promising I won't cut Teddy off, I've made sure my brother will be able to support you in the manner you wish," Devon said, "should you accept his suit, of course."

She conceded the point with a curt nod. "And secondly?"

The Strauss tune ended with a flourish. Devon rose to his feet. "I'm not only the Earl of Devonwood. One of my lesser titles is Viscount Edmondstone." He bowed over her gloved hand. "You owe me a waltz, Emmaline. And I always collect my debts."

Her mouth dropped open, but before she could speak, Lady Whitmore bustled up, her round face florid. "Miss Farnsworth, come quickly. It's your father. He collapsed in the card room. I'll fetch Mr. Theodore."

"There's no need to interrupt my brother," Devon cut in. "He's been gone from London for many months and is enjoying renewing his acquaintances. I'll see to Miss Farnsworth and her father."

Devon followed Lady Whitmore to the room reserved for whist and pique tables with Emmaline barely restraining herself from breaking into a run. Her father was propped in an overstuffed chair, his head hanging forward. Tiny droplets of red splotched the white lawn of his shirt front. He lifted his head at their approach, his eyes overbright.

He started to speak, but was overcome by a new round of coughing.

"Bring my equipage around to the rear of the property," Devon ordered one of the ubiquitous footmen, who bowed and stepped lively to obey. "There's no need to disrupt your occasion further, Lady Whitmore. Pray tell my lady mother I will send the brougham back for the rest of our party so they may return home when it suits them. Also, I believe I saw Dr. Trowbridge earlier. If you could quietly ask him to accompany us back to Devonwood House forthwith, I would deem it a kindness."

"Really, there's no need. I'm perfectly recovered." Dr. Farnsworth braced his hands on the arms of the chair and tried to stand, but it was beyond his feeble strength.

Emmaline's breath hissed over her teeth in distress. Devon bent down and scooped her father up in his arms.

He weighed far less than Devon expected, his body already wasted by consumption. It was no great effort to bear him through the Whitmore back parlor and kitchen and out to the alley where their carriage waited.

Dr. Trowbridge joined them shortly, carrying his black leather bag. He couldn't begin his examination of Farnsworth in the jostling carriage. In fact, the professor's eyes closed and he slipped into the light sleep common to sufferers of chronic illness. The doctor quizzed Emmaline on the particulars of her father's condition—its onset, past treatments, whether there had been periods of seeming remission or if he'd experienced a steady decline.

White-lipped, she answered the doctor's questions with a steady voice.

"Of course, I can't be sure until I give him a thorough examination," Dr. Trowbridge said, "but it appears to me your father is afflicted with tuberculosis."

When Devon took her hand and pressed it between his, she didn't pull away.

Chapter 18

There were no servants in residence, so the dark windows of Devonwood House peered onto the street like empty eyes. The town house seemed like a being whose spirit had flown. It was such a morbid thought, Emmaline's throat ached and tears pressed at the back of her eyes.

Stop that, she ordered herself sternly. She followed Devon as he carried her father up the three flights of stairs to the Blue Suite. Monty wouldn't be helped by a show of weepiness. She swiped her eyes.

"Turn up the gas sconce in the hall," Devon said quietly.

"Of course." Why hadn't she thought of that? Instead she'd indulged in maudlin thoughts while she let him carry Monty in the dark. She skittered around Devon and hurried up to the next landing. She stretched to reach the knob that cranked up the amount of gas feeding into the fixture.

When yellowish light flooded the hall, the butler Baxter emerged from the shadows, brandishing what appeared to be a chair leg above his clumsily bandaged head. Emma drew back in shock.

"Oh, your pardon, miss," he said as he lowered his unlikely weapon. "I thought the burglar might have returned with a few of his friends. Lord Devonwood, I am most relieved to see you. Oh, dear, has Dr. Farnsworth taken ill?"

Emmaline noticed Baxter was upset enough to set aside his stiff use of "one" for himself and spoke to them almost normally.

"Yes, he's ill. Dr. Trowbridge is behind us, so don't bash him on the head with that chair leg, Baxter," Devon said. The butler dropped the offending leg as quickly as if it were afire.

Emmaline heard the doctor's labored breathing on the landing below as he hauled his impressive girth up the three stories. "Did you say there was a burglary, Mr. Baxter?"

"In Dr. Farnsworth's room, in fact," the butler said, straightening to his usual ramrod posture and wrapping himself in his accustomed dignity. "When one returned from one's evening off, one interrupted the brigand in the middle of his theft. The professor's room is quite ransacked, milord. We'll have to move Dr. Farnsworth into the Green Room for the time being until the rest of the staff returns and we can set things to rights tomorrow."

"This way, doctor," Devon said over his shoulder to Dr. Trowbridge who was still puffing up the stairs behind them. He started down the hall toward the Green Room.

"What did the burglar steal?" Emmaline asked Baxter, knowing Monty would fear that the Tetisheri statue was gone.

"One doesn't know, miss," Baxter said. "It was dark. One didn't get a very good look at him. He was devilishly quick about giving one a clout to the head. A big chap, he was. An enormous big chap."

"We'll have the doctor take a look at your head after he sees to Dr. Farnsworth," Devon said as he laid Monty down on the jade coverlet. Then he shepherded Emmaline from the room so Dr. Trowbridge could complete his examination.

"There's nothing more you can do for him at the moment. Once the doctor is finished, we'll know more. In the meantime, I wonder what the burglar was after." Devon took her hand and led her back to the Blue Suite. "Help me discover if anything is missing from your father's effects."

Emmaline knew he was trying to distract her, but she followed him in any case with a hollow numbness in her chest. Whatever else might be missing, the only thing of real value to Monty was the Tetisheri statue. If it was gone, he would be inconsolable.

When she slowed her pace, she felt Devon's hand on the small of her back, warm and firm. She concentrated on that comforting bit of reality as he guided her down the hall.

How could he expect her to poke about in her father's things at a time like this? Why should she care what was missing?

This was the first time she'd had to face Monty's illness with a medical professional. Before, she could let him indulge in the fantasy that he'd caught a cold that lingered, or that his weight loss was the result of a vigorous life. Once Dr. Trowbridge gave his opinion, the specter of consumption would assume corporeal form, and become all too real.

Devon brought up the lights in the Blue Suite sitting room, then disappeared into Monty's dark chamber to adjust the wall sconces there. "Baxter wasn't exaggerating. It's as if a whirlwind was turned loose in here."

Emma paused to lean on the doorjamb. Dresser drawers were left pulled out and the contents were strewn across the Aubusson carpet. The double doors on the large wardrobe in the corner were thrown open and all Monty's jackets and trousers were yanked from their hangers. His extra pair of shoes was kicked aside. The mattress on the bed was askew, as if the burglar had rifled beneath it in search of the princess's pea.

"Our thief was in a bit of a hurry, it seems. He left your father's jewelry," Devon said. Despite the appalling state of the chamber, Monty's second best collar studs and cuff links were still in their small jewel box. His shaving accoutrements were present and accounted for, as were all his articles of clothing, though they'd been ripped from their hangers and might have lost a button or two. "The statue seems to be gone."

"No, it isn't. Monty didn't have it. Tetisheri is in my chamber," she said woodenly. "Or at least she should be."

Emmaline led the way through the sitting room and into her bedchamber, feeling as if she walked through gruel. Her limbs were heavy. Putting one foot before the other was a supreme effort. And she didn't care a bit what she might find when she got there.

The only thing that mattered was Monty. She hoped the doctor wasn't bleeding him. It might take him the better part of a week to recover from that kind of treatment.

Why hadn't she left strict instructions not to do it? Her tongue seemed stuck to the roof of her mouth. If she uttered one syllable more than necessary, all her fear, all her grief, might rush out of her in a cataract of such power, it would wash her away entirely.

"Nothing seems amiss in here," Devon said. "Looks as if Baxter arrived in time."

Emmaline knelt and pulled out the bottom drawer of the chifferobe and pushed aside her second-best chemise. The Tetisheri statue smiled serenely up at her.

"Father will be relieved."

"Aren't you?"

Not really. If the statue had been stolen, it would have meant Monty would have to call off the scheme and she wouldn't have to cheat Theodore.

Or Griffin. His handsome face was drawn with concern. Emma realized she was trapped. She had to go forward with the plan or Monty would have no chance at a cure. He'd continue to decline until the disease bore him away from her forever. But if she went ahead with the scheme, she'd be defrauding Griffin. Her thoughts chased each other like mice in a maze, stupid with hunger from smelling the unreachable cheese. There was no way out, no clear win to end this game.

She was unable to check her tears. They came in torrents streaming down her cheeks.

Devon took her hands, raised her to her feet, and pulled her into a comforting embrace. He held her steady while her shoulders shook. He didn't scold her for making a wet mess of his fine white shirt front, but he did make small soothing sounds, a soft shushing noise. Emma pressed her face into the wool of his jacket and inhaled.

Spicy sandalwood and citrusy bergamot and warm male.

He didn't try to console her with false hope, for which she blessed his name. It would only make things worse. In fact, he didn't say anything. Instead, Devon cradled her head against his chest with his big palm. It was a simple gesture, but it made her ache with such tenderness, the tears fell harder.

He held her tighter and she clung to him, wrapping her arms around him. Griffin was her rock, her personal island of safety while life crashed down around her in pounding waves.

He kissed her crown and she quieted in his arms, the tears abating.

Then she felt it . . . him . . . hard against her belly.

If someone came in and discovered them thus, Theodore would be desolate. She pulled out of the circle of Griffin's arms. "I'm quite recovered. Thank you, milord."

"Griffin," he corrected. "And I doubt you're recovered in the slightest." He pulled a handkerchief from his pocket and dabbed it gently on her cheeks to wipe away the last of the tears. "You don't always have to be strong, Emmaline. It's no sin to need someone, you know."

Only need? Was that all this jumbled chaos in her chest was? It felt like so much more. Sometimes when she looked at Griffin, her eyes ached at the brightness of his masculine beauty. She wanted to drink him in, engulf him, let him shoot out her fingers and toes in brilliant shafts of light.

What a thing to think! I must be losing my mind. Emmaline covered her face with both hands.

"If you won't let me comfort you, perhaps you'll allow me to attempt a diversion," he said. "I believe you owe me a waltz."

She lowered her hands and blinked in surprise. She wasn't the only one whose sanity was in question. Was he one brick short of a load, too? "There's no music."

"We don't need it. We need only our imaginations and a rhythm, which I'm fully capable of supplying." He gave her a proper bow and a devastating smile. "May I have the pleasure of this dance?"

It was a ruthlessly obvious ploy to distract her from what was happening to Monty, but she decided to succumb to it. A dance meant she'd be back in his arms, at a proper distance, of course. She could touch him again without guilt gnawing her belly.

"The pleasure is mine." She mouthed the proper response, dropped a shallow curtsey, and slipped into a dance frame with him.

He started to hum, a low rumbling approximation of a Strauss waltz. The melody didn't remain entirely in the same key, rambling with disregard for any sense of pitch. Once he lost the thread of it altogether and substituted a few bars of *God Save the Queen*, but Emmaline found his attempt charming. They moved around the room in gentle three-quarter time.

Theodore was a splendid dancer, light on his feet while telegraphing sure, capable leads to his partner. Griffin moved with the grace of a large predator, sleek and stealthy, every muscle under tense control. She felt like a helpless gazelle, mesmerized into mirroring his movements even though he might shed the veneer of civilization at any moment and devour her whole.

As they swayed and dipped, it was as if they became one entity. She wasn't conscious of being led, but she seemed to know where he was about to put his foot before he did. As they approached the carved bed post, he executed a flawless chaussée and promenade, narrowly avoiding a collision.

"My apologies, madam," he said with a sober nod to the post as they box-stepped in place for a moment. "I was so dazzled by my partner's beauty, I almost didn't see you there."

Emmaline giggled, something she rarely did.

"Now there's a sound I haven't heard before," Griffin said. "You should do it more often."

"If I did, folk would surely name me a simpleton," she said.

"Do you care so much what others think?"

A confidence artist always had to be aware of the opinion of others. If she read her mark incorrectly, the best laid plans could unravel in a moment.

A moment like this.

Suddenly, she ached to tell him everything. Since Monty had always been a bit fuzzy on the whole issue of right and wrong, he'd neglected Emmaline's theological education somewhat, but the rationale behind the church's confessional finally made sense to her.

What a relief it would be to lay her sins bare.

But Lord Devonwood was no priest. He wouldn't absolve her. In fact, he'd be far more likely to call the constabulary and see her and Monty hauled off to gaol. She straightened her posture while her soul hunkered behind stiff courtesy.

"If I care for the good opinion of others it may be because my station does not allow me to flaunt convention with impunity as yours does, milord."

His smile faded. "I thought we were past the use of titles. My mistake."

It didn't seem possible that she could injure him, but his suddenly stern expression made her think she had.

"You're a fine dancer," she offered by way of consolation. "And your humming is very . . . tuneful."

"You have the makings of a diplomat, I see. In that case, you should see me paint." His smile was back. It warmed her to her toes.

"You're an artist as well?" she said.

"Lord, no, but you should see my attempts. It's right down there with my ability to carry a tune. There ought to be a law against the way I abuse paint and canvas."

This time, she bypassed a giggle and went straight for a laugh.

"Another thing you should do more of," he said approvingly.

"Some people have a gift for levity. Alas, I am not one of them." Her life had been too deadly serious for the most part. Even the playful bits, when she and Monty perfectly executed a scheme that relieved a greedy mark of his funds, were tinged with the desperation of knowing it was either temporary success or continued lean times for them. "You, however, seem to be a man of many talents."

"A few," he said.

It occurred to her that the way the man danced was a good indication of what sort of lover he'd be. Gently controlling. Powerful. Tender.

"I've been known to get a sense about people," he admitted. "You, for example, have more layers than an artichoke and are twice as prickly, but under all that impressive armor, I suspect you're frightened most of the time."

Their waltz slowed to a crawl, and he held her far closer than propriety allowed.

"An artichoke? Thank you, Griffin," she said in a falsely bright tone. "What woman doesn't relish being compared to a vegetable?"

"I didn't mean it like that," he said, cinching her tighter yet. "I simply meant you don't have to fear me."

They stopped all pretense of dancing and stood stock still. She felt his ribs expand and contract in slow even breaths. Her own chest advanced and retreated in time with his. She turned her face toward him and tilted her chin.

"But I wonder sometimes if I should fear you," he said, yet he made no move to release her. His eyes darkened as he looked down at her.

His mouth was so close she could feel the warmth of his exhalation feather over her lips. He moved toward her by the barest fraction of an inch. She lifted on her toes and brushed his mouth with hers.

She and Monty were planning to bilk him of a scandalous amount of money. She was supposed to be considering marrying his brother. Yet she wanted him to kiss her back more than a Bedouin wants water.

"Fear me? Yes, Lord Devonwood. Perhaps you should."

CHAPTER 19

"Fear be damned." He lowered his mouth to hers.

Her heart wept. It was a trusting kiss. She didn't deserve it.

Then he slanted his lips, ravaging her mouth with a kiss that left her bruised and breathless.

Yes, Emmaline exulted, allowing herself to melt into him. That was what she deserved. A taking. A ruthless theft. She wanted him to steal her. That way she could lose herself in this man, if for only a moment.

No thoughts. No worries. No fretting over what the morrow would bring. Only blessed hot kisses, moist shared breath, and fevered touches.

He kissed down to the daring line of her décolletage, teasing his lips along the edge of the amethyst silk. Her breasts were full and heavy, the aching tips pressed hard against her stiff corset. The bodice was tight enough, he wouldn't be able to free her bosom without unlacing her.

She almost pushed her own palms against them to still the ache. Instead she arched her back, hoping to expose another finger-width of skin for his mouth's exploration.

He groaned in frustration, a sentiment she shared with her whole heart. Encased in their whalebone gaol, her nipples throbbed at the nearness of his mouth. The mere memory of his lips on them sent a zing of desire straight to her womb.

If he could only suckle her again . . .

She palmed his cheeks and kissed him, openmouthed this time. She delved in. She devoured. She couldn't get enough of his lips and tongue.

In her mind, she'd always likened Lord Devonwood to a predatory animal. Now she wondered if perhaps of the pair of them, she was the real feral beast.

His hands found her waist. Without breaking off their kiss, he raised her off her feet and deposited her on the bed. He lifted her skirts, collapsing the concentric rings of her hoops, and ran his hands up her legs. Stepping forward, Griffin forced her knees apart.

Even through the linen of her pantalets, his palms were warm as heated bricks at the foot of the bed. Pleasure danced in their wake. When he reached the apex of her thighs, where her open-crotched underthings left her sex exposed and vulnerable, she reflexively tried to pull her knees together, but his hips blocked her efforts.

He couldn't possibly mean to touch her *there*. The thought that he might sent warmth throbbing between her legs.

It would be exceedingly wicked. Sinful.

Wonderful.

It was what she'd always longed for and never realized she'd wanted. Griffin handled that secret part of her with such delicacy, such lavish tenderness, it didn't matter that she still didn't deserve his gentle loving.

What mattered was the way he made her feel.

Who knew her body held so much capacity for delight? She quivered when he teased her soft curls. She ached, swollen and needy, when he slipped a finger between her slick folds.

When his thumb grazed an extra sensitive spot, it sent heat and bliss washing over her.

"Ah, just there." The words slipped from her lips between one kiss and the next. She grasped his shoulders and held on, white-knuckled, while he continued to torment that needy bit of flesh with slow, ever tightening circles.

He kissed her neck. He suckled her earlobe. Her breath hissed in over her teeth when she remembered to breathe. She began to shake inside. Something deep within her tightened, like a cat whipping itself with its own tail, every muscle tensed for a leap.

Emma kissed Griffin back, matching his movements, nibbling his ear, sucking his neck, desperate for him not to stop the devastating game he played with her mound. Even though she knew she was still seated on the bed with her knees spread, she had the eerie sense that she was on a journey. Her soul was going somewhere. Trying to reach some place. She strained toward that unknown goal with every bit of her being.

Then suddenly, she was there.

"Griffin," she breathed his name. It slipped from her lips as power over her own body slipped away as well. The tightness inside her unraveled in a frenzied, whiplike release. Her womb pounded. Her limbs bucked and shuddered with the force of her inner pulses.

When she'd imagined earlier that if she could only drink Griffin in, his light would shoot out her fingers and toes, she'd thought she was losing her mind.

She had no idea something very like that could actually happen.

The pumping contractions began to subside. Emma's head lolled on her shoulders. She felt boneless and sated and couldn't bring herself to care about anything for the space of ten heartbeats.

She was still glowing with Griffin's light inside her.

She was vaguely aware that he smoothed down her skirt. Then he kissed her, his mouth soft and giving on hers.

Emma still didn't deserve his trusting kiss, but she allowed it anyway. Perhaps that was the point of such things. The kiss she didn't deserve was exactly the one she needed.

The sharp clack of heels on hardwood sounded in the next room.

"That'll be Baxter," Griffin said softly. "Are you all right?"

She'd never been so all right. He'd taken control of her body and stood her world on its head. A sense of well-being spread over her like warm oil, but she couldn't regain enough self-mastery to answer him immediately. She drew a shaky breath.

"Yes," she finally managed.

"Good." He helped her to her feet. "I'll stay with you if you wish while you speak to the doctor."

She'd been lost in the realm of pure sensation. Now the real world slammed back into her with his words. Monty, consumption, Tetisheri, Theodore . . . everything rushed in. She had to abandon the short respite she'd enjoyed with Griffin and plunge back into the tangled web of her life.

She had to stop thinking of him like that. He was Lord Devonwood, not Griffin. Griffin was the man who sent her soul flying and brought it safely back. Lord Devonwood wasn't her magical protector. He was Theodore's brother. Monty's mark.

"That won't be necessary," she said with only a slight quaver in her voice. She walked toward the door to meet Baxter before the butler sought them in her chamber. She stopped at the door and turned back to look at him.

She still didn't understand what he'd done to her. There'd been nothing like this in the medical treatises Monty had given her when he judged she was old enough to be educated in the ways of the flesh. She knew she was technically still a virgin, but something had definitely passed between her and Griffin.

Something special. He'd seen her spirit bared and she only now realized what it had cost him to give the experience to her without taking pleasure for himself. His chest heaved in shuddering breaths and the bulge in his trousers left no doubt of his frustrated state.

She wished things were different. She wished his brother wasn't courting her. She desperately wished she didn't have to trick him for Monty's sake.

But she did.

So she drew herself up to her full height and decided to put some distance between them. It might make it hurt less later on when he learned what she was and he was forced to hate her. "Thank you, milord. I'll see to my father by myself."

"Thank you, milord?" Devon repeated as her skirt swished through the doorway. She'd melted under his touch, then when it was done she'd gone cold as an ice sculpture. As if he'd merely rendered her a service. "Damnation."

She *thanked* him. For what? Diddling her silly? By God, she made him feel like one of those quack doctors who treated their hysterical patients by massaging them to release and calling it therapy. For tuppence, he'd go to his brother with the musky, sweet scent of her still heavy on his fingers and show Ted exactly what sort of woman he was mooning around about.

Devon strode to the washstand and scrubbed his hands. The man glaring back at him in the mirror damned him for an indecisive coward. He'd never been at such a loss for what to do next, not even in the moments after his father had died.

What was it he wanted from Emmaline Farnsworth? Relief from his gift?

There was that. Each time he touched her, normalcy flowed over him like a healing balm. He didn't understand it, but he was certain if he could only hold her hand, the fiercest *Sending* would be unable to harm his mind.

Did he merely want her body?

She'd given herself over to him completely for those brief moments, and he'd reduced her to gasping need. It made a man feel like a god to make a woman burn, then watch as her release shivered through her all on account of only his touch. If he and Emmaline actually came together in sexual congress, they'd surely spontaneously combust.

Or did he want something deeper?

He'd always imagined a happy home for Teddy, a loving wife and children scampering about. Devon knew he was obligated to wed and produce an heir for the estate, but he couldn't ever see himself happy with the shadowy figure who would become his countess. If he touched anything of hers, his gift would likely come shrieking in with a peek at their future.

Invariably, a tragic future.

It had been horrific enough to *See* his father's death. He didn't think he could bear advance warning of the death of a child. Or the death of a wife.

Especially since he was powerless to change that fate.

He'd already decided when he finally wed, he'd have to wear gloves round the clock to avoid touching anything that belonged to his bride.

But even though he'd received visions from her pencil and her fan, when he touched Emmaline he didn't fear the future breaking in. When he was with her, he lost his sense of aloneness, his sense of "other-ness." He wasn't Griffin, the monster, the freak, the one with the damnable Preston gift.

He was just Griffin.

She had sighed his name as she came, and he was reborn.

When she retreated behind distant courtesy, his solitary existence rushed up to claim him again. Years of self-enforced isolation marched ahead of him. He'd never met anyone besides Emmaline whose mere presence eased his burden. He likely never would again.

But to make her his, he'd have to betray his brother.

He walked over to her chifferobe and peered down at the Tetisheri statue nestled amid her lacy chemises and stockings. The figure's smile had seemed enigmatic before. In this setting it seemed indecently knowing.

Somehow, everything swirling in his life was tied up with that infernal statue.

Devon stretched out his hand toward it and a low thrum sounded in his head. If he touched it, he was certain a *Sending* would come.

Would it show him what he needed to do?

He lowered his hand to the cold granite.

The field of rye stretch to the horizon, the heads of grain ripe for harvest, the air dusty with motes of chaff. The sun was overbright to his English eyes. Images in the distance wavered in the heat or hovered above nonexistent pools of shimmering water.

Threshers appeared, wielding handheld scythes. The long curved blades flashed in the sunlight. The workers chanted a song of reaping. Their rhythmic movements perfumed the air with cut grain. Rasping slices of the blades filled Devon's ears. Bits of chaff worked their way under his clothing and made him itch.

The overlord of the field drove up in a gilded chariot to survey the work. Once he disembarked, he walked on two legs like a man, but his face was long-muzzled with pointed ears pricked forward.

Anubis, *Devon realized. The jackal-headed guardian of the dead.*

Anubis laughed, the hysterical cackle of a carnivore who's been reduced to eating carrion. Death hovered around him like a flock of crows. Devon smelled his fetid breath from across the amber expanse of the field.

Then Anubis pointed to one of the threshers and barked an order. The man straightened.

It was Teddy.

Devon's brother dropped his scythe and began to run, the rye wavering around him like an ochre sea. Anubis gave chase. Devon tried to run after them, but his feet were anchored to the spot. He couldn't move.

He bellowed his brother's name as Anubis closed the distance between him and Teddy with each long stride.

A phoenix appeared in the sky and streaked to intercept Anubis, but neither had the upper hand so far as Devon could tell.

Life or death. It appeared they'd both reach his brother at the same time.

Devon watched, helpless, as Theodore tripped and disappeared into the thick miasma of rippling grain.

He jerked his hand away from the statue and the vision faded. A vise tightened at his temples but Emmaline wasn't near to banish the pain. The vision was once again an allegory instead of a clear *Sending.*

Instead of showing him what to do, his gift left him with more questions.

Devon sank onto the foot of Emmaline's bed to think.

Anubis was clearly connected to the statue. Hadn't Ted's translation of the statue's base named Tetisheri "beloved of

Isis and Anubis"? If that was true, according to the *Sending*, the statue represented danger to his brother.

Clearly, he needed to get Teddy away from it. He wasn't meant to submerge himself in ancient Egypt, slogging away at his studies of dead civilizations, like the threshers in the vision whacking away at the rye.

But how could Devon persuade Theodore to give up the only intellectual pursuit that had ever captured his imagination?

And who was the phoenix?

Devon stalked back into the sitting room of the Blue Suite, his gaze fixed on his feet in concentration. The rapidly blooming migraine made his vision tunnel. Suddenly he stopped and stared at the Turkish carpet with its pair of fighting phoenixes in the center.

This was Emmaline's suite. Could she be the magical bird in his vision?

In the *Sending,* the phoenix was trying to counter Anubis, to protect Ted. If Emma was the phoenix, Theodore ought to spend more time with her. He would if he wasn't so intent on studying with Dr. Farnsworth. She saved Devon from his dubious gift whenever she was near. Could she save Teddy from being singled out by whatever malevolent force Anubis represented?

In the *Sending*, Devon hadn't been able to help his brother. His feet had been stuck fast. Ted's only hope was the phoenix. The more he pondered it, the more certain he was that the phoenix could be only Emmaline.

It was the only interpretation that made sense.

But his clear *Sending* in the carriage on the way to Lord Whitmore's had shown him that she was going to come to his bed. Tonight.

Devon sank down in one of the Tudor chairs, feeling as stolid and heavy as that age-darkened oak. Shards of pain lanced his brain. He'd known all along he couldn't betray Teddy. He didn't need the vision to urge him to do what was right. His heart had been whispering it to him all evening.

Somehow, when Emmaline came to his bed that night, Devon had to make sure he wasn't the man in it.

CHAPTER 20

"I left a special salve with Mr. Baxter and instructed him on the application of the poultice for your father's lungs. He'll relay the information to whomever you engage as Dr. Farnsworth's nurse. I recommend you hire one full time," Dr. Trowbridge explained. A strong smell of menthol and camphor oil wafted from the Green Room where Monty rested. "The poultice should give him a modicum of relief."

"Thank you, doctor." Emmaline was relieved not to hear any sound from the room. It meant the cyclic spasm of coughing had been broken. It hurt her heart to hear Monty hacking away his life, unable to stop.

"I also gave him a tincture of laudanum to help him sleep. If he finds it gives him relief, Dr. Farnsworth may continue with minimal doses. However, you should know that neither the opiate nor the poultice is a cure."

The doctor's eyes drooped at the outside corners. Combined with his heavy jowls, they gave him the appearance of an aging hound. His might not have been a handsome face, but like the Bassett he resembled, the doctor radiated kindness and compassion.

"I fear there's not much to be done for cases this far advanced," Dr. Trowbridge said.

"I see," she said woodenly. "Have you any idea . . . I

mean . . . how long . . ." Emma couldn't bring herself to finish the sentence.

"Could be a month. Could be a year. Could be another ten, but I doubt it in your father's case," the doctor said. "Tuberculosis is a deceptive disease. It's not uncommon for a patient to rally and enjoy long periods when the malady lies dormant. I've even heard it said consumption improves a sufferer's appearance, gives them an otherworldly glow. While he may at times seem hearty, unfortunately, your father's lungs are badly damaged. He's likely to weaken and succumb to the illness."

"He seemed to do much better in a dry climate," she said. *Another ten years. Please, God, would that be too much to ask?* "Suppose we returned to Egypt—"

"It would be better for him to go to Görbersdorf in the Alps," Dr. Trowbridge said. "They're having a good bit of success there, pioneering some new treatments for consumptives. Once your father is fit to travel, that's what I'd recommend."

Which meant they needed money soon, far sooner than it would take to adequately play out Monty's scheme with the Tetisheri statue. In any other game, he'd have already made up the meanings for the last of the hieroglyphs on the statue. Theodore wouldn't know the difference since everything he understood of Egyptology he had learned at Monty's feet.

But this time, their game had taken an odd turn. Monty seemed to be earnestly trying to decipher the strange lines, squiggles, and stylized beasts. It was almost as if he'd been sucked into the scheme and believed the pitch himself.

"Have you told him the full extent of his condition?" Emma asked.

"No. I will, if you wish," Dr. Trowbridge said. "However, I usually leave it to the discretion of my patients' loved ones. Some people do not wish to know they are dying. Some family members desire the opportunity to continue living with a degree of normalcy for as long as possible. In my opinion, I believe your father suspects, but doesn't want confirmation."

Emma nodded. Monty wouldn't appreciate a frank discussion of his mortality. He'd rather try to con the devil with his last breath. "Thank you, doctor."

Dr. Trowbridge smiled sadly. "I'll look in on him from time to time. Send for me at once if he worsens."

The doctor waddled down the corridor toward the staircase.

Emma pressed her palms over both eyes for a moment and drew a deep breath. She smoothed back her hair, tucking a stray curl behind her ear, and pasted on a smile. Then she pushed Monty's door open.

Her father lay with his hands on his chest. With his waxy pallor, it was almost as if he were already laid out in his coffin. Emma regretted telling Devon not to accompany her. She missed his steady strength, even if she wasn't worthy of leaning on it.

"Someone knows how to finagle a way to be waited upon hand and foot," she said with forced lightness as she drew near. The pungent smell of the medicine plastered to his chest was almost overpowering. She hitched her hip on the side of the bed and took his icy hand in hers. "Good con, Monty."

"I've done better," he said softly between wheezing breaths. He tugged his hand free and cupped her cheek, swiping at the bit of moisture beneath her eye. "My dear girl. Have you been crying?"

"Crying? No. Well, maybe a little." It would do no good to lie to Monty. A person who lied for a living could always scent an untruth in others, but she might be able to misdirect him. "You did interrupt my time at the ball, after all, and I had to leave Theodore at the mercy of a certain Lady Cressida. I fear she's set her cap for him."

"Worse luck for her then. Whoever she is, this Lady Cressida can't hold a candle to my girl." Even though the laudanum made his eyelids droop, he searched her face as if he hadn't seen her for a long time.

"You're worse than an Irishman for blarney. I'm not really your girl and you know it."

"Yes, you are, Emmaline. In all the ways that matter, you're mine." His hand dropped from her cheek as if it was suddenly too heavy for him to hold up. "Did I ever tell you why I picked you out from the foundling home?

She shook her head, not trusting her voice.

"It's because you look like your mother. You have her eyes, her sweet mouth."

She blinked in surprise. "You knew my mother?"

"Not only knew her." His eyes closed with weariness. "I loved her."

He'd never wanted to talk about the past before. Emma always figured as far as Monty was concerned, she'd burst into being like Minerva springing from the mind of Zeus on the day he took her from the foundlings home. "Monty, are you . . . really my father?"

He shook his head. "I wish I was though. Your mother, Mattie O'Sullivan, was the loveliest girl in Flatbush."

He was silent so long she thought he'd drifted to sleep, but then he began again, his words whispered as he followed the thread of a distant time.

"Her parents were moderately well-to-do, a generation off the boat, and established in their own business. Mattie was so pretty, they figured she ought to be able to marry well." He shrugged. "I wasn't cut from fine enough cloth for them."

Emma's memories of her mother were hazy at best. She

had no recollection of grandparents or any family at all beyond the thin, haggard woman who'd borne her. Now that she thought back on it, her mother couldn't have been more than twenty-five, but in Emma's memory, she seemed ancient.

"When her parents forbade Mattie to keep company with me, I left," Monty murmured. "Went west to seek my fortune in the silver mines of Colorado. I figured once I had plumper pockets, her family would relent and she'd be able to accept me."

His chest shuddered as if he might erupt in coughs again, but then he drew in a lungful of the menthol and camphor and settled into an easy rhythmic breathing instead.

"I told Mattie I'd be away for a year. Wait for me, I said." His lips twitched with emotion. "I was gone five. I guess that's a long time for the belle of the ball to wait."

"She married someone else?"

"I wish she had. No, she was bamboozled by Herman Potts, a fellow who already had a wife upstate. He got Mattie with you and that was the last she saw of him. She died alone."

That wasn't true. Emma had been there in their cheerless little tenement. She remembered the morning she'd toddled to her neighbor lady's door because she couldn't wake her mother. It was one of her clearest memories.

"She'd been gone six months by the time I returned from Colorado without the silver I went for. I made her brother tell me what had happened." Monty's jaw worked furiously. "I'm not a violent man, but I'd have done murder if Herman Potts had been nearby that night."

His chest heaved for a bit. Then he went quiet, his breathing so even and untroubled, Emma didn't dare ask any of the questions burning in her. Was her mother's brother still alive? Why hadn't her grandparents taken her in when her mother died instead of letting Emma go to the foundlings' home?

Monty's eyes popped open and he winked at her. "But I got even with him the only way I knew. First con I ever pulled was to swindle Potts out of his life's savings. It was enough to set up the bookstore. And that was enough to convince the people at the foundlings' home that I could care for you."

"I loved the bookstore, Monty." She smoothed his thinning hair over the freckles showing through on his pate. "Why'd we ever leave it?"

His shoulders lifted in a slight shrug. "I didn't want you to be a shop girl all your life. It wasn't enough for my Emmaline. So I started forging those old letters. Then you and I started our games. We've had a pretty good run of it, too." His mouth turned up in a satisfied smile. "Look at you now. Dressed like a duchess."

A duchess who'd be out on her ear if the truth about them was known.

"Theodore and me," Monty mumbled, the laudanum clearly working on him. "Did I tell you we translated another side of the base?"

"No. What did it say?"

"Herein is life long lasting, treasure beyond reckoning, for he who understands and dares to open the portal." His eyes closed and his head lolled to one side as he drifted off.

"Open the portal? What does that mean?"

"Open the door to Tetisheri's tomb, I expect. Life long lasting. Treasure beyond reckoning. We'll find it, girl. There are two more sides to the base and they're full of clues, I'll warrant." He licked his papery lips. "Tomorrow, Emma. Tell Ted to bring the books and the statue round tomorrow. I'll be . . . better then."

He slipped into the light sleep of advancing years.

"Oh, Monty. There is no tomb. There may not ever

have been a Tetisheri. It's just a con," she whispered, her lips barely moving. "Have you forgotten?"

He didn't open his eyes so his voice startled her. "I dream about it every night. We find Tetisheri's tomb in the Valley of the Kings and when the stone is rolled back, there are wondrous things awaiting us." He was quiet for so long she was sure he'd drifted off again, but then he rasped, "Maybe this con isn't just the big one. Maybe it's the real one."

"I ought to have gone home sooner," Theodore said as he handed his mother and sister from the carriage. "Why didn't you tell me Emmaline's father took sick?"

"It's been so long since you were out in Society, I didn't have the heart to pull you away," *Maman* said. "You were having such a lovely time at Lord Whitmore's; it seemed a shame to interrupt your pleasure. Besides, I'm certain everyone's fine. Devon took care of things."

Ted scowled. "Devon always takes care of things."

He ought to have been grateful to his brother, but his nattering conscience wouldn't let him. It flailed him for not taking care of Emmaline's father. Instead, he'd been enjoying himself far too much at the ball, especially when he danced with Lady Cressida.

Who'd have expected Louisa's skinny little pigtailed friend would have blossomed into such an engaging beauty? So engaging Theodore neglected to notice that the woman he hoped to wed had been forced to leave the party to tend to her father with his brother standing in his stead.

Ted was too guilt-ridden to face up to his brother's goodness.

And he wasn't anxious to explain himself to Emmaline either. It was all an innocent mistake, of course. Theodore had merely done what was expected of any young man on such an occasion. He danced every dance with the young ladies he'd been assigned.

It had been his duty as a good guest.

Lord Whitmore's ball had turned into such a successful rout; Ted hadn't even noticed Emmaline was gone till the time came for the last waltz. He was slated to dance it with her, so he searched everywhere in the press of people. When he was supposed to collect the woman who was the love of his young life, she was nowhere to be seen.

And he hadn't missed her.

It certainly made him seem like a selfish lout. Why hadn't he looked for her earlier?

He'd noticed who Cressida was dancing with once or twice throughout the evening.

Teddy cringed. That made him feel even worse. He loved Emmaline.

Why had his eye been drawn to another?

"Lady Cressida was certainly in her looks this evening, didn't you think, Louisa?" His mother asked as they approached the front door of Devonwood House.

Ted didn't hear his sister's answer. An image of Cressida had risen unbidden in his mind, all pink and gold and delicate. He tamped down the vision and conjured up Emmaline in his imagination. She was entirely lovely in a different way, but she had none of Cressida's devastating vulnerability.

Emma was such a capable sort. It was part of what drew Theodore to her, since he'd never had to be responsible for anyone but himself, and that only once he'd moved out from under his brother's shadow.

But Cressida wakened an urge Teddy hadn't realized he possessed—the desire to protect someone else. He didn't know what to make of it.

Once they were inside the house, his mother and sister pecked his cheek good night and headed up the curving staircase. The town house was dark save for a dim flicker in the parlor. Ted peeked in and found Devon sprawled on the settee with a glass of amber liquid in his hand.

"Headache?" he asked. His brother had been plagued with them on occasion for as long as he could remember. Devon usually avoided drinking to excess, so Ted figured this migraine must be a particularly virulent one.

Devon nodded and then told him what Dr. Trowbridge had had to say about Farnsworth's illness. The news was grim, not at all the sort of capper one would wish for an evening that had been filled with lighthearted fun.

"He's been sicklier than usual of late, but one always hopes, doesn't one?" Theodore crossed over to the liquor cabinet and filled a tumbler with scotch for himself. Maybe it would ease his guilt the way it eased his brother's headache. His friend Dr. Farnsworth was truly ill and Ted hadn't been there in his time of need.

The tightness that gathered in his chest surprised him. The old man had become more to him than merely Emmaline's father. Dr. Farnsworth was his partner in an adventure, his mentor, a man whose approval had become quite important as of late. Ted had still been in short pants when his own father died. In many ways, Montague Farnsworth filled the previous earl of Devonwood's long empty shoes.

"How did Emmaline take it?" he asked.

"I don't know," Devon said, a frown knitting his dark brows together. "She . . . is a very private person."

"She'll be fine," Theodore said.

Emmaline was always fine, always in control, always the smartest person in the room. Lord, how it pleased him when he discovered the rare tidbit she didn't already know.

It certainly didn't happen often.

Cressida, by contrast, had made him feel like Newton,

da Vinci and Euripides all rolled into one. Not that Cressie—she'd insisted he call her that—wasn't intelligent. It was just that she made him feel that way, too.

"Do me a favor, will you?" Devon said, his words slurring a bit.

Theodore jerked in surprise. Devon never asked him for anything, much less a favor. "Of course."

"Trade rooms with me for the night. Mine is at the front of the house and light from the gas lamps on the street blazes in. I can't bear it."

"You might pull the drapes."

"I want a bit of air." Devon leaned forward, balancing his elbows on his knees.

Even in the dimness, Theodore saw a raised vein marring the smooth plane on his brother's forehead, a sure sign he was in the throes of an unusually bad migraine. No wonder he'd imbibed enough to slur his speech.

"Your room looks out over the garden, Ted. It's cool and dark and quiet . . . it's the only way I'll sleep tonight."

"Certainly, I'll just go collect my nightshirt," Theodore said, rising.

"Use one of mine." Devon's tone was harsher than warranted as he rose and stomped toward the door, weaving slightly.

Ted chalked up his surliness to the deuced headache. "Thank you for taking care of Emmaline for me tonight."

Devon stopped and leaned an arm on the doorframe, but he didn't turn around to face Ted. "You'll take care of her from now on."

CHAPTER 21

Emmaline closed her window and slid the latch, locking out the night. The scent of jasmine in the garden below was so sweet, it made her light-headed.

Yes, that's it. Only the cloying fragrance troubled her sleep, she decided as she climbed back between the cool linens. After a few moments of fidgeting, she threw back the top sheet and coverlet.

Or maybe it's the moon.

Luminescence shafted through her window in a splash of silver. She padded across the room and tugged the damask curtains closed. Light still fingered through the slit and made a beeline across the floor to her bed.

She pummeled her pillow into the desired plumpness and lay back down.

Monty's illness was probably why sleep fled from her, but she resisted thinking about it. Someday soon, she'd have to search out information on tuberculosis, to learn what she could about the course of the disease so there'd be no surprises. She'd help him face what was ahead.

Knowledge is power, Monty always said.

She didn't want to have that sort of power yet.

Consumption was Pandora's box. She didn't dare open it for fear of the horrors that might escape into her mind. There was no way to "un-know" something.

And no way to un-do something either.

She sat up, dangling her legs off the edge of the high bed. She spread her knees to shoulder width and allowed herself to remember the way Devon had distracted her utterly with her own body. She'd never imagined she was capable of such heart-pounding joy.

She let her head fall back and admitted this was the real reason she couldn't sleep. Warmth coursed through her. The tiny muscles inside her that had rioted in pleasure earlier pulsed once now simply on the strength of her memory of his talented fingers.

Why had she allowed Griffin to touch her like that?

She'd never considered herself a sensual person, but with him, she was as randy as the highest flying courtesan.

Was she truly so weak the man could seduce her at will?

Apparently. Her shoulders slumped.

She was still a virgin, but she was no longer innocent. How much longer would it be before Griffin found a way to take her maidenhead, too?

Not long. She'd been within an ace of handing it to him. That wicked surfeit of pleasure stripped away every bit of propriety, all sense of "ought-ness" from her. His need had not been met by their indecent play and it tugged at her with as much force as her own desires. If not for Baxter's footsteps outside the door, if not for Monty's illness, she'd have dragged Griffin down beside her on the bed and found a way to cure his ills, despite her lack of experience.

In the cold light of reason, other than appeasing her appetite for the man, no good could come of bedding him. In the beguiling light of the moon, her body tried to argue with her mind.

She'd lose her only marketable commodity in the marriage game—her purity. And while Theodore had offered to wed her, Lord Devonwood seemed intent only on seducing her at every turn.

Even if she went to Griffin's bed, he probably wouldn't marry her. Society didn't censure a nobleman for dallying with a girl beneath his station. It wasn't as if her father was a powerful lord, whose future goodwill Lord Devonwood might need. Monty wasn't even wealthy enough to provide a decent dowry. Certainly not enough of one to tempt an earl.

But none of that mattered to Theodore.

Dear, sweet Teddy. He would marry her in a trice if she'd only accept him.

Or would he, now that he'd rejoined his friends in London society? It was one thing to propose under a full moon on the Mediterranean when all the world was bathed in a romantic haze. It was quite another to take a penniless bride in cold London daylight.

She glared at the moonlight streaking across her floor, knife-thin. How many lives had been upended by decisions made under the influence of that silver light?

At least Ted need not worry that Griffin would cut him off if she did accept him. He'd assured her nothing Ted might do would change his brother's standing with him. It wasn't much of a leap for her to realize Theodore cared enough about Monty to use his generous allowance to enable them to travel to Görbersdorf right away.

Monty might yet recover.

She flopped back down on the bed and slung a forearm over her eyes. She'd tell Teddy tomorrow that she'd made up her mind. Her answer was yes.

Her stomach squirmed a bit.

Teddy was a good man. If she married him, she'd be able to convince Monty to give up the long con. She'd never have to play those games again. She'd have a home—please, God!—a family, and a chance at a normal life. After his treatment on the Continent, Monty might rally and live long enough to dandle her children on his knees.

A lump of disquiet settled in her belly. Why could she not be happy with her choice?

Griffin's darkly sensual face rose in her mind.

She sat up abruptly. She couldn't wait till tomorrow. She needed to tell Teddy now. Tonight.

Better yet, she needed to seduce him. Unlike Griffin, if she and Theodore were found *in flagrante delicto*, Teddy could be counted upon to do the honorable thing since he'd already asked her to marry him.

If she waited, anything might happen. Theodore might change his mind. Lady Cressida might change it for him. Even if Emmaline hadn't overheard that lady's intention to set her cap for Ted, it wasn't hard to miss the way she flirted and flattered him. By anyone's measure, Lady Cressida was a far better match for Theodore than she.

Emmaline rose from bed and hurried to the chifferobe. She changed into her best chemise. She didn't wear scent often, even though Monty had bought her a small bottle of Eau de Cologne Imperiale, a rich citrusy fragrance with undertones of rosemary and cedar. It was an extravagance they couldn't afford, leaving Egypt in haste as they had, but he'd insisted.

Theodore had remarked on the heady scent the night he proposed. She dabbed a bit of expensive oil behind her ears and between the hollow of her breasts. Perhaps the rich fragrance would help Teddy remember why he'd asked her to marry him.

Emmaline would need all the help she could get. She slipped out her door and tiptoed across the hallway to Theodore's, her heart hammering. She spared a moment to peer down the dark corridor toward Griffin's chamber. Regret shuddered through her and it took everything in her not to walk to the end of the hall and open his door instead.

Regret is a waste of time, she reminded herself. With effort, she steadied herself with a palm on Ted's doorknob, the crystal hard and cold in her hand.

Hard and cold. Just as she had to be in this moment.

She was still a scoundrel and still full of self-loathing over it. Emma was embarking on the longest long con anyone had surely ever attempted.

She was going to seduce and wed one brother, but all the while she'd be thinking of the other.

And would for as long as she drew breath.

Devon heard the door creak, but he didn't move.

I'm dreaming, he told himself.

He was also very drunk. Devon usually avoided strong spirits because a foxed man was a weak man. A drunk gambled when he couldn't afford to lose and made decisions he'd later regret. But Devon didn't regret swilling whisky this night. The spirits deadened his pain and sent him into sleepy oblivion.

If ever he needed to wallow in forgetfulness, it was this night.

The sound he thought he heard was surely in his imagination. He tried to dive back below the surface of sleep before he came fully aware. He damn sure didn't want to lie awake *knowing* Emma had stolen into his bedchamber at the end of the hall and was being swived by his brother.

Or worse, God help him, *hearing* Emma being swived by Theodore. His chamber was several doors away, but she made the most alluring little noises when she was pleasured.

His headache flared and he squeezed his eyes tight. He couldn't think about her now, not when she was with Ted. Reliving their earlier tryst was the path to madness.

A floorboard gave with a small groan and Devon thought he heard the swish of bare feet approaching. He didn't bother opening his eyes. He was imagining it all, hoping against hope that his vision might somehow come to pass.

He rarely made an effort to derail the future, but this one seemed mistake proof. Fate would have a damned difficult time leading her to his bed if he wasn't in it.

A citrusy fragrance curled around him. That tore it. Emmaline smelled like a warm peach, not a top-tier courtesan. He was surely dreaming.

There. He heard the soft sibilance of someone else's shallow breathing.

It can't be.

Someone lifted the linens.

Whisky-soaked fantasy.

Sweat gathered at his temples as his headache raged with blinding agony.

A touch, soft as eiderdown, swept over his bare back. His pain sloughed away, as if someone had poured a pitcher of cool water over his pounding head. Anguish washed away in runnels. The blessed brush of her fingertips sent warmth and light to his battered soul.

If he was dreaming, he didn't want to wake. If this was what whisky did to him, he'd take up drinking in earnest.

By some minor miracle, Emmaline was in his bed. Real or phantom, it had to be her. No one else could banish his pain with a touch.

Euphoria swept over him. Whether from the cessation of his headache, from the alcoholic fog of Glenlivet, or from the woman whose soft breasts were pressed against his back, he wasn't sure. All he knew was that he basked in a warm embrace, blissfully free from pain.

Growing harder by the moment.

Emma's heart pounded. Why didn't Theodore turn to her? Why didn't he say something? She had no idea he'd be such a heavy sleeper.

A faint whiff of alcohol tickled her nostrils.

Oh, God, he's foxed.

Perhaps he wouldn't wake long enough to take her maidenhead and settle matters once and for all. Worse, perhaps drink would render him unable to do the deed.

Trembling inside, she wrapped herself around him. It was too dark to see properly, but there was no mistaking the fact that he was naked.

Didn't men sleep in nightshirts? Monty always did. Somehow this whole scheme would have been less embarrassing if Theodore were decently covered, if their only contact was the necessary one that would secure him as irrevocably hers. She'd heard that some husbands and wives spent their entire lifetimes and raised half a dozen children without once being in the altogether in each other's presence.

He groaned, the low feral sound of a pleased male animal. She pressed her cheek against the smooth skin of his back and heard his heart pounding like a trip hammer. He smelled deliciously male, with only a faint hint of bergamot and sandalwood.

He still didn't turn to her. Emmaline's seduction would be so much easier if Teddy was behaving like himself. She usually had to fend off his advances, to cut his kisses short and reroute his caresses. She never imagined she'd have to be the one to, well, to initiate things.

In for a penny . . .

She reached around and stroked his belly. Then her hand grazed something that was decidedly not his abdomen, something hard and thick. It was longer than she'd expected and surprisingly hot to the touch.

She slid her palm over his length. The skin was smooth and taut over a granite-hard erection. She needn't have worried that being foxed would impede his ability to take her maidenhead. He was more than capable.

Her only worry now was whether he'd remember it in the morning.

Lower down, she discovered a surprising bit of softness on this hard man. She fondled the twin orbs in a sac of skin dusted with wiry hair.

Why doesn't he say something?

Surely this sort of thing wasn't a common occurrence for him. Lord knew, it wasn't for her.

"I wish you'd—"

Before she could finish her sentence he rolled toward her and covered her mouth with his, swallowing the rest of her words. He tasted of whisky, all smoke and peat, but it was far from unpleasant.

His mouth was tender on hers, seeking.

She didn't have to try very hard to imagine that it was Griffin instead of Teddy. He kissed with the same gentle sureness.

Her body responded with the same low ache. Perhaps she could do this, after all. It was for her father, she reminded herself. She'd see him well and sort out the rest of her life later.

Then the man in the bed deepened their kiss and all thoughts of Monty fled.

He tugged up her chemise and found her sex. She was still wet from her dalliance with Griffin earlier. Still achingly sensitive. Her chest constricted as she remembered the way he'd given pleasure to her with such tenderness. Even though the room was dark, she squeezed her eyes shut.

It's him. I'll tell myself it's him. And I'll believe it till the morning light tells me different.

She'd conned so many people. How hard could it be to con herself? She tucked her soul away where nothing could touch it and ordered herself not to think.

She should concentrate on feeling. That was the only way to get through this.

There was plenty to feel. His mouth was at her breasts, tugging and suckling. Need roared inside her. Now would be the right time to tell Theodore that she loved him, that she'd be honored to be his wife, but she couldn't form a coherent sentence. Only helpless gasps and little needy sounds escaped her throat.

Or maybe it was just that she didn't want to taint the exquisite pleasure with a lie. She didn't love Teddy. And she doubted she ever would. Not when a lump of caring for his brother was firmly lodged in her chest.

He moved so his hips were positioned between her legs. She felt him at the apex of her thighs, ready to rend her. She stiffened.

He left her breasts and kissed her mouth again, teasing her with his tongue. As he slipped it in between her lips, he entered her down lower as well. Slowly. Letting her expand to receive him.

The wonder of taking him in made her forget everything else.

Then he stopped suddenly.

She knew there was more of him and to her surprise, she ached to hold all of him inside her. Emma moved her hips, wordlessly asking him to enter.

He propped his upper body on his elbows and withdrew a bit.

She whimpered with need.

Then he thrust into her hard, all the way to his base. She gasped at the sudden rending. Her insides burned. The seduction of Theodore had been filled with such unexpected pleasure up to this point, she was blindsided by the sudden agony.

She shouldn't be surprised. It was the least she deserved for this kind of subterfuge.

He held himself immobile, as if he knew what she felt.

For good or ill, the deed was done. Her future was decided. Theodore would marry her now. She ought to be happy, but a tear escaped from the corner of her closed eye and slid wetly into her ear.

"No more pain now," he said and kissed her cheeks.

Her eyes flew open. It was still too dark to see his face, but there was no mistaking his voice.

The man who moved inside her with slow sure strokes was not Theodore, not the dear boy who would marry her happily and make everything all right.

It was Griffin Titus Preston Nash, Lord Devonwood.

Chapter 22

Usually when Devon remembered his dreams, they were fuzzy and fleeting, mere snatches of images. He'd never experienced such a vivid night-phantom before, alive with all the sensations and smells and tastes of a wicked good swive.

And he'd never had a dream in which he was so aware that he was dreaming, as if he were watching himself from outside his body while at the same time enjoying every jolt of pleasure, every ache of need.

He covered her mouth with his again, unable to get enough of the honey inside. It didn't seem right that he had to cause her pain when she eased his so sweetly.

Emmaline was Devon's private poppy field. She was his mindless oblivion, his endless euphoria, and pleasure beyond his deserts.

But not beyond his guilt, unfortunately. A pang of self-reproach lanced him when a thought of his brother wandered into his mind. He slammed the door on it with force. He'd sort that out later. A man's dreams were his private business. For now, through no fault of his own, he found Emmaline, sweet and soft and gasping, beneath him.

He started to move, slowly so as not to cause her any more discomfort. Even if none of this was real, her pain seemed as real to him as if it were his own. Her body stiffened under him, though inside she was wet and pliant. He deepened their kiss and then, to his joy, she relaxed. She began to move with him, lifting her hips to meet his thrusts.

His world melted in heat and friction. The bed creaked out a frenetic rhythm. Blood pounded in his cock and pressure mounted in his shaft. His ballocks drew tight in preparation for his release.

If he'd not still been convinced this was nothing but a Glenlivet-induced wet dream, he'd have recognized the warning signs of impending release. Taking a maidenhead was one thing. Siring a bastard was another.

A gentleman ought to withdraw out of courtesy to the lady who offered up such a sweet gift. Even in a dream, Devon wanted to do right by his bedmate.

But this was Emmaline. His laudanum. His ease. He never wanted this joining to end, even if it was only a fantasy. He could no more pull out than he could stop himself from bleeding if he were cut.

The force of his climax made his back arch as he drove himself in as deeply as possible. When he growled out his pleasure, she covered his mouth with her fingertips and made a shushing noise.

Even though his body continued to riot, her "Sh!" was a dash of cold water. If this were a dream, she wouldn't try to silence him. She'd join him in noisy rapture.

He couldn't think. The thickest London fog took up residence in his mind. The absence of pain, the residual alcohol in his veins, and the sweet relief of his release conspired to drag him back to oblivion. But before he sank into the deep sleep of the thoroughly sated, one thought resonated in his brain.

This was real.

⋆ ⋆ ⋆

"Oh, please be quiet," Emmaline whispered.

His stiff member still pulsed inside her. If she weren't so afraid of discovery, the wonder of holding him as his seed spurted in hot gushes would make her cry out with him. Feeling his pleasure was an echo of hers.

But if someone else heard him and found them like this, she'd be ruined. Theodore would be devastated. Perhaps he'd even do something boyishly stupid like challenging his brother to a duel.

The thought turned her blood to ice water.

While Devon would feel honor-bound to meet a challenge, he probably wouldn't feel obligated to marry her. It would be unheard of for a man of his station to do so. If he ended up killing his brother over her, he'd hate her forever.

She'd hate herself.

Then Devon's seed stopped pumping into her and her insides contracted once in response. He sighed deeply and his full weight bore down on Emmaline.

She pushed on his shoulders, but he didn't budge.

His breathing was deep and even.

The infernal man's fallen asleep!

Irritation fizzed in her belly till it occurred to her that this was better than having to talk to him right now.

What on earth could she say?

Pardon me, milord. My mistake. I thought I was surrendering my maidenhead to your brother.

She eased out from under him. A bit of the Brussels lace at her hem ripped. She reached down to feel the tear and discovered the embellishment hadn't come completely unfastened. It could be mended.

She could not.

Emmaline tiptoed to the door and eased it open. The hall was deserted so she slipped out and hurried back to the Blue Suite and into her chamber. She turned up the gas lamp and poured water from the pitcher into the ewer on her washstand. Then she pulled off her chemise and scrubbed herself with a wet cloth.

Her inner thighs were slightly streaked with red. No amount of soap and water would fix this.

Her hands shook with delayed tremors. Her plan had gone so horribly wrong.

What was Griffin doing in Theodore's bed?

She sank into the chair before the ornately scrolled French vanity. Her reflection wavered back at her, her hair disheveled, her lips kiss-swollen. Her dark eyes, normally bright, were heavy-lidded and her gaze decidedly knowing.

Yes, she decided, *sensual experience leaves its mark.*

Deep inside, her soul shivered. It had been torn as surely as her maidenhead. Part of her was relieved, glad even, that it had been Griffin instead of Theodore in that bed. Though the mistake ruined her carefully crafted plan, there was an odd sense of rightness about how she and Griffin fit together.

She had wanted it to be him, she realized, whether it advanced any sort of plan or not.

Emmaline drew a deep breath and considered what to do. When a long confidence scheme went wrong, Monty either altered the play or folded shop and skedaddled before the constabulary took an interest in their activities. She couldn't bother him with decisions about strategy now.

Not about this.

She went to her chifferobe and rifled through her undergarments for the Tetisheri statue. Then she stood it on the burled oak piece and stared at it for a moment. The figure's enigmatic smile seemed to suggest a new gambit.

It was risky, but so was every other option open to her

at this point. After losing her maidenhead, she had very little else to lose.

She would tell Griffin the truth. About the statue. About her and Monty. About why she'd come to his bed.

About everything.

Emmaline swallowed hard. After all their carefully crafted blandishments and prevarications, she was reduced to using candor, a fragile commodity at best. Truth was most effective when used sparingly, not slathered willy-nilly like clotted cream on a scone, yet she was planning to ladle it out wholesale. Monty had taught her to mistrust truthfulness on principle, but she'd heard somewhere once that it would set one free.

She hoped that wasn't a lie.

One way or another, she'd find out tomorrow.

O'Malley finished his story and waited for his lordship to say something. It occurred to him, now that he'd already admitted to failure, that this was a message that might have waited till the morning light. He wished he'd thought of that before he talked his scullery maid doxy into delivering a note to Lord Kingsley asking for a moment of his time, despite the lateness—or earliness, depending on how a body looked at it—of the hour. At least his employer should appreciate the fact that there was little chance of anyone seeing O'Malley call at his house at this ungodly time.

The scowl on the gentleman's face did not seem at all appreciative.

Mighta saved meself the trouble.

"What do you mean you didn't get it?" His lordship slammed his fist on the desk with such force, the inkwell shuddered and black sludge oozed over the lip of the bottle and onto the ancient walnut. "I thought the house was deserted. Surely you had ample time to find it."

"The butler come back before I finished me search," O'Malley admitted, shifting his weight from one foot to the other.

He'd been surprised by the fight in the smaller man and fled the scene with a gash over his left eyebrow. The bleeding had all but obliterated the sight in one eye till he got someplace where he could clean himself up.

"The statue weren't in the professor's room," he said. "I'll swear to that."

"Then it must be in the daughter's. Devonwood doesn't keep a safe. Even the family jewels are stored off the premises in his solicitor's vault." Kingsley stood and paced like the caged leopard O'Malley had seen once at the Queen's menagerie. "When can you go back for it?"

O'Malley's mouth opened and closed wordlessly. He wasn't built for stealth. If he tried to burgle the room while the girl was in it, she'd be certain to hear him. He'd seen her earlier in the evening when the earl bundled her into a hansom. Her delicate neck would snap like a twig if he could bring himself to do it. He'd gotten away with murder once before back in Hampshire when a whore thought he was asleep and tried to make off with his purse.

But committing the same crime twice was tempting fate.

And the professor's daughter weren't no whore. Inquiries would be made and O'Malley might be tracked down. The Peelers were getting too smart by half these days. There wasn't much on earth that scared Tom O'Malley, but he was mortal afeared of the hangman's hemp.

"After a house once has a visit from a burglar, folks tend to be more particular about things," O'Malley explained. "Won't be leaving the place empty no more, I shouldn't think. The earl might even hire some extra help to guard the place through the night. At the least, Devonwood House'll be locked up tight as a drum. I'd have to break a window to get in and I don't need to tell you, that's not a quiet sort of thing."

His employer narrowed his eyes and set his mouth in a hard line. A muscle in his jaw jerked.

"You may have a point," he conceded. "The earl's household is removing to their country seat in a few days. I don't suppose you know a highwayman or two you could press into service for a wayside theft."

O'Malley frowned. What with the military traffic on the roads and the Peelers growing in force almost daily, the days when a man could make a living by ordering folk to "stand and deliver" were long gone. He couldn't remember the last time he'd heard of a successful highway robbery.

Besides, a highwayman made off with jewels and banknotes, not granite statues. What an idea! Sometimes, he wondered if his lordship was right in the head.

"I'll have to see to it myself," Kingsley said softly; then his gaze darted to O'Malley as if he hadn't intended to say that aloud. "You will hie yourself to Shiring-on-the-Green. The village is a short walk from Devonwood Park. Stay at the *Boar and Thistle.* They keep an excellent cellar, but I expect you to stay sober. If I send for you, you must come immediately."

"Where will ye be, milord?"

An oily smile spread over the gentleman's face. He picked up a neatly addressed envelope and waved it in the air. O'Malley thought he scented a light floral fragrance. "I'll be one of the houseguests at Devonwood Park, of course."

Chapter 23

A light rap at the door made Emmaline jerk awake. Last night, she hadn't dared use the bed. Not after the way Devon had pleasured her on it. Not after the way he'd taken her in Theodore's. She'd thought she would be up for hours wondering what was to become of her and Monty.

Instead, all she could think of was Griffin. She'd finally fallen asleep propped up in a chair.

She massaged her stiff neck and pulled her wrapper tight around herself. Her joints felt loose and not unpleasantly achy. Remnants of being loved to exhaustion, she supposed. A glance at the ormolu clock on the mantel told her most of the morning had flown.

"Come," she said, half surprised to find that her voice still worked.

The upstairs maid peeked around the door. "There y'are, miss," she said as she bustled in bearing a tray laden with a pot and teacup along with a covered dish. " 'Is lordship thought ye might be wantin' to take your breakfast in chambers, what with yer father—"

"How is my father?"

"Oh, the professor's quite comfy, never ye fear. After us upstairs help got home last night, Molly sat up with him and says he slept like a babe." The girl shot Emma a gap-toothed grin and removed the lid of the chafing dish to reveal a heavy English breakfast of scones, bangers and buttered eggs.

"In fact, Dr. Farnsworth was so well rested, Molly had trouble keeping him in bed this morning. Mr. Theodore's with him now or I expect he'd have ignored the doctor's instructions and tottered down the stairs to find the young master. Seems he had a . . . confound it, what was that four shilling word he used?" The girl scratched at her mobcap as if the right word might be hiding in her mass of dark curls. "A 'pipaninny?' A 'pipafanny?' A—"

"An epiphany?" Emmaline suggested.

"Ah, that's the one. Aren't ye clever?" The maid beamed at her. "At any rate, he had this Anna Piff . . . um . . . one of them 'piffy' things and wouldn't nothing do but he had to send Molly after Mr. Theodore. O' course, the young master went straight away, even though Molly had the devil's own time finding him. Seems Lord Theodore was sleeping in Lord Devonwood's chamber last night."

That explained why she'd found Griffin in Teddy's bed, but why on earth had they switched rooms in the first place?

It wasn't the sort of thing she could ask the upstairs maid, regardless of how much the help knew at Devonwood House. She reached for the tea service and was grateful to find it contained rich chocolate instead. Tea was all well and good, but Emmaline didn't share the English belief that it was the sovereign remedy for all ills. Hot chocolate was a much better candidate for that title.

Especially for the morning after she'd lost her virginity to the wrong man.

"Last I saw, your father and Lord Theodore was heads

together huddled over their papers and such like," the maid said as she began to make Emmaline's bed. "Thick as thieves, them two."

Emmaline glanced at the Tetisheri statue on the chiffe-robe. Even though she was in possession of the blasted thing, Teddy and her father had rubbings of the hiero-glyphs on the base. They worked endlessly on the transla-tions as if there really was a tomb and a treasure waiting to be found in the desert.

When the statue had first fallen into his hands, Monty had entertained no such notions, except for how he might use the tale to interest "investors." The idea of a previously unknown female pharaoh of European lineage was too outlandish to contemplate, but Monty had embellished the fable so thoroughly, it seemed he'd convinced himself of it as well as Teddy.

"Will ye be wanting help dressing after ye break yer fast, miss?"

"No, I'll manage by myself." It would be difficult but necessary. When the maid emptied the pinkish-tinged wa-ter in the washbasin, she'd assume Emmaline's monthly courses had come upon her. If she helped her dress, the girl might notice Emma made no provisions to staunch a flow. The help knew everything in Devonwood House, the countess had said. She couldn't afford having them know she'd lost her virtue. "I need to see the earl as soon as possible."

"Then there's no call to rush, miss," the maid said. "Himself already left the house this morning and didn't say when he'd be back."

The coward! Emma felt as if she'd been punched in the belly. She wasn't relishing facing Griffin, but how could he absent himself when they had so much unfinished business between them?

She ignored the bangers and eggs, slathered clotted cream on a scone and bit off a larger bite than a lady ought. She chewed without tasting it. She'd screwed her courage to use the truth with Griffin.

How was she to keep it ratcheted to the sticking point if he wouldn't cooperate and see her long enough for her to tell him all?

"Did his lordship say where he was going?" she asked.

"That he did, miss," the girl said, obviously pleased to lob a cannonball of information from her gossip arsenal. "He's off to Scotland Yard to see the Peelers."

The police! A cadre of inspectors sniffing around was the last thing she and Monty needed. If her father were healthy, she'd be all for packing their bags and heading for the hills. Last she'd heard, there were still over two hundred hanging offenses on the books in Britain.

She'd be surprised if she and Monty hadn't committed at least one of them.

The chief inspector was Sir Jasper Pennyfeather, a gaunt-faced, gray-haired fellow. With his prodigious mutton chops and half-rimmed glasses, he reminded Devon of a bespectacled Leicester Longwool.

"If you'd sent word that you required my assistance, milord," Sir Jasper said, "I'd have been only too pleased to call upon your lordship's home in Mayfair."

That was exactly what Devon hoped to avoid. Not only would it upset his mother to have the Peelers nosing about, he didn't think the official presence of the law would make his family any safer.

He wasn't ready to face Emmaline or Theodore yet in any case. After last night, absenting himself from Devonwood House seemed the better part of valor, but he couldn't stop thinking about Emmaline. Disjointed snippets of the tryst pushed to the front of his mind—the tender skin of her inner elbow, the bone-jarring way their bodies had come together, the way her breath hissed over her teeth and set his cock aching. Going to the police was merely a distraction, and not a very successful one at that.

"I thank you, Sir Jasper, but we will accomplish more if the perpetrator believes we have not sought your help. It may embolden him to commit a similar act in the future," Devon explained. "When he does, I intend to be ready."

"Very wise. The criminal mind is often brutish enough to be encouraged by perceived weakness in its victims." Sir Jasper steepled his long fingers on the burled oak desk before him. "You say your butler got a good look at the fellow."

"The house was dark, but my man Baxter may be able to give you a partial description. I'll send him round to see you this afternoon."

"Excellent." The inspector pulled out a sheet of foolscap and dipped his pen into the inkwell in preparation for taking notes. "Now, if I may, milord, with what valuables did the thief abscond?"

"None. He was interrupted before he found what he was seeking."

Sir Jasper blinked in surprise. "Have you made a thorough search? Surely the silver or—"

"Our thief left the silver and other easily portable wealth alone. I have reason to believe he was after something specific. A rare Egyptian statue, to be exact."

"How very odd. Most burglars look for something of value they can convert quickly into cash." Sir Jasper removed his spectacles and cleaned them on a white handkerchief. "Not that your Egyptian piece isn't valuable, but how would a thief dispose of something so easily identifiable?"

"I'm convinced he already has a buyer for it," Devon

said. "Have you had any reports on parties who might be interested in this sort of thing?"

Sir Jasper's eyes narrowed, further reinforcing his resemblance to an aging ram. "Let me think. Seems to me . . . " He left his thought dangling midair as he rifled through his desk drawer for a folio. He spread the folder before him and leafed through the loose pages. Each sheet had a sketch of a suspect, his criminal specialty, and a brief synopsis of his previous thefts.

Devon peered at the sheets upside down as Sir Jasper mumbled the criminals' preferred targets. "Italian art, uncut jewels, gold chalices . . ."

"Chalices?" Devon asked.

"Gold ones."

"That's a rather narrow field of interest."

Sir Jasper shrugged. "The Cathedral Bandit is a specific sort of thief. Perhaps you'll allow your Egyptian statue is pretty specific as well."

"You have me there," Devon conceded. "There's no accounting for it. No matter what a man has, it's likely another man will want it sooner or later."

"Human nature." The inspector continued flipping through the pages. "No, we have no record of a thief who specializes in Egyptian artifacts, though I suspect we'll see it soon. Seems the whole world has gone mad about the silly things. Oh, I do beg your pardon, milord. I didn't mean to imply—"

Devon waved away his apology. "Think nothing of it. My brother is the one who's interested in Egyptology."

I'm only interested in the Egyptologist's daughter.

As the inspector turned over the last couple pages, one of the sketches caught Devon's eye.

"Wait." He lifted one hand to signal a halt. "Let me see that last page again."

Sir Jasper leafed back and made a scoffing noise. "Hello.

What are you two doing in here? My apologies again, your lordship. This page was misfiled among the burglars."

He turned the sheaf around so Devon could see the artist's rendering of two perpetrators.

"Reverend Fairchild and his daughter Eleanor aren't thieves in the strictest sense, you understand," Sir Jasper said. "They're more what the Yanks call 'snake-oil salesmen.' Seems they peddled a number of fake relics on the Continent last year. More than a few folks in France were upset when it turned out their pieces of the True Cross were likely splinters from a tavern barstool instead."

Devon looked down at the pair on the page. The man's face was not as lean and he wore a full beard. Devon might not have recognized him, if not for his cohort. The woman's face was a pixyish oval, with features too angelic for anyone to suspect they masked a life of crime.

Part of Devon wasn't surprised.

"Now if you had a reliquary holding a swatch of Our Lord's grave clothes or the skull of John the Baptist in Devonwood House, the Fairchilds might be involved," Sir Jasper said as he replaced the renderings of Emmaline and her father in the correct file. "But to my knowledge, this pair hasn't ever dabbled in Egyptian gewgaws."

They have now, Devon thought with growing irritation. How could he have been so easily duped? When they'd first arrived he'd sensed a hidden agenda in the Farnsworths or Fairchilds or whatever the hell their name really was. At the time, he'd assumed they were trying to seal a fortune-hunting match between Emmaline and Teddy. Now it seemed clear that she and her father and their Egyptian statue were total frauds. They were after as much of the Devonwood wealth as they could swindle.

His neck grew hot as he went through the motions of a cordial parting with the inspector.

He strode into the gray day, heedless of the rain pelting

him like needles. He was struck by another thought that made him even angrier.

Had Emma's trip to his bed simply been part of their fraudulent scheme?

To Emmaline's delight, Monty felt up to a game of whist in the parlor that afternoon when the dripping sky kept everyone inside. He was so much his old self, he suggested playing for money instead of thimbles. She shot him a glance of reproof, but she didn't scold. She was too relieved that the doctor's pungent plasters had given Monty's chest such ease, his mind was bent in its usual larcenous direction.

Besides, Theodore was Monty's partner instead of Emma, so he had to rely on dumb luck and clever play instead of stealthy signals and palmed cards to best Lady Devonwood and Louisa. Even so, Emmaline settled herself in the corner, ostensibly reading, but in reality, watching him like a hawk. Their situation was too precarious for him to jeopardize it over winning a silly card game. Fortunately, Monty seemed to realize that as well, cheerfully losing several hands in swift succession.

She still hadn't seen Griffin. He didn't return home for luncheon and she despaired of his coming home for supper either. Her belly roiled with uncertainty about seeing him again without the gentle mask of night.

The truth took a measure of courage Emmaline still wasn't sure she possessed. It wasn't as if she'd had much practice with it after all.

Baxter appeared in the arched doorway, but didn't enter the room. While the play at the card table was going fast and furious, the butler simply stared at Emmaline as if he might communicate with his thoughts alone. He gave a jerk of his head, indicating she should follow, and disappeared down the hall.

Emmaline closed her book and slipped out of the parlor, nearly running into Baxter when she turned the corner.

"Oh, very good, miss," he said. "One was afraid more forcefulness would be required."

"Why were you afraid of that?"

"Because his lordship ordered one to fetch you, but one doesn't think you particularly want everyone to know you've been summoned by him. Especially given his mood."

"His mood?" Hers wasn't improved by the fact that Devon had sent Baxter to retrieve her like a spaniel collecting a bloody wood duck for his master's game bag.

"Oh, yes, miss. On a proper tear, he is." The normally imperturbable Baxter actually wrung his hands. "One don't think one has ever seen him quite like this . . . oh, one begs your pardon. One ought not say any more."

"Oh, really? Why is that?" Like any tale tattler, Baxter liked to be coaxed.

He straightened and looked down his nose at her. "As you know, one tries to be the soul of discretion."

"A difficult task to be sure, since you know everything that happens in this house," she said.

He fixed her with a pointed glare. She wondered if he'd been lurking in the hallway last night and seen her slip out of Theodore's room and back into her own.

"One is not privy to everything, Miss Farnsworth." He turned and led her along the hallway at a briskly efficient pace. "But one has been known to be uncannily accurate in one's guesses. Be forewarned. His lordship is extremely displeased with you."

"Oh, he is, is he?" Hackles rose on the back of her neck. She was the one who'd lost her virginity and *Griffin* was displeased? She stomped after Baxter, thinking it just might be time for another well-placed knee to his lordship's groin.

Baxter stopped before the door to the library. "Do you wish one to announce you, miss? If one is there, well, a third party's presence always encourages his lordship to temper his responses."

It was kindly meant, but she couldn't accept. What she and Griffin had to say to each other was not fit for another's ears. She squeezed Baxter's arm instead.

"Thank you, Mr. Baxter, but I believe I'll take my chances. Lord Devonwood has nothing to be upset with me about and I refuse to be bullied," she said. "It's time someone bearded this lion in his own den."

"Very well, miss. If you say so." He opened the library door.

When Emma caught sight of Griffin's face, his expression was blacker than the storm clouds roiling outside and his eyes matched the iron gray of the sky. Her courage faltered a bit and she began to wonder if perhaps Daniel had regretted choosing the lion's den, too.

Chapter 24

Griffin scowled at her, gripping the back of his chair till his knuckles went white. If she were a man, he'd have throttled her by now. No one lied to him with impunity.

His intent must have shown on his face because she blanched, her face draining of all color in a few heartbeats. Then she gathered herself and lifted her chin. "Mr. Baxter informed me you wished to see me."

Putting on a brave face, eh? Brava, Eleanor Fairchild.

"The old boy was being diplomatic. I *demanded* to see you." He never raised his voice when he was truly angry. Instead it sank into a low purr of silky menace. Most people seemed to find it far more unsettling than a loud tirade. "It's a good thing you were prompt to heed my summons. I despise being made to wait."

Almost as much as I despise liars.

Unfortunately, his body wasn't as put off by this particular liar as his reason was. The rise and fall of her breasts demanded his attention, and he couldn't help remembering how sweet the hard tips had been between his lips.

Seemingly unfazed, she sauntered toward his desk, her hem swishing against the marble floor. "Then we have an accord, Lord Devonwood. I, too, despise waiting and you've kept me in that unhappy state all day."

"*I* kept *you*?"

"Yes." She leaned across the desk and poked the center of his chest. "Didn't it occur to you that after last night there might be things we need to discuss?"

Words, words, words. At least, when a man attacked him, he knew what to expect, be it fisticuffs or business machinations. A woman could *discuss* a man to death.

Griffin scoffed. "Is this the part where you play the injured virgin and demand I marry you?"

Her eyes flared while rain drummed against the tall library windows. Then she narrowed her gaze as if she were stepping into the storm without the protection of an umbrella. "No. I entered that bedchamber of my own accord. I do not hold you responsible for the outcome."

"How very enlightened of you," he said in a tone dripping sarcasm.

Her eyes filled and her chin quivered a bit. "Why are you being so . . . so hateful?"

If she let the tears fall, he'd be hard pressed not to soften. A weeping woman was his Achilles' heel. He could've kissed her when she decided to glare at him instead.

"My feelings toward you are not hateful," he said quietly. "Last night was proof of that."

Her cheeks flooded with color. He'd have traded a year in paradise to know what part of their lovemaking was scrolling through her mind at the moment.

"Because of last night I realized something," she said. "Something I owe you."

Despite his resolve to stay upset with her, Griffin felt the fire leave his chest and settle in a lower part of his anatomy.

"You gave me a gift last night," he said huskily. "You owe me nothing."

"On the contrary, we both owe each other something."

Here it comes. She has demands, after all.

"We owe each other the truth," Emma said.

"The truth?" Griffin had just seen her truth in Sir

Jasper's files. He came around the desk and hitched a thigh on its edge, crossing his arms over his chest. "This ought to be entertaining."

She cocked a puzzled brow at him, then laced her fingers as if she were about to give a scholarly recitation. "I suppose I ought to start at the beginning."

"Perhaps you should start by giving me your real name, *Eleanor*."

Her mouth formed a perfect "O," then she clamped her lips shut for the space of ten heartbeats.

Reconfiguring her tale, he decided.

"I was born Emma Potts." Her eyes glinted like a fox, hard pressed by the hounds. The muscles in her throat worked as she swallowed before she forced more words out. "Monty is not really my father, but in all the ways that matter, he has been one to me since I was very young. I go by Emmaline Farnsworth to please him."

"So Eleanor Fairchild was what you called yourself to please him when the pair of you were cheating folks in France a while back?"

She blinked slowly. "Apparently my estimation of Scotland Yard has been too low in the past. They are remarkably well informed." The hunted expression faded and she fixed him with a direct glare. "And now, so are you. Tell me. Do you have all the women you bed investigated by the police?"

"I didn't go there with that in mind. I went to report last night's burglary," Griffin said. "However, now that we've broached the subject, the fact that you are wanted in Paris might have been something you should have brought up in conversation, don't you think?"

She laughed mirthlessly. "When have you and I ever spent much time in conversation?"

"Point taken." If his body had its way, he'd be swiving

her again now instead of all this infernal talking. But even bickering with her made him feel more normal than amiable conversation with anyone else. "We do seem to find other ways to communicate when we're alone together, ways I thought we both enjoyed. Am I incorrect?"

She shook her head and he thought she leaned toward him by the smallest of degrees. Then she straightened and edged away. "Please, Griffin, I need to get through all of what I must tell you."

"There's more?"

She nodded. "Much more, and I ask that you keep still till I finish or I may not be able to."

"Never let it be said I don't let a lady finish." Even though he'd been more than a little foxed, he'd made sure she had a ripping good time last night. Of course, that was as much for him as for her. Giving her pleasure made him feel like Prometheus, stealing fire from Olympus. He lifted a brow at her, but when she didn't smile at his double entendre, he shrugged and waved her on.

"You are right. We are wanted for fraud on the Continent. And Monty is wanted in New York for forgery." She massaged her forehead with her fingertips as if she wanted to smooth away her words as easily as she smoothed away the lines on her brow. "But that's not the worst of it."

"Most people would find outstanding arrest warrants bad enough. Do tell."

"You're not taking this seriously." She glowered at him. "The truth is we entered your house for the express purpose of swindling Teddy and, by extension, you. The Tetisheri statue is most assuredly a fake, but Monty thought we could convince you to back an expedition to discover her tomb." She sighed. "Of course, we have no intention of returning to Egypt."

"Wanted there, too, are you?"

"No," she said angrily.

"Then don't discount returning. Seems to me you're running out of places to go."

Her face crumpled. "Monty is. That's for certain. If I don't find some way to pay for him to go to Görbersdorf sanatorium . . ."

The tears he feared earlier welled in her eyes again. This time she was less successful at suppressing them. Griffin took her into his arms and was strangely grateful when she came willingly.

It occurred to him that now would be the right time to offer to pay for Farnsworth's treatment. He was inclined to do it, but contrary to what she believed, the earldom was not flush with available blunt. His father hadn't been much of a steward and when Griffin came to the title, he'd inherited a mountain of debt, the last of which he'd be able to retire only if the *Rebecca Goodspeed* ever returned to port. Every spare farthing the estate claimed was tied up in plans for repairs, invested in tenant crops and the refurbishing of the mill at Devonwood Park.

Perhaps a trip to the whist tables would provide the needed funds.

He ran his hand down her spine in long comforting strokes while she clung to him. Even knowing she'd come to swindle him, knowing his brother still intended to make her his bride, Griffin felt a shimmering mantle of peace descend over him just from holding her.

It made no sense whatever. It simply *was*.

"All this subterfuge and conniving. You, my dear, are a proper scoundrel," he murmured into her hair. "Usually, that's my job."

It occurred to him that using his gift to win at cards might be considered as fraudulent as foisting fake reliquaries on a trusting public. He and his lady scoundrel had more in common than either of them had realized.

Her shoulders shook with suppressed sobs. Griffin searched his soul for any sign of the outrage he'd felt before, but he couldn't find a smidgeon.

He pressed a kiss on the crown of her head. "Is that why you came to my bed last night? So I'd pay to send your father to treatment for his consumption?"

"No." A real sob escaped her throat. "I thought I was going to Teddy's bed."

Griffin whipped her away from his body and held her at arm's length. "You thought . . ."

Why hadn't that realization come to him before this? He'd been sleeping in Ted's bedchamber. Of course, she wouldn't suspect Griffin had switched rooms with his brother to avoid the events he'd *Seen* in a vision. She couldn't have known it was he in the bed instead of Theodore. Once again, he'd tried to cheat fate and only succeeded in helping his vision come to pass.

"So you intended to give yourself to my brother," he said woodenly.

"Yes." She pulled away from his grip and found a handkerchief in her pocket with which to dab her reddened nose. "Of the two of you, he's the only one who offered to marry me. I saw the way Lady Cressida had set her cap for him at Lord Whitmore's. You told me you wouldn't cut Teddy off if he married me; I decided I needed to do something to make sure Theodore didn't change his mind and cry off so he could court Lady Cressida instead."

"So you thought to settle the issue and make certain of the money for Dr. Farnsworth's cure in one bold stroke." Griffin's voice came out flat and colorless.

A flawless, coldly logical plan. If he hadn't bedded her and known how passionate she could be, he'd believe her the most heartless person he'd ever met. Her one saving grace was that she seemed to be motivated by the need to help the man she claimed as her father. The realization didn't make Griffin feel any less gut-punched.

She'd thought she was bedding his brother. God help him if he actually fell in love with her. It would be the cruelest of passions.

"How unfortunate for you that I was in Teddy's room instead," he said.

"I told you I owe you the truth and I won't stop now. The truth is . . . " She looked up at him, her luminous brown eyes sad and shining at the same time. Her face was taut with suppressed emotion. "I wanted it to be you. Oh, God help me, how I wanted it."

It had taken most of a fifth of whisky before he could summon the courage to try to avoid his vision. He told himself he'd tried everything to spare his brother pain, but that was a lie. He'd had a choice there in the dark and, foxed or not, half waking or half sleeping, he'd chosen to take her. He'd wanted it to be him, too.

She might be a scoundrel, but he had no stone to throw.

He stepped toward her and she was in his arms again before he could invite her. He bent and kissed her, reveling in the sweetness of her breath, in the way her twisted little soul sent a wave of unexpected freshness through his weary one. It took courage for her to admit to what she'd intended to do and what she'd done.

An honest fraud. She's a paradox with feet.

But her feet were the last things on his mind, unless he counted how she stood on tiptoe so their mouths could reach each other more easily. He'd never wanted a woman as badly as he wanted this one. When she strained toward him, his desire was honed to razor sharpness.

He cupped her bum and lifted her flush against him. She hooked a leg around his to steady herself as he deepened their kiss.

Her moan into his mouth sent his cock into a granite-hard stand and made his ballocks bunch into a tight mound. His groin clenched when she suckled his tongue. His hands roamed over her body, exploring the tender curves and bends beneath the layers of her clothing. She wrapped her arms around him, her fingertips tracing love spells on his spine.

Griffin kissed his way down her throat, undoing the little seed pearl buttons as he went.

"I wanted it to be you," she repeated, running a hand over his head. "I pretended it was you."

Griffin picked her up and set her on the desk. He swiped off the inkstand and crystal paperweight, heedless of the way they shattered on the marble floor. Then he kissed her as she leaned back into a prone position. "When did you know?"

"I didn't know it was you until you spoke."

"I was barely thinking at the time." He slanted a grin at her as he pulled up her skirt. "I don't remember speaking."

"You said, 'No more pain now.'" She cupped his cheek and strained up to kiss him again, her lips soft and pliant under his. "What else don't you remember, I wonder?"

"Don't worry. My memories about you are plentiful and vivid." He smoothed his hands up her thighs, her muscles taut beneath her pantalets. She was as high-strung as a mare in season about to be covered by a stallion.

And Griffin fully intended to cover her.

"You were right, you know," she said breathlessly as she tipped her head back to expose more of her neck to his nuzzling kisses. Her skin was salty and sweet and she smelled faintly of peaches and the musky tang of arousal. "There wasn't any more pain at all after that little bit."

Ironic, since pain was all their joining would bring—to Ted, and to each other.

Griffin shoved the thought aside. For now, he would wallow in this woman, drunk on her scent, lost in her lies, and not caring a whit.

He kissed down to the top of her chemise and corset, frustrated that there was no way to expose her breasts short of disrobing her completely. While the idea had merit, the library in the middle of a rain-soaked afternoon wasn't the place to indulge in a nude bacchanalia.

But at least there was a way to reach equally delectable parts of her.

God bless the unsung hero who designed pantalets with open crotches, he thought devoutly.

Her hidden valleys were slick and wet with dew, so soft and malleable in his hand. As his fingers slid along her sweet cleft, her jaw went passion-slack and her eyelids fluttered closed.

Griffin basked in reflected pleasure. Her little noises of bliss made his cock throb with heat. He found her most sensitive spot, risen to a hard nub, and tormented it with his thumb and forefinger.

He might not be able to enjoy her bare body at the moment, but he'd see her soul naked or die trying.

Chapter 25

I shouldn't let him do this to me.

Her mouth opened and closed a couple times, but she couldn't form a coherent word. Emma let her head drop back. It was too heavy to hold upright when all her attention was focused on the heated space between her legs.

She recognized the way her insides coiled. Griffin was sending her to that blissful place again, that inside-out, can't-give-a-tinker's-damn-about-anything place that existed in secret inside her own head and heart.

She wondered if she could find her way there without him. *No,* she decided. She might experience a measure of bliss, but it wouldn't be the same when she tumbled back to the real world if Griffin wasn't there to catch her.

How she loved his kisses. His mouth was a world unto itself, all wet and hard and smooth. His shoulders were solid, his arms comforting. And she remembered well the long male length he sported between his legs.

Her insides ached with emptiness. His talented fingers both eased and provoked her. She knew he was going to make it better, but before he did, her need would become much worse.

He kissed her breasts through the layers of her gown and she wished there was nothing separating her skin from his blessed mouth. Her nipples ached, straining against her undergarments for his touch. As tightly drawn as she was, just a suckle or two on a bare nipple would surely set her off like a Roman candle.

His fingers teased her sensitive flesh, drawing circles of torment around the intimate little spot that was the source of so much delight and anguish.

How could something feel so good and so frustrating at the same time?

Then just as her insides wound so snugly Emma didn't think she had another revolution in her, Griffin dropped to his knees before her. He shoved her gown up so he could look at her.

She resisted the urge to pull her knees together. Modesty over her body seemed ridiculous after she'd bared her secret life to him. Still, she held her breath as he scrutinized that intimate part of her.

"You're beautiful, Emma," he said. "In every way."

He thumbed her little spot and her body tensed for release. Then he leaned toward her so close she felt the heat of his exhalation on the damp curls between her legs.

No, he couldn't possibly mean to . . . He wouldn't . . . Oh, mercy! He would.

She'd thought his fingers were talented, but they were nothing compared to the raw delight of his mouth on her. Wet and soft, but with his tongue giving her spot the same lover's service his thumb had.

She crested quickly and unraveled under his intimate kiss. Her thighs shook, her insides bucked, and she dug her nails into the aged walnut so hard, she was sure she was leaving tiny curved marks in the wood under the lip of the desk.

She tried not to make any noise, but her release flowed out of her in a strangled sob.

If she expected Griffin to give her time to recover, she was mistaken. He stood and undid the buttons over his hips to drop the front of his trousers, then entered her in one quick thrust before her last inner contraction stopped pulsing.

Emma urged him in with murmured endearments, wrapping her legs around his waist and hooking her ankles together at the small of his back. She needed him so. The glory of her climax was one thing. Connecting with this man was quite another. Nothing assuaged the yawning emptiness inside like having him fill her with himself.

He drove into her with no gentleness at all. She kissed his throat in gratitude and he answered her with a feral male growl. She nipped him on the neck and he quickened his pace. Her heart bounded up to the distant ceiling. She couldn't bear tenderness from him now. Not after what she and Monty had meant to do to him and his family.

This bone-jarring swive was what she deserved.

What her body demanded.

His, too, if his desperate lunges into her were any measure. His scrotum slapped against her with such force, she wondered if he was hurting himself.

Griffin cupped her cheeks and made her meet his gaze as he plunged in and out. No pain showed on his features, only a hungry, intent determination to create another connection with her, something beyond the physical.

He wants to see me, she realized. *To know me. Oh God, given what I am, how can he bear that?*

But Griffin didn't look away. He watched her as she came again in joyous spasms and didn't turn his eyes aside when his own body stiffened and arched before spilling into her.

He wants me to see him. To know him.

She wondered what secrets an earl might have and if he'd be ready to share his truths with her as she'd shared with him. Whatever they might be, she'd accept them.

She'd even admitted she thought she was giving herself to his brother, for pity's sake, and it hadn't seemed to make a difference.

Spent, Emma let herself settle back onto the desk and Griffin laid his head between her breasts.

"I can feel your heart," she whispered. It hammered solidly through the layers of clothing that separated them and pounded through the length of him still inside her. She drew a ragged breath.

"And I can hear yours," he said.

Emma ran her fingers through his hair, reveling in the way their bodies were still connected and wondering how long they'd manage to keep it so. She began to notice her surroundings once again as her body settled—the hard, smooth walnut beneath her, the musky sweet smell of arousal and fulfillment wafting around them.

The storm outside had subsided to a gentle shower. Rain-washed air lifted the drapes to sough into the library. On the ceiling above them, Cupid and Psyche indulged in their chaste kiss.

Emmaline had been so moved by the fresco when she'd first seen it. Love in its first blush was the finest thing she could aspire to. Now it seemed pale by comparison with the force of the passion unleashed on the sturdy desk.

Was the bond between her and Griffin love? She didn't know. But shared pleasure certainly bound them together.

Why did such pleasure have to start with pain? she wondered absently. Her thoughts darted about like a school of minnows, too quick for her to snatch one up for any length of time. Then suddenly one leaped into her net and refused to budge.

"No more pain now," she whispered. Emma struggled to sit up, which was difficult since Griffin still rested his head on her.

He straightened and kissed her forehead as he smoothed

her skirts down and fastened his trousers. "I'm glad I didn't hurt you this time. I was rougher than I intended."

"Never mind about that," she said, kissing him back, then pulling away before she allowed herself to be distracted again by his mouth. "You said, 'No more pain now' before."

"I'll take your word for it. I was three sheets to the wind when I tumbled into Ted's bed."

"No. I mean, you said it then, of course. But you also said it in the hansom on the way to Lord Whitmore's when you had that . . . episode," she said. "I thought at the time you meant you'd been in pain and weren't any longer. But now, I wonder if it was something else." She laid a hand on his cheek, the prickly late afternoon stubble of his beard rough on her palm. "Is there some truth you owe me?"

Griffin inhaled deeply and lifted her down from the desk. He'd known someday he'd probably have to share the secret of his "gift" with someone beyond the confines of his immediate family. He never dreamed he'd unburden himself to a professional trickster.

It was the kind of secret that made blackmailers' mouths water, especially the bit about the way he occasionally used his abilities to win at gaming tables.

He decided to skip that part as he led her to the settee and settled beside her before the cold fireplace. Trust was earned and while she obviously trusted him, he still wasn't sure he could return the favor.

So he started with his father's death and his unwitting part in bringing his own vision to pass. To his great relief, she listened without interruption and seemed to believe every word.

"After that, I tried not to interfere with what I saw coming," he said. There had been a few times he couldn't bear not to try, but each failure cemented his belief that whatever he did would be twisted to serve Fate. "Inaction seemed the best course."

"But not one that sat well with you, I'll wager," Emmaline said, pressing her hand on his.

He leaned forward, resting his elbows on his knees, and stared at the empty hearth. "No."

"What sort of vision did you see in the hansom?"

"I saw you come to my bed."

"Oh," she said, withdrawing her hand and folding it with the other on her lap. "So that's why you traded rooms with Theodore. You didn't want me to—"

"Now just a moment. I was trying to spare my brother. Can you honestly think I didn't want you?"

"No, Griffin, but I also think you weren't trying to avoid your vision that hard. I don't believe the future is as fixed as you make it seem. Even though I came to you as you'd *Seen,* you still had a choice. If you'd spoken sooner—"

"You'd have left me?"

She sighed. "Not for worlds."

He leaned to kiss her, but Emmaline sat up straighter and turned her head away. She was responding with the time-honored response of polite society to freaks—a slight shunning.

"I'm glad you confided in me," she said, "but the fact remains that our choices have put us in an untenable position."

"Don't you mean Fate?"

"I rather think we chose this, Griffin. Whatever led to our joining last night, I didn't give myself to you by accident this afternoon. I chose you."

She laid her palm lightly on his forearm and he decided he'd been wrong. Perhaps she didn't see him as a freak.

"If we're merely playing out some preordained script, what does any of it mean?"

Her question was phrased as a philosophical argument, similar to the ones old Mr. Abercrombie used to raise. But beneath her query, Griffin thought he heard "What do I mean to you?'

He had no ready answer for her.

Yes, she was light to his dark soul, but she was also heartache for his brother. And even if Griffin could somehow find a way around that, there was still the matter of his "gift."

He'd always avoided entanglements of the heart. And he studiously avoided touching the personal possessions of members of his family. It was easier to go through life wrapped in an inviolate empty space rather than risk another *Sending* that showed him the death of someone he loved.

He wouldn't be able to maintain that distance if he fell in love with Emma.

"Damned if I know what any of it means," he said gruffly and rose, shoving his hands into his pockets. He'd already received *Sendings* from her drawing pencil and her fan. It was dumb luck her lacy underthings hadn't set off the lights in his head. He needed to be more careful around her.

And he needed to change the subject.

"If the Tetisheri statue is a fake, it's worthless. So why did someone try to steal it?"

CHAPTER 26

Emmaline felt an unspoken rebuke in his abrupt change of subject, but for the life of her, she couldn't see how she'd offended. She wanted to ask him more about his gift of foreknowledge. She and Monty had several nefarious friends who pretended to have the ability to peek into the future. They did quite well bilking the gullible out of their funds with their fabricated prognostications, but to actually see what lay beyond the next breath . . . She'd never known anyone who could really do it.

Griffin's guarded expression warned her off. She sensed he wasn't happy about his ability, but he wasn't willing to talk about it. Her brief look into his private life was over.

"Why would someone try to steal the statue, you ask? Monty weaves a spellbinding tale. He could convince people that Tetisheri descended from the clouds on a pillar of smoke if he was of a mind to," she said. "And I've no doubt the rumors floating about have further embellished his claims. Undoubtedly, our thief is unaware the statue is a fraud."

"Maybe." He paced, barely contained energy roiling off him. "Or maybe there's something about it we've overlooked."

"Why do you say that?"

He stopped pacing and drilled her with a pointed stare. "It was just an observation."

"You've had a vision about it," she guessed.

"Blast it all." The pacing resumed. "Has it occurred to you that a man resists telling a woman his secrets because he dislikes having them thrown back in his face?"

Emmaline crossed her arms over her chest. "I did nothing of the sort. I merely made a logical assumption given the information I have." Then her posture relaxed. It would do no good to meet his surliness with her own. "Don't worry, Griffin. I believe you and I won't tell a soul. Now tell me what you've *Seen*."

He gave a loud exhalation and returned to settle beside her. "All right. I've had two *Sendings* about the statue, but they weren't the usual sort."

"How do you mean?"

"Most of the time, my visions are detailed and specific. And the fulfillment of them takes place within no more than twelve hours of the *Sending*." He dragged a hand over his face. "These were like . . . trying to see through fog."

"So you're unsure of their meaning?"

"No, I'm certain they mean the statue is dangerous, but I wasn't shown why." He rose again. "Where is it now?"

"In my chamber."

"Where is everyone else?"

"I left them all in the parlor," Emmaline said. "Monty and Theodore were losing rather badly at cards to the countess and Louisa."

"Which means they'll be at it a while. Ted never concedes a game when he's behind," Griffin said, holding out his hand to her. "You and I have bared our secrets to each other. Let's go have a look at Tetisheri and see if we can uncover hers."

★ ★ ★

Griffin dropped her hand and offered his arm as soon as they cleared the library doors. In a house where the help knew everything, he considered it a point of honor to make it as difficult as possible for them to glean juicy tidbits of information about the family they served.

Sometimes, he suspected Baxter and the rest of the staff considered it a game to see who could conceal and who could most reveal the secret doings in the house of Devonwood. Fortunately, the help were all loyal in the extreme. While they might enjoy gossiping below stairs about the goings on above them, none would dream of carrying tales beyond the threshold.

Baxter ran a tight ship. As all but lord of the staff, he'd dismiss without character anyone who breathed a word of scandal about the family.

In the meantime, Griffin escorted Emmaline about the great house coolly and correctly. No one would suspect he'd just lifted her skirts in the library and lost his heart at the same time.

Griffin gave himself a mental shake. He couldn't allow himself to love her. Her life had been difficult enough before this. She deserved someone with fewer complications than he brought. Someone normal.

Someone like his brother.

No, his heart rebelled. Even though she'd been prepared to accept Theodore's suit and was willing to bed him to make certain of it, Griffin refused to imagine her with Teddy.

But he also refused to consider what her life would be like with him.

What a perfectly wicked little circle.

As they ascended the stairs together, he studied her in his peripheral vision. Alert, curious, her cheeks still kissed with color that proclaimed she'd recently been shagged senseless, she was so full of vibrant life, his guarded existence seemed pale and colorless by comparison.

"Wait here in the sitting room," she said when they entered the Blue Suite. "And leave the hall door open."

Emmaline disappeared into her bedchamber in search of the statue.

He grinned wryly after her. She knew the walls had eyes, too. Though it wasn't unusual for him to shut himself in the library and expect not to be disturbed, a closed door in the afternoon on the third floor would beg the upstairs maid to open it.

"Here it is," Emmaline said, carrying the statue back into the sitting room. She didn't bother to lower her voice. If a member of the staff was hovering, they'd see only their lord and his guest poring over the Egyptian oddity together and decide there was nothing of note to report.

Emmaline set Tetisheri in the center of the chess table and sank into one of the heavy Tudor chairs. She studied the statue with furrowed brows for a moment. "It looks the same to me as always. A carved granite figure with hieroglyphs ringing the basalt base."

Griffin narrowed his eyes at the statue. "I've seen a number of pieces similar to this at the British Museum, but I've never seen one with a base made of different material. Have you?"

Her brows shot up in surprise. "No. Now that you mention it, I haven't. I wonder if the statue was carved at one point and the base added at a later date."

Griffin wished he could pick it up to examine it more closely, but he suspected that action would result only in another enigmatic *Sending*. Standing close to it, he detected a soft hum, barely on the edge of sound.

Sometimes an object seemed to sense his presence, emitting a thrum of warning. He was certain he was the only one who could hear the low vibration. He'd long ago stopped asking "Do you hear that?" of his family and friends. It had irritated his father and made his friends cock their heads in bewilderment. Over the years, he'd learned to appreciate when an item announced it had something to tell him ahead of time. It meant he could avoid hearing what the object had to say if he wished.

"Since Tetisheri is seated, she's stable enough," he said, keeping his hands firmly in his pockets. "Why add the base at all?"

"At a guess, so the artist could add the hieroglyphs. They couldn't very well have been carved on the hem of her robes." Emmaline lifted the statue and turned it upside down to examine the bottom of the base.

"You do that very easily," Griffin said. "How heavy would you say the statue is?"

Her eyes widened. "Not as heavy as one would expect if it's all stone. Oh! Do you suppose the statue is hollow?"

"That might explain it," Griffin said.

"According to Monty the second side of the base said something about 'opening the portal.' Perhaps there's a way to remove the base and look inside."

A stifled sneeze in the hallway made his head jerk around.

"Baxter," he called.

The butler appeared in the doorway, hastily replacing his handkerchief in his breast pocket. "How may one be of service, your lordship?"

"Well, for one thing," Griffin said, "if you're that interested in antiquities, you might come in and have a seat with us instead of skulking in the hall."

"That would be most improper." Still, the man had the grace to look chagrined as he advanced into the room. Under his breath, he muttered, "One was *not* skulking. One was dusting the China Dog in the hallway niche."

"Nevertheless, I do require your assistance," Griffin said, certain dusting was beneath his butler's wintry dignity. *Pity eavesdropping is not.* "Most specifically, I require your gloves."

Baxter was never without a pair of spotless white ones. He raised a quizzical brow, but removed them without comment and handed them to Griffin.

"What are you going to do with those?" Emmaline asked.

"I'm going to see if there's a way to open the statue," Griffin said. "The gloves will give me a better grip."

And protect me from an unwanted Sending. If he thought the statue would give him any answers, he'd risk it, but all it had done in the past was give him allegorical riddles. As long as his bare skin didn't touch it, he'd be safe from another shadowy *Sending*.

"Excellent idea, milord," Baxter said, not missing a chance to toady up after having been caught spying. "That thing"—he favored the statue with a curled lip of distaste—"is thousands of years old. Who knows what sort of ancient grime it might have embedded in the crevices?"

"We're about to find out." Griffin ran a gloved forefinger around the base, feeling for any space between the granite and the basalt. There was no give at all. "Surely any sort of epoxy would have dissolved long before this. The two materials must be joined by some mechanical means."

"Maybe it's like a pickle jar," Emmaline suggested. "With threads that screw together inside."

"A pickle jar that's been closed for a few thousand years." Griffin tucked the statue under his arm and braced it against his body while he strained to see if the base would budge. After a few minutes" struggle, it turned ever so slightly.

Griffin set it down and drew a deep breath.

"If one might suggest, milord," Baxter said, "simply because the civilized world has decided that a left turn will loosen a screw, it does not signify that other peoples might not have other ideas, however misguided."

"By Gum, you're right. I may have simply tightened it up just then. Here." Griffin handed the statue to his butler. "Hold it steady and I'll try turning it the other way."

This time, over the low menacing hum, Griffin heard the scrape of stone on stone as the ancient threads ground against each other.

"Oh, it's working. You're doing it." Emmaline danced like a colt on a short tether. "Do you suppose there's anything inside it?"

"Some ancient jewelry wouldn't come amiss," Griffin said. "A golden torc hidden inside would explain why someone tried to steal the statue. Ancient gold is even more costly than newly mined ore." He shot her a pointed look. "I'd imagine it would go a long way toward paying for Dr. Farnsworth's recovery in the Alps."

Her eyes sparked with hope.

Of course, if the statue was filled with gold, she wouldn't need him any longer. Griffin wasn't sure what to wish for as he felt the base give completely. As he lifted it from the statue, the last thing he expected to see was . . .

"Sand?"

The interior of the statue was filled almost to the brim with grainy, reddish-brown matter.

Baxter reached in and rubbed a pinch of the substance between his thumb and forefinger. "I rather think not," he said, forgetting in his excitement to refer to himself as "one." "It has the texture of coarse ground meal of some kind."

Emmaline's shoulders slumped. "You mean this statue is nothing but an ancient kitchen canister?"

"Not necessarily," Baxter said. "Whatever this substance

is, we may assume it had special significance. The design of the statue is too ornate, and too unwieldy for storage of an ordinary foodstuff."

"Perhaps it's a virulent sort of poison," Griffin said, remembering the sinister aspects of his previous Sendings. The asp in his first vision and the god of death in a field of grain in the second suggested as much.

Baxter's brows shot up. "One's nephew is studying the chemical properties of natural substances at University. He's home in London for the summer. If one might be so bold as to suggest, your lordship might authorize one to take a sample of the material to him. Young Tim may be able to tell us what sort of grain it is and why it was important enough to preserve in this fashion."

"It's not my statue, so it's not my decision to make," Griffin said, looking at Emmaline, who'd collapsed into the Tudor chair, the wind spilled out of her like a schooner caught in the doldrums. "What do you say, Miss Farnsworth?"

She managed a weak nod. "Father would want to know."

"Very well," Griffin said to Baxter. "See to it, but tell your nephew to be careful. I'll see he's recompensed for his time and trouble, of course. I must also insist he keep word of this to himself."

"All we Baxters are the souls of discretion. One is sure one's nephew will be grateful for your confidence, milord." Baxter bowed and excused himself to find a jar in the kitchen for the sample.

"I'm sorry," Griffin said to Emmaline. She looked so crestfallen, he wanted to go to her and comfort her, but he was stuck holding the statue and base till his butler returned to ladle out a portion of the contents. "I wish it had held something of value."

"I shouldn't have expected anything different," she said,

her head in her hands. "After the capers Monty and I have pulled, there would be no justice in the world if we'd somehow stumbled on a windfall."

The hard shell Griffin had constructed around his heart began to crack. He'd found a windfall of his own—the woman he could love.

Unlike Emmaline, though, he'd never suffered any illusions about the way Fate balanced its scales. There was no justice in the world. Never had been.

So long as he had to hold himself apart from Emmaline rather than risk a *Sending* that showed him he'd lose her, there never would be.

CHAPTER 27

The trip to Devonwood Park was a swift one. Most titled gents, who lived part of the year in London and part on their country estates, could count on uncomfortable post chaise rides of a week or so's duration in order to reach their far-flung ancestral seats. Griffin was fortunate that his forefathers had seen fit to claim land adjacent to the sludgy worm of the Thames after they slogged across the Channel with the rest of William the Bastard's horde.

Of course, the brackish brown water cleared as the house party's ferry reached Shiring-on-the-Green. The sleepy little hamlet wasn't far from the great river's gaping mouth and the riotous North Sea. From Shiring, it was only a matter of a moderately pleasant carriage ride to Devonwood Park. How moderately pleasant depended upon whether or not heavy rains had scoured the roads to washboard roughness.

Fortunately the storm that pummeled the city had skipped over the countryside. Griffin leaned back on the tufted cushions, barely noticing the view of rolling green hills or the perfumed breath of apple orchards.

He'd avoided Emmaline whenever he could since the afternoon they'd desecrated the library desk with a coupling that had generated more heat than a midwinter's blaze. It wasn't for lack of wanting her. Rather the opposite.

He'd purposely chosen to ride in the carriage with Louisa, her friend Lady Cressida, who'd been persuaded to come early to the house party with the family, and Dr. Farnsworth. His mother was riding herd on Theodore and Emmaline in the equipage immediately behind them, along with Kingsley.

Griffin's friend had said he wanted to come early and try his hand at trout fishing in the shimmering lake on the north side of the manor. Northrop would be joining them in the morning for a few days before the rest of the guests arrived for the fortnight of foolishness. Griffin was tired of it already.

He closed his eyes. All he could see against the back of his lids was Emmaline. He forced his eyes open again. As much as he longed to be with Emma, he didn't want to be subjected to watching his brother's continued courtship of her.

Part of him wished she'd break it off with Ted, but he understood why she didn't. He hadn't given her any alternative and couldn't bring himself to.

Coward, he named himself. But no amount of internal shame would turn him. He remembered the impotent despair that followed the *Sending* that warned of his father's demise. He couldn't risk an attachment to Emma because eventually in an unguarded moment, he'd touch a teacup she'd drunk from or a bit of lace draped over her bosom and *See* her death approaching.

And he wouldn't be able to do a damn thing about it.

Better not to care. Not to love a woman like a normal man. He'd always thought eventually he'd marry for the express purpose of siring children, but he realized now that having a family was fraught with potential loss as well.

Ted would be his heir.

Lady Cressida's giggle interrupted his dark thoughts. He

dragged his gaze from the passing countryside and looked at his sister and her friend.

They burst into peals of laughter, which woke Dr. Farnsworth, who'd slipped into the light slumber of advancing years. He woke with a snort and a sputter. Griffin scowled at them for waking the old man.

"I told you," Louisa said. "He didn't hear a thing. We could be plotting the Queen's overthrow and the earl of Devonwood wouldn't hear us when he's like this. My brother frequently leaves this mundane sphere for fantastical realms in his own mind."

He deepened his frown at her. Her comment was far too on the nose for his comfort. His visions did indeed send him to worlds of his own. "If you're truly scheming against our Sovereign, I'll stop the coach now and let you walk the rest of the way."

Louisa flicked her fan at him. "Beast!"

"Patriot," he corrected.

"If you must know," Louisa said with a sigh, "we're trying to decide whether to gather the party together to play Sardines or just let everyone settle in at Devonwood Park once we arrive."

"I've no doubt the countess has already planned all the organized fun you could wish for," Griffin said.

"What if we want disorganized fun?" Lady Cressida asked, batting her lashes in alarmingly quick succession.

Was she trying to flirt with him?

Griffin made a mental note to absent himself if they did decide to play Sardines. More than one titled lord had found himself leg-shackled for life after hiding in a broom closet with a marriage-minded miss.

The carriages rumbled across a stone bridge, leading into the bailey of the ancient castle.

"In medieval times that would've been a drawbridge," Griffin said.

"In less civilized times, you mean," Louisa said.

"Or more enlightened," Griffin countered. "I understand women were regarded as chattel then and disposed of correspondingly by their male relatives without so much as a by-your-leave."

His sister stuck out her pointed little tongue at him as the carriage rumbled to a stop. Griffin handed the ladies down and then helped Dr. Farnsworth descend. The old man's skin was the color of three-day-old suet, but he coughed less the farther they traveled from the sooty London air.

Emmaline's carriage halted behind his and Theodore helped her alight. Griffin noted that the countess seemed to move a little stiffly once Kingsley handed her down. He'd always thought of his energetic mother as forever youthful. Now he was reminded that she bore more than fifty years.

"Welcome to the old wreck, Emmaline," Theodore said expansively, spreading his arms wide and turning a slow circle. "The place is a total mongrel. Every earl of Devonwood felt the need to build and leave his own stamp on it. Norman foundations, medieval Gloriette, Tudor maiden's tower." He laid a confiding hand alongside his mouth and continued in a stage whisper. "Family legend says it once housed a whole gaggle of nuns and they were reportedly more than hospitable to the warrior class when King's men passed through. And of course, there's last century's manor house all rolled into one giant monstrosity."

"I think it's charming, all higgledy-piggledy." She cast her gaze over the mismatched turrets and towers, the gargoyles and arrow loops and then met Griffin's gaze. "What have you added to the family seat, milord?"

He'd had no spare funds for grandiose projects, but he had managed to make a practical addition to the grounds. "I ordered the orangery built."

"Ah! The larger version of the one in town," she said, sending him a secret smile.

Was she remembering the evening when he'd all but forced her to join him in a tour of the town house orangery? Did it give her the same uptick in heart rate the memory gave him? She was a weakness in his blood, a sickness. If he'd had his way then, he'd have taken her on the cool paving stones that very night.

"My brother is nothing if not thrifty," Theodore said. "He was able to use the same plan, just changing the scale himself."

"Thrifty he may be, but he's also generous," Lady Devonwood said. "Thank you for hosting this party for us, dear."

When Louisa broached the subject of Sardines, the countess refused to consider starting parlor games as early as Louisa and her friend wished.

"Nonsense, girls," she said. "I have entirely too much to do. There are seating plans to draw up, rooms to assign, and then I'll need to huddle with Cook to inspect the larder, order menus for the fortnight, and prepare shopping lists. My head spins at the thought!"

"I think it will all keep till you've had a chance to rest from your travels, *Maman,*" Griffin said. "I sent word we were coming. I'm sure the staff has matters well in hand for the moment."

"A rest does sound lovely," she admitted. "I suppose I could do with a bit of a lie down. Why don't we all take our leisure this afternoon and then this evening, we'll have a few games after supper? The dressing bell will ring at seven. Dinner at eight."

Louisa and Lady Cressida agreed to this proposal without much grace.

The servants streamed into the main bailey and lined up to greet the family's return in a rolling wave of bows and curtseys. Baxter stood at the head of the line. Griffin had sent him on ahead a few days early to take charge of the country staff, leaving the town house under the watchful eye of Atkins, the young under-butler.

Griffin greeted the help, pausing to inquire after their families and calling each by name. Many of them had known him since he was a boy and several heads were more gray than he remembered from last summer. He made a mental note that something would have to be done to provide for pensioners before long.

Yet another financial quagmire his unproductive estate would have to wade through. He sent another silent prayer for the *Rebecca Goodspeed* to make safe berth in London before the end of the season. If that risky investment paid off, he'd finally turn the corner.

Lady Devonwood shepherded the women into the newest portion of the manor, the part that was a mere seventy-five years or so old, promising baths and a cold luncheon in their chambers. Footmen unloaded the carriage boots and hauled the ladies' trunks and parcels after them.

"Careful with that, Bascombe," Theodore said to the one who carried the small crate that housed the Tetisheri statue. "Come, Dr. Farnsworth." He draped an arm around the old man's shoulders. "I'll show you the library. Devon doesn't have much on Egypt, but he's assembled a fairly decent Greek and Roman collection."

The pair of them ambled off toward the Tudor portion of the castle, which housed the books and maps.

Griffin had vowed to himself that if his financial state reached the point where he had to start selling personal items to make ends meet, he'd part with the silver first and save the library till last.

Kingsley sidled next to him. "It's still impressive, never mind about the mix of architecture, Devon. Each time I see it, this place takes me back. Look at that tower there. Bet it saw the viking hordes cresting the hill."

"If it did, it was looking down at my ancestors," Griffin said with a laugh. "My family swept in with the Norman invaders, you know. If the tower was here then, and I wager it was, they found a way to breech and take it."

"The essence of nobility. *Orbi non sufficit*. 'The world is not enough,'" Kingsley said wryly. His was an old and venerated barony, but the much smaller manor house on it was a fairly recent construction, only since George IV sat on the throne. "Must cost the earth to maintain a place like this though."

"You don't want to know the half of it."

Drafty and with a roof that perpetually leaked, the Devonwood family seat was more a millstone around his neck than a showpiece. The interior hadn't been refurbished since before his father's time and was undoubtedly a bit shabby. Fortunately, he'd given Baxter instructions to see to it that the main public rooms had a thorough scrubbing. Devonwood Park had never been converted to gas. The dim glow of candlelight and whale oil lamps covered a multitude of sins.

"Well, then." Kingsley rubbed his hands together. "Shall we try our luck at the lake?"

"Maybe tomorrow," Devon said. "Go ahead if you like and take one of the grooms with you to handle the tackle. I think I'll see how the orangery fared over the winter."

"I'll go with you." Kingsley fell into step beside him on the pea gravel path that led around the newer part of the manor. "Theodore said someone tried to steal Dr. Farnsworth's statue back in town. Have you a safe place to keep it here?"

"I do, but just between us two, I don't think it's necessary. The statue may well be a fake."

Kingsley frowned. "That's not the word at White's."

"And when do the layabouts there have anything right?" He pushed open the door of the classically inspired outbuilding and breathed deeply. Several orange trees were already bearing. The sharp tang of citrus bit the moist air of the artificially warm space. "I'm surprised you have time to attend to such drivel, Kingsley. All they do at that coffeehouse is drink, gossip, and gamble."

"As to that, the wagers there are running against Teddy's betrothal now. Thought you should know."

"Do the wags at Whites say why?"

Kingsley shrugged. "The ones who're betting against the liaison say the fact that the lady hasn't said yes means she's got her eye on someone else."

"Ridiculous." Griffin snorted. "Ted's as fine a man as they come."

"And yet the lady dithers," Kingsley said slyly. "Makes one think they might be right. Still, she is a lovely creature. One can see why Ted is smitten."

Griffin gave a noncommittal "humph!"

Kingsley shot him a shrewd glance. "You fancy her yourself, don't you?"

Griffin glared at his friend.

"Don't forget, I know you, Devon. Still waters run deep and all, but your face fairly shouts it." Kingsley cocked his head as he studied him. "Has this affair progressed beyond the furtive longing stage? Have you swived the lady yet?"

Griffin snatched Kingsley up by the lapels and slammed him against the stone wall, holding him so the tips of his shoes barely touched the smooth floor. "You will not speak of her so again or our friendship is at an end."

"All right, all right. It was intemperate of me to bring it up, but you're well warned. I can see your attachment to Miss Farnsworth clearly, even though you've tried to hide it. No doubt others will, too, if they haven't already. I'd be no friend to you if I didn't bring it to your attention." When Griffin released him, Kingsley brushed imagined dust off his lapels, not meeting his gaze. "Honestly, how you do so well at the gaming tables with such an open face is beyond me."

"Let me worry about that."

"Right-o. Back to the statue, then," Kingsley said. "What makes you think it's not genuine?"

Griffin hadn't intended to tell anyone, but Kingsley was his oldest friend, except for Northrop. He ought not to have lost his temper. Kingsley might have been crude, but he was only trying to help. So he found himself explaining how he and Emmaline and Baxter had discovered the way the base of the statue came off and the fact that it was filled with a mysterious substance.

"Did Baxter take all of it to his nephew?" Kingsley's voice sounded a bit tight, as if he were coming down with a cold. A few days of country air would no doubt fix matters.

"No, only a small sample."

"May I see the rest of it?"

Griffin noted that Kingsley clenched his fists so tightly his knuckles went dead white. He was probably angry at the way he'd been manhandled and was trying to hide it. A wry smile stretched Griffin's face. He wasn't the only one who had telling mannerisms.

"Ted doesn't want anyone to see the statue until the 'unveiling' when he and Dr. Farnsworth present their paper to everyone," Griffin said. "A word to the wise. Do not invest in an expedition, no matter what you may hear."

"Hadn't considered it." Kingsley unclenched his fists and strode over to the corner where the climbing fig was running riot over the palladium window. "I was thinking about making Dr. Farnsworth an offer for the statue though. It seems an intriguing novelty at the very least."

"Only if you like hollow, formerly bearded ladies," Griffin said. "Truly, my friend, I'm trying to spare you."

"I was never one for caution," Kingsley said. "You know that. Better to attempt something and fail than never to try at something you want."

Griffin had been studying the slate pavers underfoot, but his head jerked up at that. He wanted Emmaline, but didn't want to risk the pain of losing her. His chest constricted.

Would the heavy lump where his heart should be ever dissolve? He'd made such a habit of letting life wash over him, for fear of aiding Fate in an unintended way if he acted, he was almost ready to let the woman he loved get away.

Simply because he was afraid.

Every couple on earth knows there'll come a time when one of them must stand at the graveside of the other, unless by some mercy they are taken together.

But they don't know when.

That was his hell. He feared seeing it coming. Feared the pain of unavoidable loss.

"I say, what is this green stuff twining around everything?" Kingsley pointed at the renegade vine.

"It's a vining fig."

"I don't see any produce on it. I'd have the whole lot ripped out myself. I mean, it does seem a waste, doesn't it? If your orange trees are bearing, why isn't this?"

Griffin's mouth turned up in a half smile. He and Emmaline had had an almost identical conversation. He'd explained that a specific type of wasp needed to be introduced to the orangery in order to pollinate the figs. He'd resisted doing it since no one wanted a stinging insect in the fragrant bower.

His life was just like the vine, meandering and pointless. Without the risk of pain, he'd know no joy, no growth. To love was to risk ultimate loss. There was no avoiding it.

But the joy now would be worth the pain later. New resolve solidified in his chest.

Griffin turned and headed for the door.

"Where are you going, Devon?"

"I'm going to risk getting stung."

CHAPTER 28

Emmaline opened the shutters in her new chamber and let in the late afternoon light. She and Monty were housed in different parts of the manor instead of in a suite of adjoining rooms as they had been in town. She was uneasy about being so far from him.

Suppose he woke in the night with a coughing fit? Lady Devonwood had promised to assign a valet who'd sleep in an antechamber adjacent to her father's room, so she needn't worry on that score. That wasn't the real cause of her unhappiness in any case.

All the way to Devonwood Park, she'd caught Teddy eyeing her contemplatively when he thought she wasn't aware of it, almost as if he were trying to peek into her soul. Emma didn't care if he realized that she and Monty were trying to trick him. What really worried her was the possibility that Theodore should know she'd fallen hopelessly in love with his brother.

She leaned on the windowsill. Her chamber was high enough in the manor to offer a view of a hill towering above the curtain wall. Spring grass draped over it like a velvet shawl. The country air was tinged with the green breath of growing things and a whiff of wood fires from crofter's cottages that dotted the estate in all directions.

The land around the sprawling collection of buildings rejoiced in the promise of warm summer to come.

In her heart, it was February, cold and hard. She loved Griffin, but it was a terrible love. A selfish love. A hurtful love. If Theodore should ever learn of it, she shuddered at the pain it might cause him.

Monty had shown her an old map in one of the rare books in his shop once. The edges of the continents were grossly distorted in some parts, faded and indistinct in others. A cryptic inscription near the questionable areas warned "Here there be monsters."

She was what waited for Theodore beyond the edge of the map. He deserved better.

Emmaline swallowed hard. She'd tell him so tonight. After supper, she'd find an excuse to speak with him alone and lay bare her heart. He didn't need to know she loved his brother. She couldn't bring herself to even tell Griffin since he'd scrupulously avoided her for days. The ache of that abandonment was like a fresh bruise that refused to heal, but it didn't matter. That terrible love for him kept growing inside her, filling every space.

Teddy needed to know she could never feel that awful, wonderful emotion for him.

She didn't turn at the sound of the latch behind her. It was probably the upstairs maid who'd helped her unpack. She must have forgotten something.

"I need no further assistance," Emma said.

"Then perhaps you can help me."

She whirled at the sound of Griffin's voice and the aching bruise inside her throbbed afresh.

"You see," he said, laying a hand on one of the bedposts and leaning against it, "I've discovered something rather remarkable and I'm not sure how to tell you about it."

There was an unreadable thought sparking behind his

eyes, something forbidden and wicked. She decided to erect a barrier of formality between them to keep from launching herself across the room at him.

"A peer of the realm unsure? I find that difficult to believe, milord."

He crossed the room to stand before her.

"I've lost something and I hope you can help me find it."

Something inside her wilted. He only wanted her to fetch a misplaced item. Had the man no servants? She gave herself a stern imaginary shaking and answered him with an amazingly even tone. "Of course. What's gone missing?"

"I think you know since you have it."

All the breath flew out of her lungs in a whoosh and she had to remind herself to inhale. She might be a confidence artist, but she was no thief. Emmaline drew herself up to her full height. "Since I have no idea what you're talking about, what makes you think I know where it is?"

"Because you've tempted or cajoled or swindled me out of it, somehow. You see, it's my heart, Emma."

She gulped a breath and her palm went to her chest of its own accord. To keep her own heart from leaping out.

He offered his hand and she stretched out a trembling one to take it. Griffin pulled her close. He cupped her chin and took her lips in a soft, questing kiss.

"I love you," he whispered against her temple. "My heart is in your keeping. Now I need to know if you intend to own it or if you'll throw it back."

She pulled away so she could look up at him. "I'll keep it."

She'd be his lover, his mistress, his . . . whatever he wanted her to be. She'd take him however she could have him and worry over the consequences later.

Emmaline grasped his lapels, stood on tiptoe, and kissed him with a desperation born of frustrated hope. His mouth slanted over hers and the late afternoon stubble of his beard scraped her chin. Her skin rioted in pleasure.

Their tongues played a darting game of hide and seek. He groaned into her mouth. The riot descended lower on her body to prick her nipples to taut awareness and send tingles to the already moist spot between her legs.

All impediments to their joining fled from her mind. It was the simplest thing in the world to give herself to this man. She wanted to kiss him for days, to sink into him like a pearl diver and only come up for air when she must. To touch, to tease, to strip off his jacket and work the buttons on his shirt with frantic fingers. She ached to see him in the glorious altogether.

He must have wished the same thing because he was already unfastening the last in a row of buttons that began at her throat and ended at her waist.

Then he jerked away from her and held himself at arm's length. From the stricken look on his face, their joining wasn't going to be so simple, after all.

"What is it?" she asked.

"That last button," he said hoarsely. "It started to send a vision." He dragged a hand through his hair. "Blast and damn, I don't want my infernal gift to come between us."

"Will touching *me* send you a vision?" she asked, fearing his answer.

"No. The *Sendings* only come from things, not people." His eyes darkened as he gazed at her. "When I touch you, I feel . . . wonderful, normal, as if I never had this bloody curse."

"Well, then," she said as she toed off her slippers and removed her blouse, exposing her corset and chemise. "It appears I shall have to undress myself."

Angel woman. Griffin didn't trust his voice to speak. In the undressing of a lady, there were pleasures aplenty for a man and he was frustrated at being cheated of them. But when she undid the waist of her skirt and bent to pull the voluminous folds over her head, her chemise neckline sagged and he was treated to a glimpse of the sweet valley between her breasts. He decided a man could enjoy watching a woman disrobe almost as much as doing it himself.

The wire crinoline looked awkward. But her slender arms were graceful, the skin smooth and supple, as she unfastened the hooks and wiggled out of the contraption. She lowered her gaze when she unlaced her corset and removed it. Her nipples showed dark and taut beneath the thin muslin of her chemise. He was riveted by the sight of them.

"You could be getting undressed, too, you know," she said.

Griffin set a speed record for a gentleman shucking off his clothes without benefit of a valet. He was just tugging off his last stocking when her giggle made him look up.

While he'd glanced away, she'd dispensed with her pantalets, stockings, and chemise. Venus rising from the waves had nothing on his Emma in nothing but her skin. Surprisingly, she made no attempt to hide herself from his gaze, neither her breasts, nor the neat triangle of coppery curls over her sex, but she did cover her mouth with one hand.

"Something funny?" He stood and his cock did, too. Before his experiences with Emmaline, it had been a while since he'd had a woman, but the ones he'd been with had all assured him he was remarkably well endowed. Certainly none had ever laughed at him.

"It's just that you undressed so fast," she said slyly. "I hope you don't intend to be fast about other things."

"Don't worry." He strode to her and they came together

in the hot sweetness of skin on skin. "The dressing bell won't ring for a couple hours. I intend to take my time."

He lifted her and carried her to the waiting bed. She draped her arms around his shoulders and pressed wet kisses to his neck. Griffin was treated to a glimpse of her pink slit as they passed a long looking-glass, her heart-shaped bum riding high with her knees hooked over his forearm. When they reached the four poster, she leaned down, tossed back the coverlet and let him lower her to the cool linens.

He tumbled onto it after her and even though he'd promised to go slow, he couldn't help the frenzy of kisses he lavished on her. His mouth was at the sweet hollow of her throat. He tugged on each of her breasts, suckling till she moaned. He ran his tongue over her ribs. He buried his face between her legs, rubbing the damp curls over his cheeks and chin before tonguing her to writhing fury. He lost himself in her soft wet valleys and dark cavern.

He raised himself over her and covered her, wallowing in the glide of skin on skin, the heady fragrance of her arousal, the ragged draw of her breath.

"Why did you stop?" she whimpered.

He kissed her so she could taste herself on his tongue, all musk and salt. She was utterly delicious.

Then he rolled over, taking her with him, so she lay on top of him. "I'm not stopping. We're simply taking turns."

She sat up astride his hips, the wet lips of her sex kissing his cock and making him grind his teeth to keep from finishing before they'd truly begun.

"So I should do to you what you did to me?" Her breasts rose and fell with each breath and the late afternoon sun made an auburn nimbus of her hair tumbling over her shoulders. He reached up and squeezed a nipple. She sucked in a shuddering breath.

"You should do whatever you like." He laced his fingers behind his head, putting himself completely at her mercy. "And nothing you don't."

"I won't know what I like till I try it, will I?" She arched a brow at him. "Guess I'll have to try it all."

CHAPTER 29

There was no wrong way to touch a naked man, Emmaline discovered. Feather-light or firm, open palmed or with her nails dragging, Griffin seemed to love everything she did. There were no limits, no place on his body that didn't welcome the brush of her fingers or her mouth.

It was as if no one else had ever had sexual congress before. Emma was inventing it as she moved up and down his body, discovering that his third rib on the right side was ticklish, that his brown nipples hardened when she licked them, that dangling her breasts just out of his mouth's reach would torment him beyond bearing.

Their previous coupling hadn't prepared her for the wonder of *knowing* each other. She expected to feel embarrassed at being naked with Griffin in the fading afternoon light, but there wasn't a smidgeon of shame in her. She liked the feel of his skin against hers. Liked spreading her legs over his body and grinding herself against him. Liked the way he smelled, all bergamot and sandalwood and male.

She was pure energy, pure hunger, pure curiosity.

Emmaline slid down to investigate his most male parts. "Such a study in contrasts," she murmured as she stroked his length and fondled his scrotum. "The hardest part of you is next to the very softest."

"They aren't always soft," he said. As if to prove his point, his testicles drew up into a taut bunch.

"Magical," she said. "There's no place on me that changes shape like that. Or grows like this." She leaned down to press a shy kiss on the smooth hot skin of his penis. A tiny pearl of moisture formed at the head.

"Yes, there is," he said, reaching between her legs to stroke her. She bit her bottom lip to keep from crying out in pure joy. "Just there. Feel the swell. It's a smaller change than mine, I grant you, but I love it. I love that you change there for me."

Her insides spiraled, turning back on themselves in convoluted twists to rival the Gordian knot. That place, that blessed place where she ceased to exist in her body and was nothing but light and heat and pulsing limbs, was rushing toward her again.

Was there a way for her and Griffin to go there at the same time? With effort, she moved away from his talented fingers. Then she leaned down to rub against him, his hard length fitting snugly between her breasts.

His body arced and he fisted the sheets.

So the unflappable earl can be surprised. Now to see if I can totally unravel him.

She bent and took him into her mouth.

He froze.

She swirled her tongue around the head and he made a sound indistinguishable from a growl. She took the rough bit of skin near the head between her lips and sucked.

"Are you trying to kill me, woman?" he said through clenched teeth.

She sat up. "Don't you like it?"

"I may never let you stop." He sat up and cupped her cheeks. His chest heaved. "My self-control is hanging by a thread. I don't want to scare you."

"Normally . . . I . . . admire . . . self-control," she said, kissing him between each word to give them emphasis, "but I would count it a favor if you'd chuck yours out the window right now."

"At your word."

To her surprise, he flipped her over on her stomach, lifted her bum in the air, and slid into her aching channel in one sudden thrust.

Emma's mouth gaped like a sunfish on the riverbank. Her cheek pressed against the linens. Griffin held himself motionless and she felt the throb of life flowing through his penis.

It was different holding him inside her from this angle. Deeper. More invasive.

That was it.

She'd been invaded. Conquered. Vanquished.

He withdrew and thrust into her again. Her insides tightened, pleasure sharp as a blade making her press back against him.

"If I hurt you, tell me. I'll stop if you say so," he said, his tone passion-rough. "But not for anything else."

Emma was dazed. A tear squeezed from her eye but he wasn't hurting her. It was from joy. She would trust this man with her body, with her life. She loved him. She would join with Griffin; let all the world slide by. She could do nothing else.

"Don't stop."

Friction is a drug, she decided a few moments later. *A hot, wet, illicit drug.*

She and Griffin slammed against each other with jarring force. She neared the special place again. In another few moments, her body would pump like a butter churn. Her mind would drift away to a state of complete lostness that meant she'd been found.

She was ready to go there. Almost there. Only a little more and . . . Griffin suddenly pulled out of her.

She made a bereft little noise as they rolled together in a tangle of arms and legs.

He was on her again in a heartbeat, but moving with slow purpose this time.

"Not until I say, Emma," he whispered. "Then you'll come with me."

"Oh, yes." She wrapped her arms and legs around him, and tried mightily not to hurtle toward that place without him. Each long stroke sent her closer to the edge. Holding back was an impossible task. "Griffin . . . I'm . . . I can't—"

"Now, love."

They crested together in an alternating rhythm, she contracting around him, he pulsing inside her, holding himself motionless, thrust as far in as he could.

When it was over, he relaxed onto her, careful not to crush her under his weight by supporting himself with his forearms. He kissed her softly and then laid his head beside hers on the same pillow. As Emma remembered to start breathing again and settled back into the usual expansion and contraction of her chest, she realized what she'd been given was nothing less than a blessing.

She deserved prison for her crimes. She deserved to be shunned by society for the way she'd misled Theodore. Instead, she'd found love.

Emma turned her head and kissed his cheek. "Griffin Nash," she whispered. "I'll love you till I die."

"Careful. That'll be a long time," he said with a lazy grin.

She stroked his hair. "Do you know that for certain? Have you seen a vision about it?"

"No, just hopeful. You'll grant there are certain things about the future no one should know," he admitted, raising himself up and searching her face. "In any case, my visions come with a limited time for fulfillment. Twelve hours is the furthest extent of my reach."

She knew he didn't like that part of himself, but she loved all of him. She was determined to love this about him, too. "You started to have a vision earlier when you touched a button on my blouse. Do you want to tell me about it?"

"I released the confounded thing as soon as it started to *Send*." He slid out of her and rolled onto his side, splaying a possessive hand over her belly. "I saw a flash image, nothing more."

What on earth could a button have to say to him? "What did you *See*?"

"If you must know, I saw Theodore and me. We were in a small clearing ringed with trees. Morning fog swirled about our knees."

"What do you suppose it means?"

"I don't know. I was trying to undress you at the time and I didn't want to think about my brother, much less see a vision about him." He flopped onto his back and stared at the ceiling. "But we have to think about him now."

"Before you came to me, I'd already decided to tell Theodore I was declining his suit tonight," Emma said with a sigh. She wished they'd been able to savor the sweetness of their joining a bit longer before the world came crashing back on them. "I'll be as gentle as I can. We started as friends. I'll try to see we end as such. And of course, I will not tell him about us."

"He'll have to know, sooner or later." Griffin pulled her close to his side and tipped her chin up so she had to face him. "I don't intend to lose you now."

Her heart warmed to his words. "We'll have to be discreet for a while to give Theodore a chance to heal. Monty and I haven't any money to speak of. Perhaps"—

she hesitated to ask, but she had no other option—"you could set us up in a quiet little place nearby."

"So I can court you properly without rubbing Theodore's nose in it." He nodded. "Yes, that'll do."

"Court me?"

One side of his mouth lifted in a smile. "I love you, Emma. What did you think would happen?"

"You didn't think I was a decent match for Teddy. Remember? I believe your exact words were 'the brother of an earl and the daughter of a scholar are fundamentally ill-suited.'"

"Lord, I can be a pompous ass sometimes."

"Yes, you can, but I love you in any case," she said as she teased the dark hair that whorled around his brown nipple. "Especially since in this case, you're probably right. Your Polite Society won't accept a match that bridges such a wide gap. Given the difference in our status, I assumed I'd become your mistress."

He covered her hand with his. "You assumed wrongly. I intend to make you my countess, and to hell with what Polite Society thinks."

His words stole the breath from her body. To be his before the world. Of course, there'd be endless tongue wagging, but eventually, they'd be accepted. Monty had told her once that titled lords could get away with anything short of multiple murders. The thought of marrying Griffin made her feel a bit like Cinderella.

And surely an earl could afford to send his father-in-law to a sanatorium, whether it was in the Alps or the Andes or Timbuktu!

"You may live to regret this," she said.

"A wise woman once told me regret is a waste of time." He rolled her over and covered her body with his penis hard against her belly again. "Especially when there are far better ways to waste it."

* * *

Kingsley wandered the labyrinth of the Tudor wing searching for the blasted library. He'd been to Devonwood Park a number of times before, but this section always bumfuzzled him. The way the rooms wandered into each other with few proper corridors between made no sense to his mind. For tuppence, he'd abandon the search and retire to his chamber till the dressing bell rang, but he itched to finally see Tetisheri with his own eyes.

If Theodore and that professor were in the library, no doubt the statue wouldn't be far away.

He balled his fingers into fists in frustration. How had Devon discovered the statue's secret? Kingsley's contact in Egypt had assured him it was so cleverly designed, none but the initiated would guess it hid a secret void that contained the mystical grains. Instead, at any moment now, that university student nephew of Baxter's might stumble on the true nature of the substance.

Fat lot of a chance he'd have of finagling it away from Devon then. What man wouldn't jump at the advantages the ancient grain offered?

No, Kingsley told himself, trying to control his exasperated breath and make his heart stop hammering in his ears. Some squinty-eyed scholar would never uncover the proper mix of other ingredients necessary to produce the empowering brew. The statue and its contents were meant for him and he intended to keep it that way.

But the sooner he spirited the statue out of Devonwood Park, the better.

As Kingsley approached a rounded corner he was certain he'd passed at least once before, he heard whispered voices in the next room. He stopped and cocked his head to turn his ear toward the sibilance.

"The earl? No, I'll not believe it. Himself is the finest

o' gentlemen," came a furious whisper. "Never say he did such a thing, Marta."

Kingsley held his breath. Servants" gossip was the juiciest sort to be had and it was almost always spot on.

"As God is my judge, Harriet, I saw him slip into the lady's chamber with my own eyes, not a quarter hour after all the Quality Folk arrived this afternoon," another woman, presumably Marta, said. "And what's more he ain't come out yet."

The other speaker gave a low whistle. "Gorblimey! And it bein" the middle of the afternoon to boot."

"My thinkin' exactly. Weren't bad enough the lady's meant for Master Theodore," Marta said. "But carryin' on so in broad daylight before God and everybody . . . why, it's shameless, is what it is."

"This Miss Farnsworth must be a proper highflyer, if you ask me. Temptin' 'is lordship beyond what a man might be expected to bear, so to speak. Don't y'think that's the way o' things?"

"I do, and that's a fact," Marta said. "Mark my words, we're in for a rollickin' fortnight and no mistake. But mum's the word. If Mr. Baxter catches either of us carrying tales about the Family outside the House, he'll give us the sack quick as a blink."

"I know. I know. Don't I always tell ye gossip don't do no good. A prayer to the Devil, me ol' mum used to say. Whispered words have a way of returning to bite a body in the arse," Harriet said primly. "But still . . . in the middle of the afternoon and still at it. My Oliver can blow out the candle, hop into bed, give me a poke, and be snoring before the light fades." The servants' voices receded along with their heavy-soled foot steps. "What do ye suppose they're doing to make it take so long?"

"Maybe they're just doing it so many times." The pair

dissolved into giggles and then Kingsley heard a door close in the distance and the sound was snipped off completely.

He needed a diversion to capture everyone's attention while he absconded with the statue. A little domestic scandal would do nicely. He could tell Theodore that one of the maids—Marta, he believed—was looking for him to tell him that Miss Farnsworth wished to see him immediately in her chamber. That ought to stir the pot with elegant sufficiency.

Kingsley turned and headed back through the serpentine collection of chambers the way he'd come.

Now if he could only find the damned library.

Chapter 30

Theodore bounded up the staircase, taking them two at a time. Emmaline wished to see him and he wasn't about to keep her waiting.

He'd neglected her pretty badly of late, what with all the time he and Dr. Farnsworth were spending together on their translation of the Tetisheri hieroglyphs. They were almost finished with the third side of the statue base. If they worked hard, they ought to arrive at a consensus about the rest before the other guests descended on Devonwood Park.

Deciphering the odd swirls or stylized animal forms and rendering them into coherent text was fascinating stuff, as much art as science. It was bound to cause a man to lose track of other aspects of his life momentarily. Surely Emmaline could understand that.

She'd seemed pretty distant on the trip to Devonwood Park, but a bit of time to themselves should help him smooth things over. And now that she'd summoned Theodore to her chamber, maybe the improper invitation signaled that she was ready to give his suit a positive answer.

If that was the case, he was certain they wouldn't be the first couple to "anticipate" their wedding night a bit.

I won't neglect her again, he thought guiltily. As he walked briskly along the corridor on the third floor of the newer wing, he admitted to himself that he had other things to feel guilty about as well.

Like wondering what it would be like to be wedged into a closet with Lady Cressida during a game of Sardines.

He shoved the unworthy thought aside. It was disloyal, not just to Emmaline, but to her father as well. Dr. Farnsworth had opened his eyes to a new intellectual world, one he'd never expected he'd understand, let alone excel in. His rapidly growing comprehension of hieroglyphs was a testament to his mentor's abilities. The professor deserved better from one who hoped to be his son-in-law. Perhaps Ted would feign a headache when Sardines was brought up again to avoid the possibility of an indiscretion.

Still, the thought of being tangled up with Cressie in a tight space left him slightly light-headed. Whatever perfume it was that she wore, all violets and sweetness, he couldn't seem to get the scent out of his nostrils.

And part of him wasn't sure he wanted to.

He gave himself a blistering mental tongue-lashing all the way down the corridor till he reached Emma's chamber and rapped on the door.

He heard the bed creak and then there was a rustle of bedclothes. She must have been lying down. "I say, Emmaline. Are you ill?"

"Theodore?" She sounded surprised. "No, I'm fine. What do you want?"

There was more rustling about on the other side of the door. Ted decided the best way to banish thoughts of Cressida in a linen closet would be to snatch a peek at Emmaline *en dishabille*.

"I want you, you silly girl," Ted said with a laugh. "You ought to know that by now."

Not waiting for her to open the door, he turned the knob and went in. Ted's eyes flared at the sight that greeted them.

Emmaline stood frozen beside her rumpled bed. She wasn't just *en dishabille*. She was nude. Oh, she'd snatched up a sheet to wrap about herself, but she was undoubtedly in the altogether under the thin linen.

And her bed was not empty. His brother was in it. Not bothering to cover his nakedness, Lord Devonwood swung his long legs over the edge and rose from the bed.

"Theodore, please. I never meant to—" she began but fell silent under his glare.

Cold fury swept over him. He wanted to howl, to rage, to beat someone, preferably Devon, to a bloody pulp, but his feet were rooted to the spot. "Well, brother, haven't you anything to say?"

"Nothing I say will change what has happened," Devon replied, his tone even and calm, as if he hadn't just been caught playing hide-the-sausage with Ted's girl. "This isn't Emmaline's fault."

Like hell, it's not. Very well. If that's the way you want it.

"Then it must be yours," Ted said, between clenched teeth. He straightened himself to his full height. "I demand satisfaction."

"You don't want to do that, Ted." Devon's voice sank to a low rumble.

"Yes, I do, by God. Tomorrow at dawn. The clearing north of the mill. Bring Father's pistols."

He understood now why the first recorded murder in the world involved brothers. Unlike Cain, he restrained himself from giving in to the urge to bash Devon's head in with the nearest blunt object and forced himself to be content with the only option left to a gentleman.

"You're not thinking clearly," Devon said in that maddeningly calm way of his. "Imagine what that would do to *Maman,* to Louisa."

"Evidently, you weren't doing much thinking this afternoon either." Trust Devon to try to tell him what to do. Always the bloody lord of the manor. And now he expected to reinstitute *droit du seigneur,* the practice of the titled gentleman deflowering the bride of his vassal, without a word of complaint from his loyal retainer.

Ted was done being loyal.

"Trying to hide behind *Maman* and our sister, eh? You sodding bastard." Ted turned on his heel and snarled his parting words over his shoulder. "If you want changes made to your will, I suggest you make them today."

After the door slammed with vehemence, Griffin sank back onto the side of the bed and clutched his head in his hands. "Oh, God, I shouldn't have stopped. I should have let it keep going."

Emmaline had no idea what he meant. She skittered around the bed and settled beside him, close but not touching. She stopped herself from wrapping her arms around him in an effort to console him. She couldn't be sure he wouldn't push her away and she couldn't bear that. "I'm so sorry, Griffin. I never dreamed we'd be found out like this."

"It's not your fault. It's mine," he said wearily. "I should have known. I saw it coming, but I ignored the warning, damn it. I should have held on to see how it ended."

"What are you talking about?"

"That vision I so carefully avoided when your button began *Sending* it. For a blink, I saw Ted and me in the clearing. I thought we might be out early for a bit of grouse hunting, but I should have realized there was more to it than that."

"This whole business with pistols and everything . . . surely Teddy isn't serious about a duel."

"I'm sure he is." Griffin punctuated his words with a curt nod. "Once he takes a notion, there's no turning him."

"But you're not going through with it?" she said, aghast.

"The devil I'm not." He rose and retrieved her dressing gown from the chair back she'd draped it over. His eyes glazed over for a few blinks; then he gave himself a slight shake and handed it to her curtly. He began yanking on his clothes without another glance in her direction. "Aside from the fact that a gentleman cannot in honor refuse a challenge, this duel was fixed the moment you and I tumbled into bed together. Probably even before that."

She stomped after him. "No, I refuse to believe it. You have a choice. You don't have to do this."

"I don't want to, trust me," Griffin said, tucking his shirttail into his trousers. "But everything in my experience tells me no matter what I do, I can't avoid it."

Emma threw her arms around him and hugged him tight, daring him to reject her. "You and Ted can't fight over me like this. I won't have it."

Surprisingly enough, his belly shook with a grim chuckle and he slipped a finger under her chin to tip her face toward his. "My dear, we aren't fighting over you. While I'm sure he hates the knowledge that he has lost you, that's not the reason he challenged me. What I did today offended my brother's honor. He has every right to demand it back."

He bent and covered her mouth with his, but the kiss smacked too much of farewell for her to derive the slightest pleasure from it.

"Please don't do this thing," she begged.

"We are who we are, Emma. I am a man of obligations and I always meet them. You may as well ask me to stop breathing." He disentangled himself from her arms and stepped back.

Fear threatened to close off her throat, but she managed a whisper. "Stay with me, Griffin."

He smiled sadly. "I can't. Ted gave me some good advice. I have to send for my solicitor. I want to make provisions for you and your father." He turned and headed for the door. "Then I have a pair of pistols to clean."

Emmaline spent the next half hour floundering on her bed, railing silently at Griffin's devotion to both Honor and Fate, and thoroughly soaking her pillows with tears. When the dressing bell rang, signaling that supper would be served in an hour, she sat up, decided she despised herself for being such a watering pot, and resolved to take action instead.

But she didn't ring for an abigail to help her dress for dinner. There was no chance she'd join the party for the evening meal. Her belly roiled at the thought of food. She didn't think she'd ever be hungry again. Instead she donned her nightshift and wrapper. She settled at the Louis XIV escritoire in the corner and laid out a pen and a sheet of creamy foolscap. Theodore probably wouldn't listen to her if she tried to reason with him in person, but perhaps he'd read a letter.

Explaining herself and her indiscretion in a way that might soften Teddy's heart was more difficult than she'd expected. Crumpled sheets of paper littered the floor around her. She was on the sixth draft when someone knocked at her door.

"Come," she said, leaning a cheek on her palm.

Monty blustered into the room with the pent-up energy of a summer storm. "Emma, my love, you'll never guess—why, what's this?" He stopped midstride. "You aren't dressed for dinner."

She'd have to tell him eventually, but he looked so much better than he had of late, she hated to do anything to dampen his mood. "I'm not feeling up to eating."

At least it was the truth.

"You'll feel better when you've heard my news, I'll warrant." He stroked his mustache like a cat slicking back cream-soaked whiskers.

He looked so pleased with himself, she had to ask about his news.

Monty pulled a chair close to hers and slapped a hand on his thigh. "We have a new investor for the expedition, my dear."

"Excuse me?" The search for Tetisheri's tomb had always been a fictitious endeavor, but the glint in Monty's eyes said he half believed it was real. "There will be no expedition and you know it."

"I know, I know. Sometimes, it's easy to get caught up in our own tale though, isn't it? The hieroglyphs are so compelling. I mean, just imagine if it were true—"

"Monty, you know better."

"Well, yes. But isn't this cracking good news, my love? You've been fretting over taking Ted's family for a ring around the rosy, but I'm trying to tell you, we don't have to anymore. Lord Kingsley has just offered me a princely sum to buy the statue." Monty laughed. "As if I'd part with it for a single payment!"

"What have you done then?"

"Of course, I hemmed and hawed, but hinted that he could have the thing after we've located the rest of Tetisheri's funerary treasure. After he stakes us to a sizeable amount of blunt up front, all he has to do is set up an irrevocable line of credit that we can draw on. It's a reasonable request from a man who expects to see an exponentially larger return. Once the deal is done, why, we've got an income for years!"

Monty rattled on excitedly about how he'd have to fabricate some progress reports, of course. They might need to travel back to Egypt in order to make it appear that the missives came from the right place, but they wouldn't have to remain there.

"I can gin up a dozen or so reports and leave them with a man of letters in Cairo to be sent at intervals. Then we can betake ourselves anywhere in the world we like!"

"That sounds too good to be true," Emmaline said with a skeptical grimace. Lord Kingsley seemed such a sensible sort, but her years with Monty had proven there was no accounting for who might be secretly greedy enough to be the perfect mark. "Did he actually agree to this arrangement?"

"Not in so many words, no," Monty said. "But the hook is in, deep and secure. Now I only have to reel him in. Don't look so glum, child."

He fixed her with a squinting gaze.

"What's wrong?" he asked. "Oh, I know. You're thinking that if we're traveling all the time, you can't accept Teddy's offer. I understand and sympathize. He's a fine young chap and you must be getting tired of slogging about with nothing but an old man for company."

"It's not that—"

"I know you don't believe it possible, Emma, but I remember what it was like to be young." A grin stretched his mustache across his wizened face. "Don't you fret a moment. After you and Teddy tie the knot, we'll take him with us."

Emmaline's mouth opened once or twice, but she was unable to make a sound.

"Of course, we'll have to keep the truth from him for a while, but he'll get the hang of things after a bit. Especially once there are little ones on the way and he has more to lose. Ted's a surprisingly quick fellow. He'll probably take well to the confidence game." Monty's eyes grew strangely wistful. "I hope I live long enough to see your children, Emma."

A single tear trembled on her lashes and then coursed down her cheek. "Monty, I doubt very much that will happen, and now I must tell you why."

Not because she feared Monty's illness would flare up again and carry him away too soon, but because by this time tomorrow, the only man whose children she wanted to bear might well be dead.

By Theodore's hand.

And if Griffin survived and Teddy fell, she knew he'd be burdened with such crushing guilt, there'd be no room in his heart for anything else. He might deny it, but he'd never forgive her.

She'd never forgive herself.

Chapter 31

Theodore's mount picked its way over the uneven ground in the pearl gray of pre-dawn. Since the horse seemed to know its business as they made their way through the woods, Ted was free to let his dark thoughts wander.

Behind him on a milk-mild gelding, Dr. Farnsworth clung to the pommel of the saddle, making unhappy little grunts each time his horse broke into a short trot to keep up with Ted's. The professor may have been an indifferent horseman, but he'd agreed to be Theodore's second. Since it would've taken too long to send for one of his friends from London, Ted couldn't afford to be choosy.

After all, the professor wasn't the one who'd betrayed him. That was Emmaline.

And his brother.

The first flash of rage had burned down to a low simmer, but the acidic brew of having been duped still roiled in his gut.

Gullible Teddy. So easy to fool.

How Devon and Emmaline must have laughed at him under the sheets together.

He ought to have seen it coming. Hadn't he caught them in the garden alone that very first day? Like a randy hound, Devon had been sniffing around his intended from the beginning.

Bile rose in his throat, but he swallowed it down. At least, Emmaline had never said she loved him. Perhaps she never intended to lead him on. Perhaps her reluctance to accept his offer of marriage even once they arrived in England wasn't because she was unsure of her feelings for him. Maybe it was because she'd fallen in love with his brother that first morning at Devonwood House.

The letter she'd slipped under his door last night had been so heartfelt, so desperate sounding, he couldn't fail to be a little moved by her misery. There was a smudge that might have been made by a teardrop near her signature.

The fact that she wept for his pain made Ted a little more disposed to forgive her for being weak. Though he wouldn't have believed his staunch Emmaline would succumb, it was in a woman's nature to be easily led.

But Devon knew better.

His iron-willed brother had gone into this betrayal with his eyes wide open. Emmaline begged forgiveness for Devon, not herself, but Ted wasn't in a forgiving mood.

"You know, my boy, I'm not educated on all the nuances of dueling," Dr. Farnsworth said from behind him, "but I gather there's still time to call this off."

"Not without being accused of showing the yellow stripe."

"Suppose your brother apologizes?"

"He won't."

Devon never apologized for anything. He did as he bloody well pleased and the rest of the world could go hang.

"I hear he's a crack shot," the professor muttered.

"Would you rather be *his* second?" Ted said testily and the old man grumbled his denial.

Alongside Theodore's smoldering rage, an ember of fear

sprang to life. Devon *was* wickedly lethal with any sort of firearm. His brother rarely hunted because he claimed there was no sport in it for him.

Dueling pistols had smooth bore barrels in order to hamper the shooter's accuracy and thus leave place for God to determine the outcome in a contest of honor. Even so, a few years ago, Ted had watched Devon pick off a squirrel on the far edge of the clearing with one.

If his brother wanted to kill him this fine morning, he'd be dead before breakfast.

"Cheer up, Devon." Northrop had arrived in time for supper last night. After finding no one but Lady Devonwood, Louisa, and her friend Lady Cressida at table, he'd helped himself to the well-spread board and unfettered feminine companionship, then after a suitable interval, went in search of Griffin. The pair of them had emptied several bottles of more than passable port while Griffin let the whole sordid tale spill out. Till well after midnight, they reviewed all possible scenarios for the impending disaster, but ultimately decided there was nothing for it but to see the game played out. "Theodore may not show."

"Yes, he will," Devon said with certainty. He was beginning to think of himself solely as his title again. The time of being simply Griffin was gone.

"How can you know that?"

"Because if I were in his place, nothing could keep me away," Devon said.

"He has to know you can outshoot him."

"Sometimes that doesn't matter." Devon wished he'd held onto Emmaline's button a little longer so the vision it had tried to *Send* had scrolled out to its conclusion. Maybe then he'd know whether what he intended to do was the right thing. He'd done so little of the right thing lately, it was hard to be sure.

But he'd cut off another vision after that as well and it continued to plague him though he didn't understand why it should. When he'd handed Emma her dressing gown, he'd *Seen* her in the eerily sharp lines of a *Sending,* seated at a table, sipping from an ornate china cup. It wasn't the most earth-shaking of visions, but the image niggled at his brain with dogged persistence.

"Where the devil is Kingsley?" Northrop said.

Their friend knew about the duel. Every man in Devonwood Park knew about it, even among the ranks of servants. By tacit agreement, no one had told the women of the household and Emmaline had kept to her rooms, so she wasn't about to upset Lady Devonwood by carrying the tale.

Devon had considered asking Kingsley to be his second, but according to Baxter, he hadn't appeared for dinner last night either. Before Northrop showed up, Devon had resigned himself to drafting his butler into service as his second. Now that worthy domestic was serving as the impartial referee, taking exquisite care to load the pearl-handled pistols so each would be exactly the same. Baxter had also arranged for Dr. Walsh, the physician from Shiring-on-the-Green, to be present in case of injury which required his care.

The fact that Dr. Walsh also served as the hamlet's undertaker did not escape Devon's notice.

"Kingsley's probably still abed," Northrop said. "He's turning into quite the odd duck these days."

"Odder than someone about to duel with his brother?"

Northrop shrugged. "I didn't ask last night because you were too upset, but how in hell did you let this happen?"

"It's quite simple. I fell in love with the lady. It blinded me to other things." Devon removed his jacket and handed it to Northrop. He'd never allowed his heart to rule his head like that before. "I won't let it happen again."

"You should," Northrop said. "I rather think that's how love is supposed to be."

"No, it's not." Love wasn't supposed to upend a family and destroy lives. "I shouldn't have—"

"Aren't you the one who always says the future's fixed? If that's the case, there is no room for 'shouldn't have.'"

Devon nodded in gruff acknowledgment of his friend's logic, but something in him still cried out that he ought to be able to change what was coming. Everything in his experience argued for a predetermined fate. Everything in his gut demanded that a man's choice should rule the day.

"What's done is done," Northrop said. "Let it alone."

Ted and Dr. Farnsworth broke through the woods and entered the clearing. Northrop clapped a hand on Devon's shoulder.

"Besides, you have enough *now* to worry about without bothering about what's past." His friend jerked his head toward the approaching horsemen. "And maybe this is a good time to give you something to fret about for the future."

Devon raised a quizzical brow.

"I'd like permission to court your sister."

"Louisa?"

"You don't have another female sibling hidden in the attic, do you?" Northrop drawled. "Of course, Louisa."

"You're asking my permission?" Devon narrowed his eyes at his friend. "That's a strangely honorable request coming from you."

"It is, isn't it? Ordinarily, I'd seduce the girl and be done with it. I confess to surprising even myself with my unusually honorable intentions," Northrop said with a charming smile as Theodore and his second dismounted and headed toward them. "Of course, since this is an aberration in my character and behavior, one must hope the honorable bent continues, but I cannot guarantee it."

"If you do anything to shame my sister—"

"I make no promises. I simply advise you to make sure you're here to keep me on the side of the angels." Northrop's smile faded. "Live out the day, Devon. Do what you must, but live out the day."

Emmaline stood by the tall window in her chamber and peered in the direction of the mill. The lowering sky brightened by the smallest of degrees as the sun tried unsuccessfully to break through thick clouds. It was a dawn without sun.

Almost time.

She hadn't slept. She'd found herself talking to God most of the night, asking a deity she'd largely ignored for most of her life for the biggest favor she could imagine—for both brothers to be spared after this dance with insanity. She wept. She prayed. Now she was an empty husk, filled only with the hollowness of waiting.

No one stirred on the third floor. Not even the maids had come to scrub the hearths yet, but Emmaline had dressed herself in a serviceable traveling suit without assistance. If someone came over the hill with news of the duel's outcome, she intended to make a beeline to the castle portcullis to greet them.

Though perhaps the only thing worse than not knowing would be . . . knowing.

When the door opened behind her, she didn't turn at first, thinking it was the maid. Then she realized it would've been odd for her not to knock.

She glanced over her shoulder, unwilling to leave the window for a moment. "Lord Kingsley, what are you doing here?"

"It's not in the safe. It's not in your father's chamber." His face was taut with frustration. "Where is it?"

"What? You shouldn't be here. I insist that you leave immediately."

He pulled his hand from his pocket and Emma found herself staring down the snub-nosed barrel of a derringer. "I have no time for your games, girl. Where is the statue?"

She'd brazened her way out of confrontations with angry marks before but none of them had held a loaded gun. "I believe my father explained that he wouldn't sell it to you before he uses it to discover Tetisheri's tomb and recovers the rest of her funerary treasure."

"I'll show you funerary if you say another word. As if I'd be taken in by the likes of your father. Now bring me that statue and be quick about it," he said, leveling the barrel at her midsection. "I'm told a gut shot is a particularly nasty way to go."

CHAPTER 32

Devon walked to the center of the clearing with the eerie sense of having lived through this moment. Low-lying mist swirled around his knees and the edges of his vision blurred. He met his brother in the middle of the miasma with their seconds, Farnsworth and Northrop, a step behind. Baxter stood between them, sweat trickling from his temple to his cheek despite the chill in the morning air, and holding open the case that housed their father's pistols.

Theodore's face was pale, bloodless as a vampyre, but his jaw jutted in determination.

"My lords," Baxter said, his glum expression making him resemble a repentant hound who'd soiled the rug, "is there any hope this matter might be resolved without gunplay?"

"No," Theodore answered before Devon could speak.

He allowed his brother to choose a firearm first. Then Devon hefted the pearl-handled piece that remained and turned his back to Ted.

While Baxter intoned the rules for the engagement, Devon was remembering the time when Teddy had taken a tumble from the big oak at the far end of this very clearing and broken his arm. Devon was supposed to have been watching out for his little brother that day. He'd felt so wretched about the accident, their father hadn't even punished him over it.

"One." Baxter's voice echoed back from the woods as if he had a doppelganger hidden in there mimicking him.

Devon took a mechanical step forward. The scent of honeysuckle drifted by, filling his nostrils with such sweetness, the back of his throat ached.

"Two."

Another step. A breeze stirred, setting all the hairs on his forearms at full attention. Dew-wet grass tugged at the soles of his shoes and damp, fecund earth squelched beneath them.

He took another step, and then another, reveling in the way muscle, bone, and nerve moved in concert to propel him across the clearing. Strange to think this body, so crackling with life now, might be reduced to cooling meat in a matter of moments.

He was suddenly glad he hadn't *Seen* the whole vision about the duel, after all. It was freeing not to be burdened with the future. He could cling to the hope that things might yet turn out all right for another few heartbeats.

Baxter called out another number and Devon stepped. He was losing count. He forced himself to attend to his butler's voice, but the shimmering beauty of the woods, all bearded with mist, made his chest ache.

Thank God, he thought, *that the sun is not shining.*

A dreary gray day in England was glory enough for any man. He couldn't have borne the thought of leaving it if the morning had been spangled with light.

Theodore marched with grim purpose, setting his heart like flint to what he was about to do.

Damn Devon for bringing us to this.

He tamped down the flicker of fear. It wouldn't help his aim and he needed his hand to be steady. Devon could probably outshoot him, but blast it all, he had right on his side, didn't he?

"Twenty!" Baxter's voice was rimmed with a hysterical edge.

Ted pivoted and froze. He knew his brother was devilishly fast with a firearm, but he was unprepared for just how fast that was. Devon's arm was already outstretched, the barrel of his pistol leveled at Ted's chest.

He hadn't even had time to raise his gun.

"Don't move," Devon said. "And I will not shoot."

Ted's face burned. Even now, his brother shamed him, holding him motionless, impotent.

"Before these witnesses, I acknowledge that I have done my brother Theodore a grave hurt," Devon said in a firm, clear voice. "I do not regret loving Emmaline Farnsworth. Love is rare enough that when it comes, we ought not shove it away because it does not come neatly or conventionally or conveniently. But in loving Emma, I have injured one whose life and happiness are dear to me. My brother Theodore. For that offense, I do humbly ask his pardon."

Theodore swallowed back his surprise that Devon had stooped to apologize publicly for his private wrong, but he wasn't ready to forgive. "You demand forgiveness while you hold me at gunpoint?"

"You're right," Devon said. "A penitent ought not to demand."

Devon pointed his pistol skyward and pulled the trigger. The shot rent the morning quiet and reverberated against the distant hill. Then he spread his arms out, baring his chest to Ted, presenting the largest possible target.

"I am at my brother's mercy."

Murmurs of "well done" and "good form" came from the men gathered on the side to witness the duel. Even though Devon was clearly in the wrong, he'd found a way to come out on top. Again.

It was so grossly unfair.

All his life, Ted had felt the sting of being the spare heir, the second best. When he'd proposed to Emmaline, he felt at least he'd come out ahead on the race to the altar, though Devon always made it clear he wasn't interested in that contest.

But he was interested enough to find his way into Emma's bed.

"I'll forgive you, Dev," Theodore said coldly, "if you survive my shot."

After all, that was the point of dueling, wasn't it? To stand before another man and not flinch. He owed it to his brother not to cheat him of his full moment of bravado. He raised his arm and squeezed the trigger, not taking the trouble to aim.

If God wants to kill my brother, let Him do it.

The pistol left behind an acrid puff of smoke. When it cleared, his brother was still standing.

But a hideous patch of red blossomed and spread on the white lawn of Devon's shirt.

"You have the statue," Emmaline said as she and Lord Kingsley waited for the London ferry to arrive at the Shiring-on-the-Green quay. "I don't understand why you need me."

After she'd retrieved Tetisheri from its hiding place in the drawer containing her undergarments, Kingsley had ordered her to stuff it into a hatbox. Then he'd forced her to accompany him to the stable and into a gig and made her take the reins. They stopped briefly at the inn in Shiring-on-the-Green to collect a great hulking brute who went by the name of O'Malley. The big Irishman had driven them the rest of the way to the port on the

Thames, while Kingsley kept the derringer in his pocket turned toward her at all times.

"I choose to keep you with me because you're the only one who knows I have the statue and frankly, I don't need anyone interfering at the moment," Kingsley said, his voice the low rasp of a serpent gliding through dead leaves. "Later, of course, it won't matter so much, but you needn't concern yourself with that."

That sounded ominous. "I'll be missed."

"No one saw us leave the stable. The men are occupied with their silly duel and once the ladies deign to rise, they'll be anticipating the arrival of the rest of the guests this morning." He narrowed his gaze upriver where the ferry was just coming round a bend. "No one will find it odd that you've kept to your chamber again today. Especially once word of the scandal breaks and trust me, it will." Kingsley turned to O'Malley. "Take the gig back to Devonwood Park and try to ease it in along with the other equipages that will be arriving today so it's not remarked upon."

"Right ye are, guv."

"Watch Devonwood Park till evening to make sure we are not followed."

"And if ye are?"

Kingsley shot him a withering glance.

"Oh, oh, I see," O'Malley said. "Make sure they don't get far, right?"

He lumbered away from them, whistling a tuneful Irish ditty.

"Mr. O'Malley enjoys his job far too much," Emma said dryly.

"Indeed. Pity he's witless as a bag of hammers," Kingsley said, "but O'Malley has his uses."

"Lord Devonwood will come after me and he won't let Mr. O'Malley deter him," Emmaline said with more conviction than she felt. The Irishman was a monstrously big chap.

"If he's still alive. And if he is, I doubt he'll thank you for making him shoot his brother."

They'd heard the pair of gunshots as they bounced down the disreputable country road to Shiring-on-the-Green. The hollow dread of not knowing returned to Emma's chest.

"If Devon doesn't emerge the victor," Kingsley went on, "I doubt the hapless Ted will be anxious to see you, one way or the other."

"My father—"

"Your father is a charlatan of the first water and we both know it." Kingsley looked down his long nose at her. In repose, his aristocratic face might have been austerely presentable, but now he resembled a thin-faced weasel. "Once Farnsworth realizes he's lost the statue, he'll slink away looking for a new set of willing sheep to shear, devil take the hindermost."

"If you're so convinced my father and I are frauds, why not let me join him? We'll not trouble you. One scoundrel cannot very well complain to the authorities about another."

"Clever girl, but I think not. I need you yet."

The ferry wallowed up to the quay. They stood aside to allow the passengers to disembark. Kingsley pulled the brim of his hat forward to obscure his face, obviously concerned about being seen by anyone who knew him.

Emma scanned the passengers, hoping she might recognize someone she'd met at Lord Whitmore's ball. Lady Bentley waddled down the gangplank surrounded by a bevy of friends. She looked right at Emmaline once through the milling crowd, but showed no sign of acknowledging her or Lord Kingsley.

"Why do you need me?" she asked.

"You may as well know." Kingsley bared his teeth in a feral smile. "You see, that substance you and Devon discovered inside the statue has . . . unique properties when taken in a tea of sorts. But since I'm not sure how it all works, I'd rather not be the first person to test it. I'll explain its benefits once we determine whether the potion lives up to my expectations. Or rather, if you live through drinking it, my dear."

Emma's insides shivered. He intended to use her, to experiment on her like a pitiless vivisectionist. She started to dart away from him through the crowd, but he snaked out a hand and snatched her back.

"Let me go," she said.

"Do not make a scene," he whispered through clenched teeth, his lips barely moving. "Have you forgotten I have a gun trained on you?"

"Whether you shoot me now or use me as a laboratory specimen later makes very little difference."

"Keep your voice down." He yanked her close and hissed into her ear. "Do you see that mother with the pram boarding the ferry now?"

Her gaze followed the young mother and baby accompanied by an older woman who must have been the child's grandmother as they moved up the gangplank.

"If you don't behave, I'll put a lead ball in *her*. Do you understand me?"

Emma drew a shaky breath and then nodded.

"Good." He offered her his arm, his hooded eyes demanding she take it.

She would have sooner touched a toad, but he seemed so dangerously unhinged, she deemed it wiser not to antagonize him. She slipped her hand into the crook of his arm.

"Don't forget your hatbox, my dear," he said, loud

enough for passersby to hear. "Wouldn't want to mislay your treasures."

The lead ball striking Devon's flesh caused surprisingly little pain. At first. Then the burn started in his left bicep where the sticky red stain spread. Blood trickled down his arm to his fingertips and fell in great droplets on the green grass.

"Devon, Dev," Teddy shouted and barreled across the clearing toward him. "I didn't mean it. Truly, I didn't. I didn't even take aim. How bad is it?"

Dr. Walsh and the rest of the men plowed toward him, but it seemed as if they were running through pudding, their progress strangely sluggish. The sun broke through behind Devon and each blade of grass was edged with its own sharp shadow.

The doctor tore Devon's shirt off to expose the wound. Everyone was talking at once, tugging at him, asking him if he was all right.

"No, I'm not all right," he said testily. "My little brother just shot me."

"You all but dared me to," Ted countered. "It's not serious, is it, doctor?"

"Any time lead insults flesh it's serious," Dr. Walsh said, clucking his tongue against his cheek. "But the ball appears to have gone clean through. We need to staunch the bleeding."

Devon cocked his head and peered down at his arm. It seemed to belong to someone else. He bunched and flexed his fingers. He could control them, but the numbness remained except for the bolt of fire that burned along the path of the pistol ball.

"I'm sorry, Devon," he heard Teddy say, his words cutting through the stillness and thudding into Devon's heart.

"That makes two of us. Next time, take aim. I'll be safer." He punched his little brother with his good arm while the doctor bound up the other one. Ted punched him back, and they laughed together as if they were much younger and this had been only a schoolyard scuffle. Then Devon's laughter died. "I won't give her up, you know."

"I'd think you mad if you did," Ted said.

Something broke over Devon in shimmering waves, an emotion he'd felt so seldom, he scarcely recognized it. He inhaled deeply. Peace.

The doctor finished tying off the bandage. "There. That's as good a field dressing as I can manage. I'd like to see that arm in a sling for a week or two." He stooped to pick up Devon's bloody shirt. "There's no help for this. The stains will terrify Lady Devonwood if she sees you returning in it."

"And Devon without a shirt will scandalize the arriving guests good and proper," Northrop said with a laugh. "Plenty of port, twenty paces at dawn, and an earl caught in a public state of undress. I knew this party would be worth attending."

"Never fear, milord." Baxter scurried back to the horse he'd ridden and rummaged through the saddle bag. He pulled out a slightly rumpled, but otherwise clean shirt. "One has brought a change of clothing for both you and Master Theodore."

"I say, that's forward thinking of you, Baxter," Teddy said.

"As was the fact that Dr. Walsh is also an embalmer and would be just as efficient tending to his lordship if he'd cocked up his toes," Northrop said. "You've a brutally competent butler there, Devon."

Baxter shot Northrop a tight-lipped glance. "One tries to anticipate all eventualities."

He helped Devon into the fresh shirt, taking care with

the bandaged arm, and the party mounted and rode back to the castle.

Ted rode beside Devon most of the way. Dr. Farnsworth and Northrop kept up a running diatribe debating the comparative merits of true Scotch whisky as opposed to the distilled liquor of the same name from the Yank's Kentucky. The brothers didn't speak.

There was no need. Devon felt the bond between them healing with each measured step. It would take time to mend the rift completely, but he and Theodore would emerge from this whole.

And so would he and Emmaline.

She must be sick with worry.

He urged his gelding into a trot. When Dr. Walsh complained that he'd open the wound again, he broke into a canter. The need to see Emma was sharper-edged than the brightest blade. If it made him bleed, so be it.

When he passed under the portcullis and reached the bailey, he found Lady Bentley and a gaggle of matrons descending from a hired coach.

"Oh, Lord Devonwood, I see you've tried to stop them. To no avail, I gather," she said breezily. "It's no shame to you or your brother, of course. They had such a head start, you know."

"My apologies, Lady Bentley," Devon said as his mount side-stepped near her. "You have lost me."

"I saw them in Shiring-on-the-Green. *He* tried to hide his face with that top hat of his, you understand, but *she* was standing there bold as brass at the ferry landing. Met my eye without a blink, too, the cheeky girl. Off to Gretna Green for the pair of them, I shouldn't wonder." She made tsking sounds. "One shouldn't be surprised, Theodore, dear. Blood will out, you know."

"Who are you talking about?" Ted asked, still mounted.

Lady Bentley's eyes widened. "Oh! Oh, so you don't

know. My word. How to tell you? It's simply so shocking to see a young lady and an eligible peer without a proper chaperone. It's simply not *done*. However, I assumed she'd jumped at the chance to have a title. Oh, Theodore, I do apologize, I didn't mean to imply—"

"Are you talking about Miss Farnsworth?" Teddy interrupted.

"Of course, who did you think? Honestly, it's too bad of her after the way she dangled you along and all, but I suppose she figured Lord Kingsley controls the chinks on his estate and can give her a heftier allowance."

"Kingsley!" Dr. Farnsworth said. "I wonder . . . Mr. Baxter, would you please betake yourself to Emmaline's room and see if the Tetisheri statue is missing." He leaned in the saddle toward the butler and whispered. "It should be in the drawer with her unmentionables."

Lady Bentley gave a little squeal of shocked delight over this juicy tidbit. Mentioning "unmentionables" brought out her fan and set it aflutter.

"You think Emmaline would have taken it?" Devon asked.

"No, but Lord Kingsley might have. We almost came to an agreement for me to sell it to him last night, but I guess he didn't like the terms." While Baxter dashed into the newer wing of the monstrous edifice, Dr. Farnsworth explained Kingsley's intense interest in the statue. "So I think he may have absconded with it and if that's the case, I don't think my Emma would have gone with him willingly."

"Agreed," Devon said and started to turn his gelding's head so he could bullet away down the long drive, but Theodore reached over and grabbed the reins.

"Hold a moment," he said. "We don't know that the statue is missing yet."

"I don't give a damn about the statue," Devon said, yanking the reins back. "All I care about is Emma."

"Begging your pardon, your lordship"—Baxter came back at a run—"but the statue may very well be at the crux of the matter. It *is* missing and what's more, a letter arrived from my nephew this morning. Seems he's had time to analyze the sample of the substance we sent him."

He handed the letter to Devon who ripped it open and ran his gaze over the small, precise script.

"What substance? What's this all about?" Theodore asked.

"The statue is hollow," Baxter said. "His lordship and Miss Farnsworth discovered it was filled with an ancient sort of grain. One might speculate that Lord Kingsley suspected as much and it is this that motivates his actions."

"That makes sense. He's been a balmy bastard of late," Northrop said. "Gone a bit queer in the head over that occult stuff. Tried to get me to go to some of the meetings with him. After the first time, never again."

"Why?" Teddy asked as Devon continued to read the letter from Baxter's nephew.

"I was expecting a new incarnation of the Hellfire Club," Northrop said.

Devon was listening with half an ear. *Trust Lionel to be intrigued with a society dedicated to unbridled debauchery.*

"Instead, there was plenty of hell," Northrop went on, "but none of the fire, if you know what I mean."

Lady Bentley emitted a little squeak of titillated horror.

"You never said anything about Kingsley being involved with that sort of thing," Devon said.

Northrop shrugged. "You're his friend, too. I figured you knew. Besides, I'm not given to carrying tales." Then he leaned down to Lady Bentley who was hanging on every word of their exchange. "I believe Lord Devonwood has pen and ink in his study if you'd care to take notes for future reference, milady."

She puffed up like a fat grouse on a crisp fall day. "Well, I never!"

"I don't doubt it, madam," he said with a wicked grin. "But having none of your own may be why you are so interested in the affairs of others."

Her eyes widened and she sputtered in search of a retort, but found none. Instead, she wheeled and chugged through the open front doors, calling for Lady Devonwood as loudly as she could.

"That tears it," Teddy said. "*Maman* will know everything now."

"Not everything," Northrop said. "I didn't mention that Kingsley is mad about brewing potions and elixirs and is always going on about how best to 'infuse this' or 'distill that.' That news would have given Lady Bentley at least another hour's worth of material."

A muscle ticked in Devon's cheek. The vision of Emmaline sipping something from a teacup rose up in his mind. "Baxter's nephew says he gave the grain to one of his laboratory rodents. It became frenetic, then aggressive and then . . ."

"Then what?" Teddy and Dr. Farnsworth asked in tandem.

"It went mad."

CHAPTER 33

The rope cut her wrists and ankles if she struggled at all against her bonds. Emmaline tried to relax, but the straight-backed chair was not built for comfort even if she hadn't been lashed to it.

She was held in a musty cellar beneath Lord Kingsley's London town house. In happier times, it had probably held hogsheads of beer and great rounds of cheese, and perhaps had woven strings of onions and garlic dangling from the heavy black beams of the ceiling. Traces of the pungent scents still hung in the air.

Now the walls were covered with signs and symbols from a dozen different mythological systems—ankhs and pentagrams, yins and yangs, stars and daggers and many-tentacled beasts. Kingsley had cherry-picked his way through multiple belief systems, lifted out the most fantastical elements, and synthesized them into something that was wholly his own.

Lord Kingsley boiled water for a pot of "Old Sticky," the popular name for the Earl Grey blend of tea and bergamot. Then he fussed with the ingredients steeping in a stone vessel over a small kerosene burner that would have been more at home in a laboratory than a cultist's lair. He consulted a moldering grimoire from time to time.

"I apologize for the wait, my dear," he said as if he were preparing a spot of tea for her. "These things are delicate and cannot be rushed."

"I'm in no hurry."

He laughed. "No, I'd imagine not. I really can't guarantee the efficacy of this potion since it's the first brew. But if the effect is what I hope, you'll enjoy a benefit beyond your wildest dreams." He cocked his head and considered her with a slightly elevated brow. "There's no point in preternaturally long life if one hasn't someone with whom to spend it. If you play nicely, perhaps I'll share my limited quantity of grain with you."

"I have no intention of playing with you, nicely or otherwise." She wiggled her fingers, trying to keep circulation stirring in them.

He narrowed his eyes to slits. "It's just as well. You may be my taster then and nothing more. I'll find a more worthy consort, no doubt, once I've amassed the wealth and power the potion promises as well. Perhaps I'll acquire two of them, variety being the spice of my very long life. A man grows weary of the same woman after a while, you know. However, I do intend to have a bit of sport with you after our little experiment. Can't let Devon have all the fun now, can we?"

Emmaline looked away from him in disgust. Her gaze fell on the Tetisheri statue, lying on its side next to the steeping teapots with its base removed. Lord Kingsley had transferred the contents to a "more reliable" set of Mason jars and sealed them tightly. If he were thinking clearly, he'd realize that the design of the base with its threaded seal proved beyond doubt the statue was a modern fake. The enigmatic smile on Tetisheri's face mocked her.

Kingsley wouldn't believe anything she said. She was a huckster, a confidence artist, a fraud, and he knew it. Why should he believe her even when the evidence was right before him?

His lordship poured steaming tea into one of the china cups he'd set out, then ladled an equal amount of liquid from a stone vessel. He set the tea on the table before him and the other brew in front of Emmaline.

"I didn't want you to drink alone, my dear. But you will have to go first." He lifted the cup to her lips but she jerked her face aside. He grasped her head in a long-fingered grip and turned her back toward the cup.

"I have no intention of drinking at all if you force me."

"You will when I hold your nose and you have to open your mouth to breathe," he promised, jostling the cup beneath her lower lip.

"I will spew it out immediately and you'll have wasted some of your precious grain. Once it's gone, it's gone, you said." When murder glinted in his watery eyes, she lifted her chin and adopted a more conciliatory tone. "However, if you untie my hands so I can manage by myself, I will drink."

He frowned at her, considering. "Very well. That's a civilized attitude. Never let it be said that we are less civil than a Yank."

Kingsley set the cup down and untied the knots at her wrists. She rubbed the raw scrapes and flexed her fingers.

"Your hands are free. Drink."

Emma raised the cup to her mouth and sniffed. "It smells bitter. I never drink tea without a lump or two. It would be a shame if I couldn't bear to swallow it because of the taste. Might I have some sugar to make this more palatable?"

"A reasonable request. I'll take mine with a lump as well," he said and turned away to rummage in his cupboard for the sugar bowl.

Emma leaned across the table and reached for the cup of tea in order to switch it with hers, but it was slightly out of her grasp. She managed only to turn the cup in its saucer so the handle pointed in the other direction.

The clink of china against china made her jerk her hand back, turning her own cup slightly as well. He whirled around at the small sound.

"You exchanged the cups," he accused.

Emmaline adopted her most serene charlatan's face and smiled at him. It was time to execute the best "bait and switch" of her life. "Perhaps I did."

It was important not to lie directly. Even the best of liars had little tells that gave them away.

"Would you care to join me in a drink to find out?"

Griffin stood at the ferry's prow, leaning into the wind, as if he could make the little steamer go faster by sheer strength of will. After that brief moment of sun following the duel, clouds had swallowed up the sky and now threatened rain. The ferry's two-man crew was snug in the wheelhouse to the rear of the craft. Theodore and Northrop had descended with the rest of the ferry passengers to the salon below to make the short trip in relative comfort.

There could be no comfort for Griffin. Not as long as Emmaline was in danger.

A ship's bell sounded on the starboard side and Griffin turned to survey the other traffic on the broad river. A merchantman was making its way up the Thames under full sail, pulling even with the ferry and overtaking it in the favorable tide and stiff breeze.

"I'll be damned," he muttered. "The *Rebecca Goodspeed*."

Finally, the ship on which he'd pinned so much of his hopes had come in. Riding low in the water, her hold was filled to the brim with trade goods that would guarantee his estate's solvency for years to come. He could set Ted up in whatever endeavor he pleased, give Louisa the Season she deserved, and keep his mother and retainers in comfort.

Even more important, he could marry Emmaline and send her father to that sanatorium to regain his health. And keep the old man out of trouble.

But he had to find Emma first.

He turned at the sound of footsteps, thinking Ted or Northrop had come to join him, but found a monstrously big fellow advancing on him instead.

"You shouldn't oughta have followed 'is lordship," the man said. He grasped Griffin's collar and tried to throw him over the rail into the churning sludge of the Thames below.

It was difficult to fight back with his arm in a sling, so Griffin slipped out of it and wrapped the length of cloth around the big man's neck. His ruddy face turned an alarming shade of purple, but he clawed at the cloth and managed to tear it off his neck.

The men separated, circling for best position. Once more Griffin found himself with his back to the rail. The man charged him. This time, Griffin bent forward and used the man's own momentum to heft his attacker at the last moment. He tossed him over his back, over the rail and into the water. The man sputtered to the surface, then disappeared beneath the ferry's keel.

"Devon!" Theodore came running toward him, with Northrop at his heels. "We heard sounds of a scuffle. Are you all right?"

"Bugger," Northrop said. "You're bleeding again."

"Could be worse. I could be swimming." Devon looked into the murky water. "It must have been the fellow Baxter caught trying to burgle us a while back. Big chap. Hope he misses the paddle wheel."

"That's charitable," Northrop said.

"No, it's practical," Griffin said, grim-faced. "A fellow that big could gum up the works and leave us dead in the water. And since his attack proves we're on the right track, we haven't a moment to lose."

Kingsley's smile stretched unpleasantly across his face. "You may be common, but you are also uncommonly entertaining, Miss Farnsworth. Very well." He dropped two lumps of brown sugar into each of the cups and stirred. "What shall we drink to? Our health, perhaps?"

"Sounds good to me." She forced a slight smile and lifted her cup to touch rims with his. Then she brought the cup to her mouth without hesitation and tipped it so the liquid lapped at her lips.

"No, wait!" he said and set down his cup.

She peered over the rim at him, straining against the urge to do the same. He mustn't think her the least anxious about the contents or in any hurry to remove the cup from her lips.

"We'll switch cups," he said.

"Are you sure?" she asked, letting her brow wrinkle slightly in what she hoped was convincing, though surreptitious, evidence of worry.

He took the cup from her and gave her his. She stared down at the innocuous tea before her and bit her lower lip.

"You don't want that one, do you? Yes, I'm sure," he said with a laugh. He raised his cup and drained it in one gulp. "Now it's your turn."

She hesitantly reached for the tea.

"Don't be shy. Drink up."

She let her hand tremble a bit as she lifted the cup to her mouth.

"Careful. Don't want to waste a drop. Drink. Drink. What are you waiting for?" He spoke faster and his voice had gone up at least half an octave in pitch. His pupils widened to engulf his irises. "Come now, I drank, didn't I?"

He began pacing and wringing his hands. Whatever it was that had been in his cup acted with amazing swiftness, though he seemed unaware his behavior bordered on frantic.

Emma decided it wouldn't do to give him time to notice. She took a small sip of the Earl Grey and swallowed with deliberateness.

"Again. Again. Again." His eyes darted around the room as if he couldn't keep them focused on her.

She finished the contents and set the cup down.

He plopped down in the chair across from her and then almost immediately rose again. "How do you feel?"

She pressed her lips tightly together for a moment. "No longer thirsty."

He slammed a fist on the table. "No!"

She flinched at his sudden violence. His head jerked several times as if he had a bit in his mouth and an invisible hand were controlling his movements. He sucked in a deep breath and slid into the chair again. His fingers drummed the tabletop.

"How do you feel?" he repeated. "Any palpi-palpi-palpitations? Shortness of b-breath?"

"I feel . . . fine," she said, allowing her shoulders to relax. "Stronger. As if I could fly."

"Good. Good. Oh, yes. That's as it should be. Yes, indeed as it ever shall be. W-world without end. Amen, and all that r-rot." He cackled out a laugh and then leaned forward to study her face.

She forced herself to meet his gaze.

"Your eyes, they're brighter. By gum, you're absolutely positively glowing. There's a light behind your eyes that's *absoltively, positutely* ethereal-ereal." He leaned down and rested both elbows on the table, cupping his face in his palms. "I wonder how it looks from the other side. Pop out your eye, why don't you, and give me a peek."

Emma's jaw dropped.

"You should see your face." He giggled like a twelve-year-old girl. "Never mind. I believe it's time, yes it's time, I said it was didn't I, for me to join you."

He turned back to his stone pot and ladled out another cupful of the dark draught. He cursed when his hand shook convulsively and a tablespoon or so splashed on the cupboard shelf.

If one dose of the stuff disoriented him this much, Emmaline didn't want to be present when he consumed a second batch. She bent down and worked at the knots restraining her ankles, while Lord Kingsley drained another cupful of the Tetisheri potion.

She yanked the rope from around her ankle and stood just as he turned around.

"Oh, you've slipped your bonds," he said with an idiot's grin on his face. "No matter. I'd have had to untie you in any case."

"Of course, you would," she said trying to maintain a reasonable tone with him. With any luck, the potion had rendered him suggestible. "Since you're going to let me go now."

He made a rude spluttering noise. "Not a chance, ducks. Unless it's off the roof."

"What?"

"You said you felt you could fly," he said. "Me, too. Let's go up to the widow's walk and test it out, shall we?"

His head jerked to the side and he seemed to continue the conversation with someone Emmaline couldn't see. "Yes, we shall. Because I said so, that's why!"

His gaze swung back around and fastened itself on her. "And since I'm always a gentleman, when it's time to leap off the roof . . ." He dipped in a low bow. "It'll be ladies first."

Why on earth was she fighting him? She struggled so on the stairs, he'd finally had to slap her and throw her over his shoulder as if she were a sack of wheat.

Or Egyptian rye, he thought with a grin. That's what the grain was supposed to be after all. The splendiferous, glorious secret ingredient that made him strong as an ox.

Now that he thought on it, he could probably have carted an ox up the winding staircase, through the attic, and out over the rain runnel that divided the butterfly roof that capped his four-story town house. Of course, the way Miss Farnsworth screamed and pounded his back and carried on, an ox might have been less trouble.

His butler Farley had appeared briefly to investigate the unholy racket the woman was making, but when Kingsley snarled at him—quite ferociously—Farley had retreated back down the stairs, his eyes swollen to the size of dinner plates.

"Yes, they were too that big," he said to the scarlet imp bouncing on Miss Farnsworth's heels. "I am not exaggerating in the slightest."

"Lord Kingsley, you're not well," the infuriating woman said, as if he'd been talking to her in the first place. "Put me down and we'll—"

He swung her down from his shoulder and dropped her near the front parapet. She landed on her backside with an "oof." Her skirts hitched up, baring her legs to the knees.

She had well-turned ankles and comely calves.

His cock swelled at the sight and for a moment he lost track of why they'd come to the roof. The trio of chimney pots on the next house leaned over and made noises of disapproval that sounded remarkably like his stern old nanny. He shot them a glare and they straightened, pretending they hadn't been hovering over him like a clutch of old biddies riding herd on debutantes at a ball.

The red imp that had ridden on Miss Farnsworth's ankles was joined by three more little gargoyles bounding across the rooftops and leaping over the wrought iron railing that edged his parapet. He rather liked them and didn't care if they spied on him so long as they didn't try to argue.

"Lord Kingsley," she said, tugging down her skirt. "We should call a physician for you."

"I don't need a doctor," he said as fire began creeping through his veins. He rubbed his forearms, trying to extinguish the slow burn. Now he remembered why they were on the roof. "I need to see if you can fly."

"No!" She wailed when he hauled her to her feet and started manhandling her toward the railing.

"Emma!" A voice came from the street below.

Kingsley leaned over the wrought iron and peered down. *Damn.* It was Devon. He was clambering out of a hansom with his brother Theodore and that wastrel Northrop in tow. The earl bounded to Kingsley's front door and began pounding on it as if he'd tear it from the hinges.

"Such a fuss over nothing," Kingsley said. "Fly down there and tell him to stop it, there's a good girl."

He lifted her over the rail and dropped her.

CHAPTER 34

Emma twisted and grasped at the wrought iron as she went airborne. She was able to wrap the fingers of one hand around a picket. The smooth metal slid down her palm till she came to an abrupt stop where it met the brick façade of Kingsley's town house. She felt a sickening crunch at her wrist and her shoulder wrenched painfully, but she steeled herself not to let go.

"Hold on, Emma," Griffin shouted from below her.

The sound of his voice gave her the strength to swing her other arm up and grab the bottom of a more substantial post topped with a spear-like finial. She hung suspended above the street, her cheek scraped against rough bricks, her skirts billowing in the breeze.

"Oh, Miss Farnsworth, I'm so disappointed," Kingsley said from above her. "And you thought you could fly. You know what this proves, don't you?"

She didn't dare look up. She hardly dared breathe for fear of losing her grip, but she heard Kingsley scuffling around above her as if he were tussling with someone. It couldn't be Griffin. She could still hear him bashing at the door below.

"Don't rush me, I'll tell her. I said I would, didn't I? Get off, you demon spawn!" Kingsley's voice rose to a hysterical pitch, then dropped to maddening calm as he knelt to peer through the rail at her. "You're simply not worthy, my dear."

A crackle of splintering wood reached her ears. Griffin had broken through. Hope shot through her like a second wind, but her palms were clammy. Her grip slipped by a hairbreadth.

"No! Not them," Kingsley yelled and leaped suddenly to his feet. "There are hundreds of them. Thousands. They're spewing out of the Dome of St. Paul's and heading this way. You've got to fly, Emmaline. They'll be on you in a moment."

He knelt down again and tried to uncurl her fingers from around the post, bending back her nails and scratching at her skin. She pleaded with him to stop, but even when he kicked at her fingers, she wouldn't let go.

"You've got to . . . I can't stop them . . . there's no help for it . . . they're here!" He shrieked and leaped on top of the iron railing, balanced between earth and sky. "Save yourself!"

Then with an unholy wail, he propelled himself into space, arms windmilling as he fell. A dull thud cut off the scream abruptly. She made the mistake of looking down and saw Kingsley's body splayed obscenely on the cobbles below.

Her groin tingled with the sense of impending destruction. If her grip gave, she'd be next. Emmaline squeezed her eyes shut and focused every bit of strength into her fingers.

Someone was grappling through the bars, grasping her forearms and trying to uncurl her fingers. Panic clawed her belly. Whoever or whatever had chased Kingsley from the roof was trying to send her to her death as well.

"No, stop," she begged.

"Emma, sweetheart, let go. I've got you."

She looked up into Griffin's handsome face, drawn with equal parts concern and determination. He had a firm hold on her forearms so she forced herself to release the iron and clutched at Griffin's strong wrists. She scrabbled her feet against the brick, trying to help him pull her up, but there was little need. Griffin had her safely up and over the iron railing again by the time Theodore and Northrop pounded up the stairs and onto the rooftop behind him.

She sagged into his arms, burying her face in his chest. Oh, the smell of him, all warm and male and safe. Always safe.

"I've got you," he repeated as if he scarcely believed it himself. "And I'll never let you go."

"You'd have to drive me away." Emmaline squeezed him tightly. She'd never want for anything else as long as she could be near this man, listening to his great heart hammering beneath her ear.

"Griffin, what are you doing here?" Emmaline knuckled her eyes to make sure she wasn't dreaming. His smiling face didn't waiver. Dawn streaked in through the leaded window behind him, silhouetting his nude form with light and rendering him fair as an angel.

Except that his wicked grin wasn't the least angelic.

"Don't you know it's bad luck to see the bride before the ceremony?"

"I couldn't wait." He threw back the covers and slid in beside her. "In a few hours, we'll be married, but once the household wakes, you'll be surrounded by women clucking over you."

"They'll only be clucking to make sure I'm dressed and pressed and decked out like a bride worthy of you."

"A lot of bother for nothing." He covered her mouth in a possessive kiss.

She wedged her arms between them and pushed on his chest. "Come now, a girl wants to impress her bride-groom."

"You want to impress me? Take off that nightshift."

Her lips curved in a feline smile. It would be some time before the upstairs maid came to her chamber to begin her wedding day toilette. Then after the ceremony in the Devonwood Park chapel, they'd be surrounded by family and well-wishers till well after midnight. She wouldn't be alone with Griffin again for hours.

Emmaline wiggled out from under him and then pulled the nightshift off over her head.

"We've been so poisonously conventional for the past fortnight," she said between fevered kisses. "Are you sure you want to ruin our streak of unusually good behavior?"

"Absolutely."

After the death of Lord Kingsley, there'd been a brief inquiry by the Peelers. Once Emmaline showed them the reddish brown substance hidden inside the Tetisheri statue and Griffin produced the letter from Baxter's nephew describing the adverse effects of ingesting it, the authorities were willing to accept their account and ruled his demise an unfortunate accident.

"St. Anthony's fire, eh?" the constable said. "I've heard tell of the like. And it comes from tainted rye, you say. Makes a body want to swear off bread, indeed it does."

The tale lost nothing in the telling once they returned to Devonwood Park. The house party guests were spell-bound in horrified fascination as Theodore and Northrop relayed the particulars. The early morning duel was never mentioned since everyone assumed Griffin had injured his arm during the course of Emmaline's rescue.

And of course, the merry company of guests completely understood when her affection transferred to Lord Devonwood from Theodore. He had led the charge up to the roof and snatched her from the brink, after all.

"Yesterday, I overheard Lady Bentley nattering on about the fact that there may be another wedding in the family soon," Emmaline said as Griffin kissed his way down her throat. His lips made her skin shiver with pleasure.

Griffin's flat belly jiggled in a low chuckle. "It's like to be at the point of a shotgun if Teddy gets caught with Lady Cressida in another game of Sardines."

"No, it wasn't—" Emma's breath caught when his lips teased over a nipple without stopping to suckle it. "She meant Louisa and Lord Northrop."

"Louisa's leading that dog a merry chase, but he may yet run the vixen to ground." His dark head disappeared under the sheets and found a place to rest between her breasts. "Fortunately, it'll be Teddy's problem in a week."

Theodore had volunteered to step up and deal with the issues associated with the estate while Griffin and Emma went on their honeymoon. First, they'd escort her father to Görbersdorf for treatment and while he convalesced there, the happy couple would tour the capitals of Europe—always taking care to avoid the ones which had an outstanding arrest warrant for the bride, of course.

That meant Ted would see to the disposition of the influx of funds brought to the estate by the timely return of the *Rebecca Goodspeed*. It also meant he'd be stepping into Griffin's shoes with respect to their sister.

"Teddy's going to be very busy," Emmaline said breathlessly. The way Griffin teased her breasts while his warm breath swirled over them made her toes curl. "Perhaps Lady Cressida is safe for a while yet, then."

"Yes, but you aren't." He rose up and traced the thin line of gold at her throat. He circled the locket with her mother's picture inside it that Monty had given her as a wedding present and suddenly his eyes glazed over. A vein bulged on his forehead.

Emma cupped his cheeks. "Griffin. Come back."

He moved his fingers away from the locket and rolled onto his back.

"You had a vision," she guessed.

He nodded.

"Oh, Griffin, I'm sorry. I know you hate it when the future presses in on you. I shouldn't have worn the locket to bed and—"

"No, it's all right," he said with wonderment. "Did I tell you that I *Saw* you drink some of Kingsley's tea?"

"I put the cup to my lips, but I didn't drink. Your vision was wrong."

"No, it was incomplete," he said. "You had a choice about what to do and you exercised it, something I couldn't *See,* no matter how clear the *Sending* seemed. The future is not fixed. We have a choice. In the past, the problem has always come when I tried to choose for someone else."

She ran her hand over his chest, enjoying the crisp dark hairs that whorled around his brown nipples. "Do you want to tell me about this new vision?"

A smile curved the corner of his mouth. "We're going to have a child within a year."

Emmaline sat up. A husband, a home, a baby to love. Her heart threatened to burst out of her ribs. "Will it be a boy or a girl?"

He leaned on an elbow and splayed his other hand protectively over her belly. "I think I'll let you be surprised."

"Oh, you!" She rolled on top of him, pinning his long body beneath her. "You're going to live to regret that."

He grasped her hips and slid into her. "Regret," he said with a wicked grin, "is a waste of time."

Have you tried the other titles in Mia's series?

Touch of a Thief

London's most talented criminal is about to be fingered . . .

Lady Viola Preston can relieve a gentleman of the studs at his wrists without his being any the wiser and pick any lock devised by man in less than a minute. But she's careful to wear gloves when she steals jewels. Because when Viola touches a gemstone with her bare skin, it "speaks" to her, sending disturbing visions—visions almost as unsettling as the sight of the cool-eyed stranger who catches her red-handed.

Now Viola will only be stealing at Greydon Quinn's behest. And even more daunting than the violent history of the red diamond he's after is the prospect of a night in the devastatingly handsome lieutenant's arms. Touch has always been Viola's weakness, and the full body-to-body contact Quinn has in mind is about to shatter her defenses and set her senses reeling.

Touch of a Rogue

He can keep her safe . . . or be her very ruin . . .

Jacob Preston has three requirements for a woman desiring access to his bed: She must be enthusiastic in affairs of passion, jaded in matters of the heart, and—to ensure the first two qualifications—she must be married.

Lady Julianne Cambourne has all the makings of a passionate lover, and she certainly shows no signs of sentimentality . . . but her unmarried status should render her firmly off limits to Jacob.

Instead, it proves only a temptation. One that grows stronger when she comes to him in desperation, looking for the kind of answers only he can give. For beyond his rakish reputation, Jacob is known for the mysterious—even otherworldly—power of detection he commands through his sense of touch. And Julianne, surrounded by long-hidden secrets that threaten to ensnare her in a deadly trap, will do whatever it takes to recruit his skills . . . using every form of persuasion at her disposal. . . .